FOR LOVE
& COFFEE

A MATCHMAKERS' BOOK CLUB
NOVEL

NICOLE VIDAL

COPYRIGHT

TABLE OF CONTENTS

Copyright 2

Table of Contents 3

Keep in touch with NV 6

Prologue 8

Chapter One 13

Chapter Two...23

Chapter Three...32

Chapter Four 39

Chapter Five...53

Chapter Six...67

Chapter Seven 84

Chapter Eight 98

Chapter Nine 112

Chapter Ten..124

Chapter Eleven 136

Chapter Twelve 149

Chapter Thirteen 161

Chapter Fourteen..175

Chapter Fifteen..188

Chapter Sixteen 204

Chapter Seventeen..221

Chapter Eighteen..229

Chapter Nineteen..239

Chapter Twenty..248

Chapter Twenty-One..258

Chapter Twenty-Two 264

Chapter Twenty-Three 275

Chapter Twenty-Four..288

Chapter Twenty-Five 298

Chapter Twenty-Six 308

Chapter Twenty-Seven..322

Chapter Twenty-Eight..328

Chapter Twenty-Nine..342

Chapter Thirty 351

Chapter Thirty-One 358

Coming Soon..364

My Books 365

KEEP IN TOUCH WITH NV

Visit me on social media or online to learn about my newest releases:

Facebook (http://fb.me/NicoleVidalAuthor)

Instagram (http://instragram.com/nicolevidal_author)

My website (www.nicolevidal.com)

Goodreads (https://bit.ly/NVGoodreads)

Amazon (https://amzn.to/2XCLSlR)

Pinterest (http://pinterest.com/NicoleVidal_Author)

PROLOGUE

LOIS

ONE YEAR AGO

"I would like to call this meeting of the Matchmakers' Book Club to order. Let's get the business out the way and then focus on the fun."

The ladies' chatter decreases upon my announcement, and they gather around the dining table.

I continue, "For those of you who are new to our group, allow me to share our purpose. Initially, our group started as a gaggle of nurses and EMTs to de-stress from the rigors of our professions with book club and girls' night in. Over the years, it evolved into a girl gang of epic proportions. Not only do we host charity events for the local children's charities, but we keep tabs on the most eligible bachelors in our community. Our club and list of eligible bachelors was created in good fun, and the tradition has continued for the last five years. Along with the purpose of our group, the rules for inclusion on the list has evolved.

"Smoking hot is a must," one of the newest members shouts from the back of the room.

The remaining members laugh at her statement.

"I agree. As I was saying, inclusion is a few factors balanced against one another. First, as our sister stated, a handsome face and strong physique are a must. Also, candidates and admitted bachelors must be a member of our first-responder community, including police officers, firefighters, and EMTs. Most importantly, those included on the list are kept secret until after he has been legally wed."

Chatter erupts around the room.

I silence them by introducing a new face. "This evening, I would like to welcome our newest member, Willa Cappelli."

A chorus of "Welcome, Willa" echoes around the room.

"It has come to my attention that a few younger members of the YPD are aware of our group and have attempted to learn the inner workings. So far, they've failed. The secrecy must be maintained. The last thing we want is our fun to be thwarted. Now I open the floor to all members to suggest changes."

Carly, a bubbly blonde member, speaks first. "I suggest we add female first responders. While there aren't many of them in our area right now, there's at least one in each department who may warrant discussion and inclusion."

"All in favor, raise your hand," I request.

Each voting member raises her hand.

"The motion is carried. Please put forth your name for each department," I request.

"Lacey Ransom for the EMT list, Mia Arden for the fire department, and Piper Montgomery for the police department," Carly replies.

I open the floor to objections, I ask, "Any issues with those nominees?"

The room is silent.

"The motion to add women is carried, and those three are the inaugural honorees. As a side note, the list shall be expanded to five per department. One of which must be a female. In the event there are no eligible female honorees, the spot shall remain vacant. Agreed?"

"Agreed," the members reply in unison.

I now open the floor to suggestions for our next person to be matched.

"Landry Reed," one member suggests. "He would be the first fire firefighter we've attempted to match."

I look for further nominations.

"I suggest Zachary Smithson," Kelsey adds. After a group discussion, we decide to vote silently on the way out. The chairperson will then enlist members to foster the selected honoree.

"There's one last bit of business. I'll be stepping down as chair of this group to free up time for travel. I nominate Carly Reed as my replacement. All in favor?"

All members vote positively.

"Congratulations, Carly!" I motion for her to join me at the head of the table.

"Thank you, Lois. The members and I will carry on this group you created to give us an outlet—a group that has also given rise to lasting friendships and marriages along the way. Let's raise our glasses in celebration of Lois and our amazing group."

"Hear! Hear!" We clink our glasses together and dish on the latest dating gossip and our book selection.

"Before I go, I'll add the newest members to the list, recite the names, then turn the book over to Carly," I state before inscribing the three female members into their places in our book.

"The current list for the York Police Department reads as follows: Santino Gugliotti, Zachary Smithson, Lachlan Hagen, Donovan Davis, and Piper Montgomery. Former honorees are William Ramirez, Grant Washington, and Luca Cappelli."

Kelsey Ramirez, Maggie Washington, and Willa Cappelli smile as I read their husbands' names.

"The York Fire Department list includes Bradford Collings, Alden Rhodes, Aidan Madden, Landry Reed, and Mia Arden. No former honorees to date. Lastly, the EMTs in York County include Séamus Penn, Jude Pascal, Hollis Booker, Lexington Soren, and Lacey Ransom. No former honorees to date. It has been a pleasure spending time with you ladies. I look forward to peeking in on you in the future. Best of luck." I wander around the room and hug these women who have become my friends despite our age disparities and differences in opinions over popular books.

CHAPTER ONE

ZACHARY

Today's patrol shift was boring and makes for a long day. I shuffle into the locker room before heading home.

"Hey, Smithson, got plans tonight, or you coming out with us for some burgers and brew?" Craven slams his locker closed. Craven is a solid guy and has been with YPD for more than two years at this point.

"Yeah, I have things to get done."

"No worries, man. Next time." We bro hug, and I exit the precinct quickly, hoping I don't run into anyone else.

Until recently I would've joined Craven and the guys. However, none of the guys know what's going on in my personal life.

My mother was diagnosed with Alzheimer's about a year and a half ago. Given my hectic schedule and need to be on call frequently, my sister, Nadine, has been handling most of our mother's care. Unfortunately, my brother-in-law, Trevor, took off recently. Now single, my sister can't manage our mom's care, her twins, and her two jobs. We moved our mom into my townhouse a few months ago and hired a caregiver.

"Hi, Gladys. I'm home." It's a bit later than usual. My schedule is anything but consistent and predictable. Ideally, I arrive home by six each night, especially since I haven't gone out since Mom moved in.

Gladys accepted the job as my mother's caregiver with the slimmest of margins—just two days. Two days before I would've needed to take time off from work to care for her myself. She provides care around the clock and uses one of my guest bedrooms. However, she's only contracted for three months. I have yet to find a suitable replacement, and I'm rapidly running out of time.

The guys have taken to ribbing me about Gladys's daughter leaving here early in the mornings when I'm not on shift. Essie stops by once or twice a week to refresh Gladys's meds or bring things she needs from her apartment. While Essie is gorgeous, with caramel skin and pin-straight hair, she's also married. A sparkly diamond band surrounds her left ring finger—a fact I'm surprised my coworkers, who should be keen on details, seem to miss.

"Hello, Zack. How was your shift?"

"Not bad. How is she doing today?"

Gladys drops her head. "I'm sorry, Zack. She's been asking for your father all day."

I scrub my hands down my face. "Not your fault. Thank you." My parents, Saul and Carol, were childhood friends who fell in love. Most of the time, my mother does recall her husband of nearly thirty-five years passed away about four years ago.

Rounding the corner, I greet my mother, who is sitting in a chair in the living room. "Hi, Mom. How was your day?"

Typically, I get only two responses these days. Either she doesn't recognize me at all, or she sees my father. Except for my imposing stature, I look more like her than him.

"It was a good day, Saul. How was work at the plant?" My father used to work at a steam plant long before I was born.

My chest tightens. There's nothing more I can do for her as far as her deteriorating mind is concerned. "My day was good. Did you eat?"

"Yes, your daughter brought me a lovely dinner from the diner down the street."

There's absolutely no chance her memory is accurate. The diner is near our childhood home, and Nadine lives thirty minutes away.

"Great. I'm going to wash up. I'll be back soon." I exhale sharply and leave the living room. I can only imagine how difficult being trapped in your mind must be for her. I take the stairs two at a time, strip out of my clothes, and shower. Gladys is working with Mom on her nighttime routine when I sit down to eat.

Once I finish, I boot up my laptop and scan my email for replies to the job posting for an overnight caregiver. There are two responses. I return both inquiries and set up phone interviews for tomorrow on my lunch break. Content I can't do anything else, I trudge upstairs to bed, though there's no guarantee I'll be able to sleep all night.

Thankfully, the night passes peacefully, and my alarm shocks me awake at five. I tug on running clothes and shoes before peeking in on my mom as I pass by. I'm not the praying type, but I hope she has a better day today. I slip out the front door and run toward the exit of my complex.

It's a bit chillier than normal for this time of year, but I don't mind. Early spring temperatures are hard to predict. Some days the weather is downright frigid, others it's balmy. Shortly after five in the morning, there are only a few diehards I may see along the trail. The converted railroad track is a four-mile loop. With the added distance from my front door, it's a tad shy of six miles. As I round the corner, I encounter the first diehard.

Captain Ramirez is running at a decent pace with two dogs beside him. Bear and Knox are their names, if I recall correctly. Cap and his wife, Kelsey, live on the far side of the loop with their two kids, Benjamin and Valentina. Kelsey owns the Perk, a coffee shop and catering company. "Morning, Cap."

"Smithson," he replies and continues past me toward his home.

I check my watch and slow my pace to near seven minutes a mile. I don't need to be exhausted before my shift starts. In the last quarter mile of the loop, Washington and I acknowledge one another but keep running. He and his wife, Maggie, met at a traffic stop. They have two kids as well. I finish my run and down a water as I approach the entrance to my complex. I climb the front steps and hear screaming. I step inside and join them in her bedroom.

"No, no, no! You aren't my Nadine." My mother is shouting at Gladys. Her arms are flailing, her head furiously shaking side to side.

"Easy, Carol. Let's take a seat and regroup," Gladys attempts to soothe her.

"Morning" is all I can muster.

Mom's head snaps in my direction at the sound of my voice. "Zack, you're home. Where is Nadine?"

"Mom, Nadine doesn't live here. She's lives with her husband and kids. We can call her after breakfast if you want."

"Okay." Her voice is soft, childlike even.

Placating her was almost too easy. My arrival was clearly at the tail end of her episode this morning.

Given the relief rolling off Gladys, I'm likely correct. "Thank you."

"You're welcome." I would like to say I'm a stellar son and I'm able to care for my mother. I'm not. Handling her personal care is not something I'm equipped to do. After her diagnosis, she was adamant about not spending the end of her days in a memory care facility. Nadine and I agreed to keep her home as long as possible. I'll admit, she's been here for two months, and the strain on me is significant with a full-time caregiver. How my sister survived with her kids and work is beyond me. Despite our promise, I don't know how long I can keep her here with a nurse. It isn't about the money but about the quality of care and providing a safe space for her. Hopefully one of these interviews pans out for a night nurse.

"Go ahead, or you're going to be late for work," Gladys ushers me away.

I immensely appreciate her understanding of my career demands and my lack of ability to care for my mother's personal needs. It's one thing for me to be present and spend time with her. The rest is something else. I nod and bound upstairs.

Within twenty minutes, I'm showered and clad in my uniform for the day. I hustle into the Perk and take my order from Becca. "Thanks, Becca. Always on point."

"Have a good day!" Becca smiles.

I leave as quickly as I arrived at the quaint coffee shop. I have a standing order for the same time every morning. Kelsey bills me monthly. If I don't arrive within ten minutes of it being ready, they put the next customer's order on my tab.

I park and take my place at the front desk. Each of us takes at least one monthly shift at the desk to interface with the public. Normally, I don't mind it, but my brain is still working on finding a caregiver for my mom. I send a quick text to my sister before the line grows.

> Me: I may not have asked before, but how did you handle it for so long? This is hard. She's not really there.
>
> Nadine: It wasn't easy. I know, it's heart-wrenching. Her condition has deteriorated more rapidly in recent months from the reports I've read.
>
> Me: I'm interviewing two people at lunch for the night shift.
>
> Nadine: Good luck. Love you.
>
> Me: Thanks. Love you back.

I exhale and handle a few complaints from concerned citizens. After a lull, the stream of people increases until I'm relieved by Greyson for lunch.

"Hey, Rook. Thanks for the assist." Probably shouldn't call him "Rook" anymore. He's officially off probation.

"No worries. Go, I've got this," Greyson informs me.

I don't wait for him to change his mind. I grab my jacket and hustle outside to the food trucks.

Once I have my food in hand, my phone rings. "Hello."

"Hi, this is Michael. I'm calling about the night caregiver job."

"Great. Thank you for your prompt call." I explain the duties of the job, including the live-in requirement, which was clearly stated in the ad.

"I can't live with you," he states emphatically.

I bite back an annoyed comment. "I appreciate your time, but the job requires overnight hours." Once I end the call, I drop my head. In the following fifteen minutes, I scarf down my tacos and hope the next call is better.

I answer on the second ring, and she's already talking. "Hi, my name is Valerie. I read about the job. Are you the same Zack who helped me with my car accident last year?"

How did she connect me personally, my job, and this ad? "I don't know." I set for the parameters of the job.

"Like all night?" Her response isn't promising.

"Yes, the job is from 6:00 p.m. to 6:00 a.m."

"Yeah, I can't do that and keep my other job too. Sorry." She ends the call abruptly.

Me too. Distraught and frustrated, I chuck my trash and meander back inside to relieve Greyson.

"Hey, Smithson, Cap wanted to see you before you take over for me."

I acknowledge him and make my way to Cap's office. "You wanted to see me?"

He motions for me to take a seat. "Everything okay with you?"

"Sure, why?"

"Over the last few months, you've been arriving on time by the skin of your teeth, and you're out the door as soon as you can. What's changed?"

Perhaps I should've shared with Cap sooner. "My mother moved in with me a few months ago. She was diagnosed with Alzheimer's about eighteen months ago. Until recently, she was living with my sister and her husband. He took off, and my sister asked for help."

"I'm sorry," Cap offers.

"Thank you. I'm in the process of finding a permanent night nurse. I've been striking out though."

Cap steeples his fingers like he does when he's considering each possibility for a scenario. "Have you tried posting for a student nurse at the hospital?"

"No, that's a great idea. Who handles the postings?"

"Willa Cappelli." The look on his face shows he's tickled he can help.

"I'll give her a call."

"Next time, please give me a heads-up. I don't like wondering if my guys are okay."

"I hope there isn't a next time, but if there is, I'll let you know." I leave his office and immediately dial the hospital.

"York Memorial. How may I direct your call?"

"Willa Cappelli, please."

"May I ask who is calling?" the perky receptionist asks.

"Zack Smithson."

Hold music, which I believe is Vivaldi's "The Four Seasons," plays while I wait for her to answer.

"Hey, Zack. Everything okay?"

"Hi, Willa. Yes and no." I explain what I need, and she indicates she'll get the post out today.

I thank her and return to the front desk. Even though the job isn't filled, I feel slightly unburdened.

CHAPTER TWO

SCARLETT

I slam my alarm again and note I snoozed too many times. *Damn! I'm going to be late!* I jump into a pair of scrubs, tie my hair into a messy topknot, and hurry out the door with a coffee prepped by my roommate bestie and a protein bar.

"Have a good day," she shouts as the door closes. Lia and I were instant friends when I arrived in town. At first I was skeptical, but moving here was the best choice for me.

I hustle into the hospital and throw my bag and phone into my locker. I closed the Perk last night as a favor to a coworker. Now I'm regretting it. The money is nice, but I need to find a higher paying job to knock down my loans a bit. I refuse to allow Savi to pay them off simply because she can. When we moved here, I learned Savi was paying for my schooling under the guise of me earning scholarships. I put a stop to it. She shouldn't have to pay my way despite her motherly role and her husband's substantial wealth.

"Nice of you to join us this morning, Scarlett." Stacey, my supervisor, scowls at me.

I pull to a stop at the back of my group. "I'm not late yet." Snarky maybe, but I'm here just in time instead of fifteen minutes early.

Stacey brushes off my comment and runs down our patients for the day. After she finishes, she states, "Scarlett, a word please."

I drop my head and follow her to the nurses' station. "Stacey, I'm really sorry. I closed last night for extra money. It won't happen again."

"Relax, Scarlett. You weren't late. I need to make an example out of you since you're the top student in this class. Plus, Willa wants to see you."

Willa Cappelli is the staff coordinator for the hospital. Her job encompasses the student nurses as well. As I walk to her office, I mentally tick off my actions for the last week. By the time I reach her door, I still haven't come up with a possible reason for this meeting.

"Come in, Scarlett," Willa answers.

"Good morning, Willa. You wanted to see me?"

"I can hear the concern in your voice. You aren't in trouble. Please have a seat," she offers.

The tightness in my chest loosens a bit. True, I'm one of the top students in my class, but school isn't over for another few months.

Willa continues, "I received a call late yesterday regarding an in-home, overnight nurse position. The family needs a nurse to assist an Alzheimer's patient. Given your aptitude while you worked in our memory care facility, I thought it would be a good fit for you. The hours are six to six, and you'd have a private room. The family would provide you with an extensive history. The current nurse, Gladys, is only round the clock temporarily. Would you be interested?"

I consider the offer. It's perfect except… I would need to stop working at the Perk.

I inquire, "When does the position start?"

"He didn't say. What is your concern?"

"I'm interested. It would be an amazing opportunity for me, and I did love my time with the memory patients, but I can't quit on Kelsey." I don't need to go into more depth. The Perk is a York Beach staple. Willa and Kelsey are friends as well.

Willa considers my statement. "Call Zack and see if he can wait two weeks for you to give Kelsey proper notice." She hands me a piece of paper with his contact information on it.

"Thank you. I'll call him on my break."

"You're welcome. I hope it'll work out well for both of you."

I get the feeling she's talking about more than the job, but I ignore the innuendo and return to my floor. With his chart in hand, I visit my first patient of the day. He's having surgery on his rotator cuff, an injury he received playing football with his buddies. "Morning, Mr. Glenn."

"Well, aren't you gorgeous?"

I glance at his chart and note his marital status and her name. "Thanks, but I think Naomi might not appreciate your comment. I'm Scarlett, your pre-op nurse. I'm going to get a set of vitals and send you off for surgery." If a patient isn't hitting on us, they're trying to fix us up with their sons or their grandchildren, at least in my case.

His face falls, and he apologizes for his remark—a rarity, but I'll take it. Fifteen minutes later, he's off to the operating room. I spend the next few hours ushering patients from pre-op to the operating room and back to post-op. During lunch, I grab my phone and jacket and step outside into the ambulance bay to make my call.

I dial the number, and he answers on the first ring.

"Hello." His smooth and velvety voice surrounds me like a fluffy, warm blanket.

"Hi. I got your number from Willa about the overnight nurse job."

"Thank you for calling. I want to be upfront, as most of the other candidates didn't seem to understand. The job requires you to live in my townhouse to care for my mother, Carol. There are occasions where I'm called in overnight, and I need someone present for her."

"I understand. Willa mentioned she has Alzheimer's. You're looking for someone to handle her nighttime routine and be on call should she have an episode in the middle of the night."

"Yes, that's precisely what I need. She was officially diagnosed about a year and a half ago at stage four plus. Now Mom is closer to stage five since the medications don't seem to make a significant difference." He explains the salary and gives a brief history of his mom's care and prognosis, which frankly isn't great.

Taking this job will help me determine if I can handle working with patients like Carol for the rest of my life. The disease wreaks havoc on a person and their family, physically and mentally. It's heartbreaking. "When are you looking for someone to start?"

"As soon as possible, why?"

"I have a job in addition to nursing school, and I would need to give notice. I won't quit."

He exhales sharply. "It shouldn't be a problem. I'll discuss with Gladys, her day nurse, if I need coverage for the next two weeks. Can you meet me at my townhouse tonight?"

"Sure, what time?"

"Seven," he replies. "By the way, what's your name?"

"Scarlett."

He gives me the address and ends the call.

I consider waiting, but I don't see myself not taking the position. The salary is more than I make at the Perk, and it's in my field. Not living with Lia will be an issue only to the extent of my decreased bestie time. It's temporary though. I exhale and dial Kelsey's office.

"The Perk, Kelsey speaking."

"Hi, Kelsey, it's Scarlett."

"Hey, what can I do for you?"

"I'm calling to give you my notice. I have a second interview for a job tonight, more like a 'make sure it's a good fit' meeting, and I won't be able to do both."

"I appreciate the call, Scarlett. I'll see what I can do with the schedule for you."

"Thanks, Kelsey. It has been a pleasure working for you, but the new position is in my field."

"I completely understand. It was only a matter of time with graduation rapidly approaching. You'll be missed behind the counter. Good luck," Kelsey states and ends the call.

I gobble my lunch and hustle back inside. As I put my phone back into my locker, I note a preview of a message from my sister. It'll have to wait until later.

I slip out of the locker room and back to the surgical floor. Mr. Glenn is resting comfortably with his pain medicine drip, and the emergency case from right before lunch is coming out of her anesthesia.

"Hi, Ms. Josten. How are you feeling?"

She was in a car accident, which required her arm to be reset and a pin put in place. "I've been better, but I'm alive and I'll make a full recovery eventually."

"Good perspective. How is your pain level?"

"I'm fine. Thank you."

"You're welcome. You should be out of here before dinner."

I make my way to the nurses' station. I spend the rest of my shift filling in my patient charts. Right after five, I head out to my car and reply to my sister's text from earlier.

Savi: Hey there! How are you?

Me: I'm good. I have an interview for a new job tonight. You?

Savi: You're leaving the Perk?

Me: It's an in-home nurse position.

Savi: Makes sense. Good luck. We should see each other soon. The kids miss Auntie Let.

Me: Thanks. I miss them too. I'll let you know.

I rush home and take a no-shampoo shower before heading to my interview. What I mean is, I don't have time to wash and dry my hair. Pinning my hair up, I wash the hospital smell off. I opt for jeans and a light sweater. I verify the directions and head to the interview with a sandwich to go.

Right before seven, I arrive and knock on the door.

An older woman, probably in her upper fifties, answers the door. "Hello, can I help you?"

"Yes, I'm looking for Zack. We're meeting about the overnight nurse position."

She studies me carefully before speaking. "Scarlett?"

"Yes." She's still sizing me up, though I'm not sure why.

"He was held over at a call. Would you like to wait inside? I can give you a synopsis of Carol's routines."

"Thank you." I step inside. The townhouse is modern but comfortable. It appears Carol is using the first-floor office as her room. Stairs must be an issue for her.

Gladys introduces me to Carol. "Carol, this is Scarlett. She's going to be helping out in the evenings."

Carol looks up and notes my presence.

I extend my hand to her, but she doesn't take it. "Pleasure to meet you, Carol."

Gladys walks me through Carol's nighttime routine, which will be my responsibility. Step by step, Gladys shares everything from her meds to her preferred sleeping position. She also explains her morning routine for reference in case Carol wakes early. Generally, she wakes after six, which would be after shift change.

"What is her history? Who does she routinely ask for?" I inquire.

"I'll let Zack share his family information with you."

"I understand."

We back out of Carol's room and take seats in the kitchen.

"Would you like a beverage?" she offers.

"A water would be great."

We chat at the table about her expectations of me and mine of her—a set of guidelines for Carol's care, if you will. What I'm responsible for, what Gladys is responsible for, and what the elusive Zack handles.

CHAPTER THREE

ZACHARY

I arrive home well past eight. I didn't expect Scarlett to be here waiting, so as I step into the kitchen, I'm taken aback. She's stunning. Her raven hair is tied into a ponytail. Wide blue eyes meet mine. *We've met before—only once.*

The precise moment is etched into my mind. About two years ago, I met the guys at the Perk before shift to grab breakfast. This was before my standing order with Kelsey was in place. I spilled my coffee on a gorgeous woman who was waiting in line with her sister, her brother-in-law, and niece. She mesmerized me. I was dumbstruck to the point Cap and Kelsey spoke for me. *I'm screwed. She's more beautiful now than she was then.*

"Thank you for waiting," I address Scarlett.

"You're welcome." She extends her hand to me.

When I take it, heat streaks up my arm. I almost release her instantly. Instead, I relish the softness of her hand in mine and how well it fits. It wouldn't be a huge leap to believe Scarlett feels the same warmth as she hasn't pulled away either.

"I'll let you talk," Gladys announces, breaking the tension in the room. "It was a pleasure meeting you, Scarlett."

"You as well."

Reluctantly, I release her hand. "Thank you."

She leaves the kitchen, and I'm alone with Scarlett. "Have we met before?" I wonder if she recalls too.

"Yes, you literally ran into me on my very first day in York Beach and spilled your coffee all over me at the Perk."

"Please allow me to apologize now. I don't recall properly conveying my regret then." Hell, I was tongue-tied.

A small smile graces her face. "You're forgiven."

"I'm sorry for being late to our meeting as well. I was on a call."

"It's no problem. It further shows why you need help in the evening. Can you tell me about your family history and who your mom's triggers are?"

"Sure, are you hungry?"

"No, thanks. I grabbed food before I arrived. Feel free to cook while we talk. I'm sure you're starving," she suggests.

"I appreciate your accommodation." I step into the kitchen and pull out ingredients for a quick stir-fry. While I cook, I share about my family. "My parents were married for over thirty-five years. My father, Saul, passed away about four years ago."

"I'm sorry," Scarlett murmurs.

"Thanks. My mom lived on her own for nearly two years until my sister noticed she was forgetting trivial things, like closing the garage door or my name."

"Your name isn't trivial," she adds.

Warmth cascades through me. She certainly understands Mom's disease and its impacts. "Nadine started to worry, and she took her for testing. It took almost a year, but she was diagnosed as having early-onset Alzheimer's. I surmise my father was covering for her for a while before he passed away. It took some strong persuasion, but we convinced her to sell our childhood home. At the time, we were discussing care options, she adamantly refused a memory facility. My sister and I promised it would be our last resort. She moved in with Nadine. The kids loved spending time with her, and given my schedule, she was the logical choice."

"Kids?" Scarlett asks.

I plate my dinner, grab a water, and join her at the table. "My sister has ten-year-old twins, Tanner and Tallie, short for Tallulah. Until about three months ago, everything was going well. A nurse spent the day with Mom, and Nadine handled the overnights. Her husband took off with his coworker. Nadine needed to find a second job to make ends meet, so she couldn't handle the overnight anymore."

"That's terrible. Please eat before your food turns cold."

I take a few bites before sharing more. "Most of the time, Mom confuses me for my father or doesn't know me at all. Her last serious episode was soon after she moved in here. She woke up screaming for Nadine. It took Gladys and me over two hours to calm her down."

Scarlett sets her hand on mine. "I'm sorry. Her disease is terrible and unpredictable. What stage is she now?"

The warmth of her skin on mine is heavenly. Her touch is meant to be comforting, yet it feels more intimate. *No, she's off-limits.* Slowly, I slip my hand away. Purposely I grab my water to make it known it isn't that I don't want her to touch me. I do, more than I should, but she's going to work for me. She'll be here to care for my mother. "She's solidly in stage four at this point. Lately, she has been exhibiting more signs of stage five though, like forgetting I'm her son and becoming disoriented."

"How do you handle her doctor visits, and does she have visitors? Is there a list?"

"My sister and I handle her doctor visits together. We schedule them when we can both take the time away from work. No one visits other than my sister and her kids. On rare occasions, the guys stop by, but they haven't since... my coworkers don't know my mom is here." I rise from my chair and grab my phone from the island. I scroll through my phone until I find a recent photo. "Here, this is my sister and her kids, so you have an idea."

She glances at the image. "Thanks. Why don't your friends know about your mom?"

"I'm a private person. I don't share much about my personal life with the guys."

"I understand. It might help to talk to someone though."

I stare into her sparkling eyes longer than I should. "What about you?"

"Sure. I'm willing to listen."

Danger. Warning! You can't spend extra time with her. My admonishments are having the opposite effect. Instead of a warning, I'm more like a bull charging toward the red flag.

"I have a shift at the Perk tomorrow night. Kelsey said she would do her best to cover my shifts over the next two weeks. I'll let you and Gladys know which nights I have to be there or if she wants to leave near nine, it's up to her."

"You're going to take the job?" Surprise laces through my tone.

"Is there a reason I shouldn't or you don't want me to?"

Shouldn't—no. I want you to take the job a little too much. "No, not at all. Again, I appreciate you waiting for me. Let me get you a key, in case Gladys is indisposed when you arrive, and the alarm code."

"Do you have a contract for me to sign or something?"

"Yeah, I'll have it ready in the next few days. Willa sent your basic information already and confirmed your background check was clear." I hand her a key and go over the alarm code with her. "Do you have any more questions?"

"No, I'm set for now."

"Have a good night, Scarlett."

"You too. Let me know if Gladys wants to leave late tomorrow or not."

"I will." I escort her to her car and wait until she pulls away. Scarlett is walking temptation. Not only is she smart and gorgeous, but she's willing to take on my mom's care. I drag my fingers through my hair and step back inside.

While I wash the dishes, Gladys returns to the kitchen. "She's a looker."

"I guess." My reply comes out as nonchalant as I can manage.

"Don't think for one second I didn't see the tension between the two of you, young man," Gladys calls me out.

"We met a few years ago, once. It was recognition, that's all." *Liar.* My words don't ring true to my own ears. I share with Gladys about Scarlett's current job. She agrees to work the nights Scarlett needs to be at the Perk. I'm grateful for the accommodation for me, my mother, and for Scarlett.

Gladys checks on Mom again and turns in for the night. I consider watching a movie but, instead, clean up and fall into my bed. Before I think better of it, I text Scarlett.

Me: I talked to Gladys. She'll work the nights you need..

Scarlett: Great. Please thank her for me. I'll let you know the rest of my schedule once Kelsey finishes it.

Me: Thank you. Good night, Scarlett.

Scarlett: Night, Zack.

With that settled, I close my eyes and hope to get some sleep. As if I needed something else to keep me awake at night, my mother's nurse, with a perfect hourglass figure, invades my thoughts. I sleep fitfully until right before five. Resigned, knowing my chance for sleep is over, I lace up and take off running.

CHAPTER FOUR

SCARLETT

Last night when I arrived home, Lia was still working her shift at the brewery. I fell into my bed after a text exchange with Zack. Attempting to sleep proved difficult. A disgustingly gorgeous man with a chiseled jaw and intoxicating smile thwarted my efforts.

Near five, I wake before my alarm and get out of bed. I'll be early today despite knowing it will be a long day closing the Perk. Surprisingly, Lia is already awake.

"Morning," she grumbles.

"Morning, we need to talk."

Lia looks over her cup at me.

"I got a new job, and it's overnight. I'll be moving there during the contract."

"Oh, okay. What kind of job?"

"I'm working as a private overnight nurse for a patient with Alzheimer's."

"Good for you. I'll miss you, but it isn't forever, right?"

"Of course not. I just won't be sleeping here. I'll be here when I'm not on shift at the hospital or at school."

"I'm happy for you. You may love memory care."

"Thanks, Lia. I'm lucky to have you as my bestie!" I glance at the clock and hustle out the door to class.

I stow my bag and silence my phone. Days at school aren't terrible, but they are long. After two classes, I hide away in the library to focus on my classwork. A few hours later, I stroll toward my last class of the day to find Lia waiting for me.

"Hey! Wasn't expecting to see you again today."

"My lab got out early. When are you starting your new job?" she asks.

"I'll know more after my shift at the Perk tonight. Probably in the next few days, why?"

Lia shrugs. "I want to be prepared not to expect you home."

"You're the best ever, Lia!"

A huge smile graces her face. "I know." She winks, hugs me, and walks away.

Telling Lia went easier than I thought it would. I wrap up my third class and head over to the Perk. The line is out the door when I arrive.

"Did I miss a giveaway or something?" I ask Becca as I join her at the counter.

"I don't think so, and it's too early for tourists."

"True." York Beach, Maine, is a small beach town with quaint shops, an amusement park, an arcade, and an old-fashioned restaurant that pulls saltwater taffy in the window. The tourists don't usually arrive until spring break and then are in full force early to mid-June. We dispatch the line within twenty minutes.

"Phew."

"Exactly. Hopefully, we'll be good for the rest of the shift," I mutter.

"Why on earth would you curse yourself?" Becca asks.

"What are you talking about?"

Becca gives me the side-eye. "Is this your first job in food service?"

"Yes. First and only, why?"

Becca's head drops and shakes side to side. "You never, ever comment on the number of customers or lack thereof."

"Noted." I finish cleaning the counter and move to the tables in the café area before Kelsey calls me into her office.

"You wanted to see me," I ask at the threshold.

"Yes. I covered all but two of your shifts. You're still on Saturday night and then next Wednesday."

"Thank you, Kelsey."

"You're a great worker, and I'm sad to see you go. However, I'm proud of you too. Your move here was abrupt, but you've thrived."

I round her desk and hug her tight. "I couldn't have asked for a better boss than you."

Kelsey smiles, and I step out of her office. The rest of the shift is blissfully quiet. After I close up, I head to my car and drive home. Lia is on shift tonight at the brewery. I pour a glass of white wine and pack up a few days' worth of clothes. I'll be able to come home on Saturday to do laundry and gather more clothes.

Before I collapse into my bed for the night, I text Zack my schedule.

Me: Kelsey was able to cover all but this Saturday and next Wednesday.

Unexpectedly, he answers right away.

Zack: Great. I'll update Gladys. How was your day?

Me: Good. You?

Zack: I had three calls back-to-back today.

Me: You must be exhausted.

Zack: I am. Thanks for the info. I'll see you tomorrow.

Me: Night, Zack.

Zack: Good night, Scarlett.

I sigh. Nothing in our exchange was anything over the top, but I'm drawn to him, and I don't know why. Sure, he's gorgeous, but looks aren't everything. Yet I've never felt the prickles of awareness beneath my skin with any other guy simply from shaking his hand.

My alarm shocks me awake. Apparently, I was tired too. I hustle through the shower, tug on my scrubs, and head off to work with coffee and a muffin in hand. Not only am I starting my new job, but today I'm working on the pediatric floor.

Stacey directs me upstairs as soon as I arrive. I report to Judith, and she hands me three charts. Trial by fire it is.

I step into the first room to find the patient's dad still sleeping on the pull-out bed. My patient, Mariah, puts her finger to her lips to make sure I let him sleep.

I tiptoe over to her bed and introduce myself. "Hi, I'm Scarlett. How are you feeling today?" I whisper. I scan her chart. She's here for a leg ulcer, a complication of sickle cell disease, but should be released today.

"Nice to meet you. I'm good but ready to go home. Dad is tired. I've been in and out of hospitals my entire life. You would think he would be used to it by now. He doesn't sleep well when I'm here."

I stifle a laugh as I check her vitals and her leg. Her vitals are normal, and her leg looks much better based on the notes in her chart. "Completely understandable. He's worried about you. Although, you're looking good. I'll see what I can do about springing you."

"Thanks."

"You're welcome, Mariah."

I smile and leave her room. Next up is eleven-year-old Keegan. His chart indicates he has leukemia and finished a round of a new treatment two days ago. He's slated to go home tomorrow unless there's a reaction to his regime.

"Good morning. Well, look at you. Your breakfast is gone."

"Hi. You're pretty." Keegan's voice quiets as he speaks.

"Thank you. I'm Scarlett. Were you starving?"

He motions for me to come closer. "Truthfully, I ate super quick so Mom would have to leave the room to get her own breakfast."

"Why?"

"She needed a break." My heart splits wide open for this cutie, caring for his mom while he's fighting a horrible disease.

"She's lucky to have you."

"It's definitely the other way around." Keegan smiles.

I smile back as I check his vitals and meds to update his chart. "Let me know if you need anything."

"Will do, Nurse Scarlett."

I attempt to check on my third patient, but he isn't in his room. At the nurses' station, I note he's having a procedure and won't be back for a few hours. The rest of my day moves smoothly, at least on the outside. However, my stomach is in knots. The mere thought of Zack causes uncontrollable butterflies to take flight. They only increase when he's nearby, a state which will be tested tonight for the third time.

I exit the hospital, grab a deli sandwich, and make my way to work. When I arrive, Gladys is serving Carol dinner.

"Hi, Gladys. Hi, Carol."

Gladys replies, "Hello, Scarlett. Let me finish this, and I can give you a rundown of her day."

"Thanks. If you could direct me to where my room is, that would be great."

"You should probably hold off until Zack gets home. I'm not sure if he cleared out the second guest room yet."

I shrug. "No problem." I set my bag on the floor off to the side in the living room and join them in the kitchen.

"Zack updated me with your schedule. I'll be here for those evenings. I appreciate you starting early."

"I'm grateful you're willing to stay on for those evenings."

"I committed to the three months of nights because Zack needed the help. I'm an old lady. Full-time, live-in care is a lot of work. It's meant for young, spry women like yourself."

I giggle. "You're not old."

Gladys shakes her head. "Yes, I am. I own it. Sixty-two qualifies as old in my book."

"Well, perhaps it does, but you look spry to me."

Gladys laughs and finishes with Carol's dinner. "Let's get you to the chair for the news, Carol."

Carol nods, takes Gladys's arm, and follows. I wash the dishes and load them in the dishwasher.

"I could've done those," Gladys states when she returns to the kitchen.

"It's no problem."

"Carol had a good day. She wasn't triggered today."

"Glad to hear it."

Gladys pushes off the island. "I'll leave you to it. Please call if you run into any problems before Zack gets home. I don't live too far away. My number is by the phone."

"Thank you." I grab my notes and take a seat near Carol in the living room. As her shows end, I guide my patient toward her room. "Ready, Carol?"

She nods weakly and replies, "Yes. What is your name again?"

"I'm Scarlett." I don't know why my parents selected my name, other than it starts with S like my sister's.

"Like the old movie character?"

"Exactly."

"She wasn't as pretty as you," Carol offers.

"Thank you."

We shuffle to her room and make progress changing her clothes for bed. Halfway through her personal care, Zack arrives home. He leans against the archway and greets his mother.

"Hi, Mom. How was your day?"

"Saul, it's great to see you, my love," Carol replies.

It's impossible to miss the flash of pain in Zack's eyes. I catch his gaze before he steps away. I finish up with Carol, verifying the rails of the bed are up and she's comfortable before leaving the room.

"Hey, want to talk about it?" I ask.

He looks up from preparing his sandwich. "No, but thanks for offering."

"Okay. Gladys indicated I should wait for you to ask about my room."

His face scrunches up in discomfort. "About that, I only have one guest room. True, there are three bedrooms, but only one extra bed. You can use mine until Gladys is done with her overnights, and I'll sleep on the couch."

Oh, okay. No. "Zack, it's fine. I'll take the couch. It's only for a week or so."

He shakes his head vehemently. "No, I didn't think it through. I'll take the couch, Scarlett. Like you said, it's only a week or so."

"I can't take your bed. You need to sleep. Isn't that the whole purpose of my presence?"

He raises an eyebrow at me. "You don't?"

There isn't a response, but there may be a solution. "We can trade off."

"Meaning?"

"Every other night, one of us uses your bed and the other sleeps on the couch, deal?"

"Fine, I can live with a compromise." He takes his food, sets it on the table, and leaves.

Confused, I simply wait for him to return.

"Here's the contract for Mom's care. It's for three months and will automatically renew unless you give me notice at least a month in advance. Please review it."

I take the paperwork and sit across from him. Skimming the contract, I sign my name on the last page beside his and date it. We sit in silence while he finishes his dinner.

"I'm going to clean up. Why don't you bring your stuff upstairs and get settled?"

I retreat to the living room and grab my bag. Before I can take a step, Zack reaches for the bag. "Thanks."

I follow him upstairs. *Holy hell!* You would think being behind him wouldn't be appealing. You would be wrong. His shoulders are broad and taper to a lean waist, and his ass is a sight and a half. He has manners to boot.

"Scarlett."

Hearing my name pulls me out of my lust-filled stupor. "Uh-huh?" I lift my gaze to meet his.

He smiles, and it lights up his entire face. If I'm not mistaken, a hint of red creeps into his cheeks as well. "Why don't you put your stuff in the guest room and change? After I clean up, I'll head back downstairs, and my room is yours."

"Okay." I slip into the guest room and close the door. I set my bag on the floor in the closet and hang a few things to avoid extra wrinkles. I shuck my scrubs and exchange them for leggings and a thin hoodie. The entire time, I admonish myself. *I'm here to work, not lust after my boss. But he's… sexy as hell, and his breathtaking smile makes my heart race.* I attempt to push unprofessional thoughts about Zack out of my head.

The knock on the door steals my attention.

"Scarlett, you okay?"

"Yeah, why?"

"I assumed… never mind. The towels are in the hall closet if you need one to wash up."

A weak "thank you" is all I can manage. *I'm screwed. More like I want to be screwed.* Before I think better of it, I text Lia.

Me: Holy crap! My boss is smoking hot!

Lia: Isn't that a good thing?

Me: No, I can't date him.

Lia: Why not?

Me: Oh how I love you mostest. It isn't right, right?

Lia: You never know when you'll meet someone with potential.

Me: You're wise beyond your years, my gorgeous friend.

Lia: I know. Love you. See you in a few days.

Me: Love you. See you.

I settle myself and return downstairs. After I peek in on Carol, I find Zack scrolling through the channel guide.

"Any requests?" He looks in my direction.

"Don't worry about me. It's your television. You pick."

He shakes his head and selects *The West Wing.*

I take a seat as far away from him as possible with my back against the arm. "How long ago did you start rewatching?"

"I'm a few episodes into season two, why?"

"Cool. You're only a few behind where I am."

He turns his gaze to me. "You're rewatching too?"

"Yup. I like a few current shows, but late nineties shows are my jam."

"Are you old enough to say that?"

I give him the side-eye. "You know how old I am. My sister was my main caretaker, and she chose the shows. I may have been too young before, but I'm not now."

"Why was your sister caring for you?"

I inhale sharply.

"You don't have to share."

"I feel as if I could share everything with you. Other than with Lia, I haven't really shared my story. Never wanted to before. I was raised by my older sister, Savannah, when our mother died in childbirth."

"I'm sorry."

"Thank you. Our father was around, but he mostly checked out due to his grief and alcohol addiction. My parents were inseparable outside of work, at least that's what my sister shared with me. Savi did everything from first-day-of-school pictures, to scraped knees, and boy crushes. While we were entrenched in our life, I didn't see the sacrifices she was making for me. Almost three years ago, my sister met and fell head over heels in love with Sam Morgan. They moved here to give their family a more peaceful life away from the spotlight of the big city. They have a daughter, Emerson. She's almost three, going on twenty-three, and a son, Bennett, who is six months. I made a poor choice or two with the people I chose to hang out with during my days at NYU. Luckily, Sam and his friend Cruz were able to pull me out of it. I enrolled here in the nursing program, and I'll finish in May."

"Thank you for trusting me."

"Thank you for listening. I'm comfortable talking to you."

Before starting the episode, he asks, "What current shows? Let me guess, *Yellowstone* and *Jack Ryan*."

"Spot-on actually."

He flashes his megawatt smile in my direction, presses play, and leans against the back of the couch.

Halfway through the episode, I grab a tennis ball out of my purse and roll my arches on the carpeted floor.

"Feet hurt?"

"Yeah. Almost daily."

"Give me your foot." He extends his hands in my direction.

Reluctantly—in my head at least—I scooch forward and set my foot in his hands. His thumbs move along the arch of my foot with precision and the perfect amount of pressure. So much so, my eyes roll back into my head involuntarily. Within a few minutes, my foot feels looser and more flexible.

"Damn, that feels fantastic! You're really good with your hands." *If I could reel back the second sentence....* It's true but inappropriate.

His eyes snap to mine, but he says nothing about the unintended innuendo. He releases my foot and gets to work on the other. Zack methodically massages my foot while the episode plays.

"Another?"

I glance at the clock. Sleep is overrated. "One more."

He stops rubbing my foot near the beginning of the second episode, but he doesn't move my foot out of his lap. Instead, he takes both and absently draws circles on the tops of my feet with his fingers. It's soothing.

As the credits roll, I carefully draw my feet in and twist to stand. Zack stands at the same time. I'm tall for a woman by most standards, but he makes me feel small. He stands north of six feet, and I need to tilt my head up to see his eyes. The room crackles with sexual tension. It's thick and heavy, palpable.

Gathering my wits, I manage, "Good night, Zack."

"Night, Scarlett."

CHAPTER FIVE

ZACHARY

She's tempting me, and she doesn't realize it. What am I going to do with her? I couldn't keep my hands to myself earlier. Nothing about her screams she needs protection, but the wariness she tries to hide spikes my radar. I'm not suggesting she's purposefully hiding anything. I have an overwhelming urge to protect her, and I don't know why. It makes no sense at all. She's unassuming, smart, loves the same shows I do, and she's sexy as sin. Absolutely nothing about her clothes was revealing. Yet I found myself cataloguing every curve of her statuesque frame.

I punch the pillow I brought down to the couch, hoping I can sleep instead of imagining Scarlett snug in my bed—alone.

Near five, I sneak upstairs into my bedroom. Scarlett is a goddess, but peacefully asleep with her hair awry on my pillow, she's more so. I tiptoe into my room because I forgot to grab a pair of socks last night.

"Morning," Scarlett mumbles.

"Morning. Sorry, I didn't mean to wake you. I forgot socks."

"You didn't. I pressed snooze. Your bed is cozy."

I grin at her. "It is and was worth every penny. I'll be in the gym in the basement for a bit. Help yourself to coffee and breakfast."

"Thanks."

I force myself to leave without taking a second longing look at her in my bed. I hustle downstairs, grab a water, and get my workout in. I only work through two sets, hoping to see Scarlett again before she leaves for work. Not the smartest move, but I'm drawn to her.

As I crest the stairs, I hear Scarlett talking to my mom.

"Do you know what day it is, Carol?"

"It's Wednesday. No, it's Friday."

"Good job. Let's get you some breakfast," Scarlett states and follows Mom into the kitchen. She's fully dressed in light pink scrubs that leave nothing to my imagination. The images of Scarlett traipsing through my sex-deprived mind don't require any assistance.

"Hi, son. You need a shower," Mom points out.

Scarlett giggles.

"Go, your wife can handle breakfast."

Wow, that's unexpected.

Scarlett's gaze catches mine.

"*I'm sorry,*" I mouth.

"*Don't be*," she mouths back. "Oatmeal work, Carol?"

"Don't forget the coffee, Scarlett," Carol adds.

"I would never." Feigned disgust drips from her words. Scarlett busies herself making Mom's breakfast while I grab a cup of coffee for myself.

"I'm sorry about her," I reiterate.

"It's no problem. However she needs to process my presence in your home is fine. You know as well as I do correcting her will likely cause an episode."

"Yeah, but I don't want you to be uncomfortable."

"Don't worry about me."

I can't seem to stop myself from worrying about you. Thinking about you. "I should get ready for work. I'll see you tonight."

"See you tonight," Scarlett replies.

I take the stairs two at a time and refuse to exhale until I get into my bedroom. My wife. That's a big leap. Although she does make me smile, which hasn't happened in quite some time. I shove those thoughts away and hurry through getting dressed.

I'm wholly disappointed when I retreat downstairs and find Scarlett already gone. Even though I knew she should be, I didn't want her to be. That in and of itself is telling.

"Hi, Gladys. Bye, Gladys. Bye, Mom."

Gladys laughs.

"Make sure you get flowers for your wife," Mom calls after me.

I respond without a second thought, "I'll see what I can do, Mom."

Gladys looks at me with a question in her eyes but doesn't voice it. "I'll be right back, Carol." Gladys follows me to the door.

"What is that about?"

I scrub my hand down my face. "I think she's confusing me and Scarlett with Nadine and Trevor. She called Scarlett my wife earlier."

"Oh. Okay. Have a good day."

"You too." During the drive to work, I attempt to push my thoughts and feelings about Scarlett out of my head. Even if I was successful, Greyson brings her back to the front of my mind as soon as I arrive.

"Dude, who was the smoke show leaving your townhouse early this morning?"

"Greyson, do you have any respect for others, especially women?" Not only is he disrespecting Scarlett but me as well.

"Of course." His tone sounds slightly offended.

Unfortunately, I need to address his question. "She's none of your business."

"She isn't yours?"

Honest question. I may want her to be mine. Not may. I want her to be mine.

Before I can answer, Greyson continues, "Can you give me her number?"

"Not without her permission and before I ask if she has a boyfriend."

"How was her relationships status not part of the interview? It should've been your first question."

"I would not disrespect her or any other person who came to an interview by asking that question. It's none of my business or yours. Have a good day." Irritated, I walk away and stand in line for roll call. Swimming in my thoughts, I don't hear anything until Cap addresses me.

"Smithson," he calls.

"Yes, Cap?"

"My office when we're done here."

"Roger." I know better than to get worried. I haven't done anything wrong. I've been making it to work on time since we spoke about my mom. I have no idea why he wants to talk to me today. After we're dismissed, I grab a fresh coffee and then make my way to Cap's office. Lightly, I tap on the door.

"Come in, Smithson."

"You wanted to see me, Cap?"

He motions for me to take a seat. "How is your mother?"

"She has her good days and her bad days. The last few have been good."

"Glad to hear it. On your last performance review, you indicated interest in the detective division. Are you still interested?"

"Yes, I am."

Cap reaches behind him and thrusts three huge books in my direction. "Between you and me, there will be a slot opening in the next six months or so. The exam is in five months. If you want the position, you need to study and pass the exam."

I'm floored. Promoting within the department has always been my preference. I want to build my life here. "Thanks, Cap. I won't let you down."

"I know. I'll start rotating you in with the division periodically in a few months."

"Thank you. I'll come back for those later with my bag." I point to the books.

"Understood."

I leave his office and make my way back to the break room to temper my reaction to Cap's offer. There's one person I want to call, but it makes no sense at all. I barely know Scarlett, yet she's the only person I want to share this news with. I quickly consider all the reasons it's a horrible idea and dismiss them.

Me: Any chance you can meet me for lunch?

I pocket my phone and get to work. The next few hours pass with no answer from Scarlett. I feel rejected, which isn't logical. I grab lunch at one of the vendors outside the precinct and promptly return to my desk.

The rest of the day sails by, and despite not getting an answer, I rush home. The only reason is she'll be there. As I pull into my garage, my phone vibrates with a text.

Scarlett: I'm sorry I missed your text. We can't have our phones during the day. I'll be there in a little while.

Relief rushes through me, and it makes me wonder if we should address the tension between us.

Me: See you soon.

When I step inside, my home is unusually silent. I peer into Mom's room and find her sound asleep. Evidently, she had a rough day.

"Hi, Gladys. How bad?" The wariness in her eyes makes my chest constrict.

"Pretty terrible. She was fine until she saw an ad on television for a bridal gown. She freaked because she couldn't remember the details of your wedding to Scarlett."

"Because there wasn't one," I reply.

"I know and you know, but she doesn't."

"I need to talk to Scarlett when she gets here, don't I?"

"Yes, I believe so. You two are going to have to keep up with the charade, unless you want to correct her."

I want to date her for starters. "I'm torn as to what the right choice is. Lying to her seems wrong, but if it keeps her episodes at bay or lessens them somehow…."

"I'm sorry, Zack. Her disease is progressing rapidly. She's staying more near stage five instead of waffling between four and five."

"It's not your fault. I don't want to impose on you or Scarlett. In this case, Scarlett more so than you."

"Take some unsolicited advice from an old widow. Tell Scarlett you like her. It's obvious, at least to me. If you choose to play this charade out for Carol's sake and not date, you both need clear boundaries."

"Thanks, Gladys. I'll talk to Scarlett tonight if I can."

"Good luck, Zack," Gladys offers as the front door swings open.

I greet her as she joins us. "Hey, Scarlett."

"Hi, Gladys. Hi, Zack," she replies, taking a seat at the table. "On a scale of one to ten, how drained is Carol?"

Scarlett is perceptive and exceptional at her job.

"A solid nine plus. She's been sleeping since about five," Gladys replies.

Scarlett frowns. "Poor Carol."

If you only knew.

"I'll leave you to it." Gladys leaves the kitchen.

I move behind the island and start searching for ingredients for dinner. "Did you eat?"

"No, can I help?"

"Sure."

She rounds the island as well and washes her hands.

The space feels smaller and warmer with her in arm's reach. "We can go with chicken and veggies in a cream sauce or pasta with spicy shrimp."

She turns to face me before replying, "Either works. I'm sorry about lunch. Was there something you wanted to discuss?"

Yes, I want you. I opt for the chicken dish. "Can you slice the veggies while I prep the chicken?"

Scarlett starts cutting beside me. I barely know her, but my heart and body yearn to know her marrow deep.

"I got some good news at work today. The moment I stepped out of Cap's office, I only wanted to share it with one person... you."

Her hands hover over the mixed root vegetables. She sets the knife down and turns in my direction. "It isn't just me?" Her words are almost inaudible.

I eliminate most of the space between us but refrain from touching her despite how much my body aches to feel her skin beneath mine. "Can you repeat that?"

Blue orbs of emotion that conceal nothing, at least to me, lift to mine. A myriad of emotions flutter through her irises unfiltered. "It isn't just me?" She restates loud enough for me to hear her this time.

"No, I feel it too." I slide my hands around her flawless face and lower my lips near hers.

A tiny gasp passes between us before she rises slightly on her toes to meet me. Her soft, supple lips feel heavenly against mine. After a few tentative kisses, I draw back.

Her eyelids open before she says, "Zack, kiss me again."

I slide one hand down her arm, bracket her waist, and draw her flush against me. Her curves melt into me with precision. Her lips warm mine before she opens for me. Our tongues twirl in an exquisite dance. It's as if I've been kissing Scarlett for years. She draws my lower lip between her teeth before pulling back slightly. We gaze at each other until our breathing slows to normal. My heart rate, however, is going to take more time.

When I finally grasp the gravity of the last five minutes, I manage, "I've wanted to do that since I first laid eyes on you."

The look on Scarlett's face is nothing short of dumbfounded. "Are you a good cop, Zack?" She pauses before clarifying. "I don't mean good as is not corrupt. I mean good as in capable of digging for information."

I laugh, knowing Cap recommended me for the detective exam. "I would like to think so, why?"

"You could've found me if you truly wanted to," she suggests.

"You're right. If you recall, I was mesmerized by you to the point I couldn't speak. Cap spoke for me. I wasn't looking for my potential someone then either."

Without a moment of hesitation, she asks, "Are you now?"

"Yes. Are you?" Given her age, she may not be yet.

Instead of a verbal response, Scarlett kisses me slowly and with an intensity I've never experienced before. The rest of my thoughts fall away until I need to get a grip on my self-control. My mind goes blank to every solitary thought other than how she feels in my arms. The knowledge she wants to date me as well makes pulling back harder.

With a bit of space between us, Scarlett gets back to work. "How much did Gladys sugarcoat Carol's day?"

I hang my head. "You're exceptional at your job, aren't you?"

"I love it, and I care about each of my patients as if they are family. Was it your dad or something else?"

"It was us."

A confused look graces her gorgeous face.

I finish seasoning the chicken and set it to cook while collecting my thoughts. I'll add the veggies in a bit. No reason for me to temper my words. She's either in with the charade or she isn't. "She spent much of the day frustrated and upset she couldn't remember the details of our wedding. She's confusing us with my sister and her husband. As you know, I use the term loosely for Trevor. To Mom, they're still together."

"How do you want to handle her misunderstanding?"

"As I said to Gladys, I don't want to make it worse or impose on either of you. However, given our mutual interest in one another, faking the depth of our relationship wouldn't be overly taxing. Right?"

"No, but we should get our story straight."

I chuckle. "Meaning what?"

A smile cracks on her face. "We should be on the same page about how long we dated before we got married, what our wedding looked like, etc."

"Makes sense." I add the veggies to the pan in the oven. "Water, iced tea, soda?"

"Water, please," she replies.

We take a seat on the couch to talk about the details of our fake marriage and courtship. Unlike the first night, she's right beside me with one leg bent between us. Her knee is against the back cushions, and she's facing me. It's the first time I allow myself to experience the subtlety of her perfume. Even after working all day, she smells like citrus and floral at the same time.

"How long did we date before we got married?" I ask to break the ice.

She taps her index finger on her lips. "I would say we dated for almost two years before we married. Does that work?"

"Reasonable, plus it closely mirrors my sister and Trevor's courtship as far as length before they got married. How did we meet?"

"I think our actual first meeting was perfect."

Me too.

She continues, "Only, in our fake relationship, you would need to speak to me."

"Very funny," I reply as the timer expires in the kitchen. We plate our food and continue to talk details of our fake wedding over dinner. Scarlett wants an elegant, small, beach wedding for only close family and friends. I agree with her. Hopefully it's enough details to pass with Mom. I don't want to overstep before we get to one of those points in our actual, new relationship.

"What was the good news you wanted to share? You could use some right about now," Scarlett asks.

She's spot-on there. "Last year, maybe the year before, I indicated to Cap I wanted to move into the detective division. He wants me to sit for the exam in a few months."

"Congrats! That's amazing!" She leans across the table and brushes a sweet kiss across my lips.

"Thanks." We head to the kitchen to clean the dishes. She washes, I dry, and then we take a seat on the couch.

"What is your schedule tomorrow?" I ask.

"I'm going to do laundry, study, and then work at the Perk. Why?"

"Can I take you to lunch?"

"I would like that."

"Me too."

I scroll through the queue and start the next episode of our show. Two episodes later, we peek in on Mom before we turn in for the night. Scarlett takes the couch, and I take the bed. Chances are we're going to have an incredibly early morning.

CHAPTER SIX

SCARLETT

Near four in the morning, Carol is calling for Zack. I step into her room and greet her. "Morning, Carol. How are you feeling?"

"Oh, Scarlett. You were such a lovely bride."

"Thank you." I turn toward Zack's footfalls.

Zack joins us, tugging on a shirt. *Focus on Carol!* The glimpse of his abs is nothing short of mouthwatering. Apparently, my *husband* sleeps without a shirt on. It makes me wonder if he slips beneath his ultra-soft sheets naked.

"Morning, Mom."

"Hi, Zack. How was your honeymoon?"

He moves beside the bed and slides his arm around me, his hand gripping my hip possessively. I like it... too much. "It was lovely. It rained a few days, but we made the best of it," Zack replies and winks at me.

I can feel my face heating at the insinuation of his answer—an insinuation I could get behind in real life sooner rather than later. Well, the trapped inside together part of it. "Ready to start your day?" I ask her.

"Sure. I'm hungry. Son, could you make us some of your special pancakes?"

"Absolutely. You good?" Zack asks me.

Special pancakes? "Yes, we've got this. Right, Carol?"

"Yes," Carol replies and throws back her covers.

Given her episode yesterday, she's still dressed in her clothes. While she sits on the edge of the bed, I locate a set of clothing for her and escort her to the powder room in the hallway. Carol can still handle most of her personal tasks. However, given the recent deterioration and progress through level five, her capabilities may change in the near future. The main concern right now is a fall. About ten minutes later, she emerges from the bathroom dressed, and she attempted to fix her hair.

"Want me to finish that?" I point to her hair.

"Yes, please. You're so sweet. Zack is lucky to have you."

I gently smooth her hair and reply, "Thank you."

We walk to the kitchen. Zack is busy flipping pancakes and scurrying around. I wait for Carol to be seated and join him.

"How can I help?"

"Can you make coffee, please?"

I busy myself preparing the coffee. When the first cup finishes brewing, I ask him, "How do you take this?"

Carol immediately responds, "A wife should know how her husband takes his coffee."

Crap! I guess Zack and I need a deeper crash course in basic information later today. Thankfully, he rescues me. After setting a pan in the sink, he slides his arms around me from behind and presses a kiss to the curve of my neck. The warmth of him surrounds me. Tingles run down my spine, and stifling a moan is harder than I anticipate. I fail miserably.

"Noted, beautiful. I take my coffee with cream and one sugar," he shares, kisses the same spot again, and moves away.

I pause before continuing to make sure to school my features before turning around, for our sake and for Carol's. I walk over to the table with the three cups in my hands.

Zack takes the cups one by one, sets them on the table, then pulls out my chair.

"Thank you."

A huge smile is on Carol's face. Zack serves me, then Carol, and finally himself.

I take a bite of the pancakes. *Ohmigod!* "Babe, these are amazing, as always." I've never had Zack's special pancakes before. I don't know the secret yet, but I'm going to find out. These are light, fluffy, and have a hint of something I can't place. They're downright delicious.

"Thanks."

Breakfast passes with no more mishaps by me. I escort Carol to the chair in the living room and turn on the morning news before heading back to the kitchen. Zack and I each drink a fresh cup of coffee while we wait for Gladys to arrive.

"I'm sorry, Zack. I wasn't thinking," I admit.

"Nothing to be sorry for. Pretending isn't the perfect solution but likely the most logical to prevent additional episodes by correcting her. Plus, I did learn a few more things I like about you already this morning."

"Such as?"

He eliminates most of the space between our bodies. "You love physical proximity, you like being called something other than Scarlett, and you take your coffee like I do. A well-placed kiss to the curve of your neck, which smells delicious, makes you shiver." I've never been a nickname person, but I'll allow it from him, only him.

"Zachary." My tone is meant as a warning. I note him shift when I use his full name.

"Yes, beautiful?"

I have nothing. He's absolutely right. "What time will you..." I peer around him to verify Carol hasn't moved, "be picking me up for lunch?"

"Can I come over as soon as I finish getting ready?"

"As long as you promise to let me get through the study guide at least once," I request.

"I'll do my best," he states. "In fact, I'll bring the books Cap gave me."

"Sounds good. We'll study together." I scoot out the front door after greeting and updating Gladys and saying goodbye to Carol. I can't wipe the smile from my face. Is it my smartest choice dating Zack, working with Carol, and pretending we're a married couple? Perhaps not, but I'm in to date him. The tiny glimpse of his abs earlier makes me want to strip him down and explore every inch of him… with my tongue.

I park in my spot and let myself into my condo. It's eerily quiet. Lia doesn't appear to be home. I look outside the window and realize her car isn't here either.

Me: Everything good?

I make my way to my room, shuck my clothes, and gather my laundry. My phone chimes with a response.

Lia: Yeah, why?

Me: You aren't home.

Lia: Remember my classmate I like? We fell asleep watching a movie after the group study session.

Me: Okay, just checking on you.

I don't pry into Lia's love life, and she doesn't pry into mine. I start the washer and search for clean clothes. When I finish tugging on my leggings and a tee, there's a strong knock on my door. I check through the peephole, and Zack's hazel eyes stare back at me. I whip open the door. "That was fast."

"Do you want me to leave and come back later?"

I laugh. "No, not at all. Come in."

He steps inside and sets his heavy bag on the floor beside the ottoman. He tugs me against him and kisses me softly. When he releases me, he looks around before commenting, "Cute place."

"Thanks. Lia is more the decorator than me."

"Lia?"

I scrunch up my face. "Lia Cappelli is my roommate. She's not here right now." I moved into this condo overlooking Short Sands Beach when I first arrived. During the spring and summer months, it's busy, but in the offseason, it's peaceful and serene. Lia moved in a few weeks after we met on the first day of classes. It's the only reason I have the master with access to the private balcony.

"Good, now I don't have to worry about checking the security here," Zack admits.

"Meaning?"

"I'm absolutely confident Luca not only checked the building but the windows, doors, and added a security lock."

"That's disturbingly accurate in every detail. He's with the state police. You know him?"

"Yeah, he was YPD until a little more than a year ago."

"I probably could've figured that out myself. Do you want coffee or water?"

"Water please."

We settle on the couch with books strewn all around us. About thirty minutes later, the washer buzzes.

"I'll be right back." I stand, switch the clothes into the dryer, and start a load of scrubs. When I return to the living room, I take a seat on the floor beside the ottoman. After scanning the pages, I find where I left off. This exam is for the nurse management class. It's boring. The material will be useful later on in my career, not so much now.

"I feel you staring." I steal a glance in his direction.

He rapidly shifts his eyes back to his book, attempting to cover. He looks back almost instantly. "I am. You're amazing and stunning."

I rise, steal a light kiss, and take a seat beside him on the couch. Immediately, he hauls me into his lap. "Thanks. You're not so bad yourself, and your hands might be magical."

"Oh really?" He skims his free hand from my knee along my outer thigh upward until he's cupping my face.

It takes every ounce of resolve not to succumb to the sparks of heat chasing his fingers. My imagination spins, picturing Zack shirtless and hovering over me. As expected, his eight-pack is droolworthy. I clamp my eyes closed. The heat pooling between my thighs is significant given we're fully clothed and I barely know him. Although, his reaction to me is impossible to miss.

"Scarlett." His voice is velvety smooth. "Where did your thoughts go?"

I exhale slowly. "Too far from appropriate for how long I've known you."

"You should tell me and let me have a vote," he says with a sexy, panty-melting grin.

I smirk before leaning forward to kiss him. Instead of sharing my lusty daydream, I act part of it out. I dip my fingers beneath the hem of his shirt and find hard ridges and valleys. At least my glimpse and active imagination are accurate. Zack tightens his arm around my waist and lowers me to the couch before moving over me. I snake my hands between us and cup his jaw. I'm a mere inch away from kissing him again when the front door swings open.

"Scar, I'm…."

Zack rocks back onto his heels and pulls me to sitting. The lack of his warmth around me is startling. He was spot-on about my physical proximity preference. I didn't realize it myself before he mentioned it.

"Hi, Lia."

"Hi, Scar. Smithson." Realization crosses my roommate's face. She lifts her eyebrow, and I reply with a tight chin drop.

"Would you two like me to leave the room so you can talk about me?" Zack asks.

We laugh.

"Nah, we're good," Lia replies. "I need to get going. My shift at the brewery starts in an hour. Will you be home tonight, Scar?"

"Yeah, I'll be here after my shift at the Perk."

"Cool. We'll talk more then."

"'Kay," I reply.

Once she leaves the room, Zack brushes a kiss across my lips. "Did you get through the study guide at least once?"

I laugh. "Not quite. Ready to get some lunch?"

"We can stay here if you want to finish. I make a mean grilled cheese," he suggests.

"I probably should, but what about you?"

"It's fine. I can study tonight. I was wondering how you pull it all off."

My mouth curls up into a half smile. "I'm over-the-top organized. There's no other way for me to make sure everything gets done. The final semester is a bit easier with student nursing and less classes."

"Get back to work. I'll handle lunch."

"On it," I reply and curl up in the corner of the couch. My phone chimes with a text, but I ignore it. Nearly thirty minutes later, Zack is finished making lunch.

I take a seat beside him and marvel at the food on our plates. "This is a grilled cheese?"

"Grilled cheese with ham, and tomato soup."

"We had tomato soup?"

Lia rejoins us in the kitchen. "Yes, it's a must have in your pantry."

"Exactly, what she said," Zack states.

"I'm out, Scar. I'll see you later tonight. Bye, Smithson."

"Bye, Lia," I reply.

"Later, Lia," Zack adds before taking a bite of his sandwich.

I follow suit. It's melt-in-your-mouth delish. "Zack, this is yummy!"

"Thanks. Eat so you can finish studying before work," he demands.

"Okay. Pushy."

He laughs and continues eating. "What time do you need to be at work?"

"I need to be there at three." I take the last spoonful of soup, gather my dishes, and prepare to wash them. Before I can get my hands wet, Zack places a decadent row of kisses along the back of my neck, his fingers bruising my hips possessively. "Your sexy kisses aren't going to get me back to my study guide quicker," I murmur.

"Yeah, I didn't think it through. I wanted to distract you from the dishes. Go study. I've got this."

I turn, press a kiss to his cheek, and walk away before I don't finish before work. A little while later, Zack silently takes a seat on the side chair and skims the exam requirements for his test. I clean up and stow my books when the timer expires for the dryer. I fold the load and switch my scrubs to the dryer before exchanging my tee for a Perk shirt and pulling on sneakers.

"All set?" he asks.

"Unfortunately, yes."

"I'll walk you out. Please call me when you get home tonight." He grabs his bag and follows me out the door.

"I will. Please try to study yourself."

"I will. I wouldn't dare watch our show without you snuggled against me." Zack opens my door and leans in to kiss me before backing away.

"I'll talk to you later."

He closes my door, and I back out of my spot. The ride to the Perk isn't long. I park and scan my messages.

Savi: Hey. Give me a call when you can.

Me: I'm closing the Perk. I'll call later tonight.

Savi: Maybe we'll stop by.

Me: Okay.

I step out of my car and join the new hire behind the counter. "Hi, Mike. How are things?" Mike is a high school junior looking for some extra cash to pay for prom.

"Hi, Scarlett. Good, you?"

Amazing! "I'm good. Thanks for asking." As much as Becca hates me for thinking it, weekend nights are generally slow. Usually only one person works those hours, but Mike is new, so there are two of us tonight. We have a few customers, which I handle while Mike cleans the tables and restocks the sugar and creamer.

Near six, Savi and Emme step through the front door. "Auntie Let, it's been so long since I see you. Ben won't know you if it isn't soon."

She's calling me out hard. "I'm sorry, Emme. With school, studying, and working, I barely have enough time to sleep. Bennett will know me. I promise. Can I get you something, Savi?"

"Yeah, I'll take a chai latte and a scone. The reason I messaged you earlier was the gala. Are you attending this year? It's the second weekend in September."

An image of Zack in a tux flashes through my mind. Of course it's fictional, but my brain is creative. I would love to spend hours in his arms on the dance floor.

"Earth to Scarlett." Savi pulls me out of my thoughts. "Who is he and do I know him?"

"Yes, I want to go, but I would like to ask someone to be my plus-one first."

Impatiently, Savi asks, "Again, who is he?"

I consider how much to share. "Do you remember the guy who spilled coffee on me the first day I was in York Beach?"

"The cop, right?"

"Yup, him. Although it's very new."

"That's sweet. I need to know in two weeks if you want to attend. Then we can talk to Kelly about a dress," Savi adds.

"Auntie Let," Emme interrupts.

"Yeah, Emme?"

"I want to go to the dance too," she asserts, crossing her arms over her chest. I feel for Savi and Sam when she's a teenager.

"I think you're too young. I'm sure Mommy will find someone great for you to stay with."

Emme shrugs and asks, "Can I have a cookie?"

I glance at Savi, who gives the okay. "Sure, which one?"

"The biggest chocolate chip one. Kelsey's cookies are the best!" Emme adds.

"I'll talk to Zack about the gala and get back to you."

"Sounds good."

"Can I have a hug, munchkin?"

Emme launches herself into my arms before she and Savi leave.

"Is she your mom?" Mike asks.

A moment of sadness passes through me. I never knew my mother, but the stories Savi shared are ingrained in my heart. "No, she's my older sister." I have no intention of sharing my life story with Mike. I've barely shared enough with Zack. I smile inwardly at the thought of him. I check my messages and note Lia is hanging out with her niece, Ellie, tonight and won't be home. It's "hanging out" when your niece is a teenager and only needs a babysitter because she isn't old enough to be home alone overnight.

The rest of my evening at the Perk passes uneventfully. When I get home, I park in my spot and make my way upstairs. I find a note addressed to me and a single rose on our doormat.

> *Me: I'm home. Thank you for the rose. I'll call you after a shower.*

> *Zack: You're welcome. Talk soon.*

I turn on the dryer to unwrinkle my scrubs before I take a shower to rinse off the smell of the bakery. It's less offensive than hospital antiseptic, but a shower is a must. I pull out my scrubs and hang them immediately before slipping into a pair of shorts and a tee and climbing into my bed. Once I'm settled, I dial Zack.

He answers instantly with a video call. "Hi, beautiful."

"Hi. Did you get any studying done?" No one has ever called me anything but my name. I kind of love it.

"Yeah, some. I think Cap gave me more than I need to study for the exam. Two of the books are procedure, most of which I already know from the academy. I only need to refresh those sections and learn the detective portions of the procedure."

"Makes sense. Savi stopped by tonight to remind me about the gala. Will you be my date? Before you answer, it's black-tie and in New York City."

"Why would any of those details make me hesitate?"

I shrug.

"I want to take you on numerous proper dates before then. However—"

"Our schedules are nuts."

"Exactly," he replies.

"A date doesn't necessarily require leaving the house. We can hang out and watch a movie or finish our series instead. I don't need to be wined and dined."

"Maybe not, but you deserve it." Zack's reply is sincere and unwavering.

"I'm a realist. We can fit in lunches here and there though, right?"

"Consider me penciled in whenever we're both available."

We can make an "us" work if we try. "Same for me."

"Will you share some normal first-date stuff with me?"

I wrinkle my nose in response.

"That's cute."

"Like what? My favorite color?"

"Sure, start there. Mine is blue."

"Yellow. Tell me something about you no one else knows."

He pauses a few moments. "Only Nadine knows this about me. I paint in my free time."

"What do you paint?" I ask.

"Mostly landscapes. I visit one spot and paint it for each season. I've drawn a few people, but not painted."

"The four paintings along the staircase are yours?"

A proud smile materializes on his face. "Yes, they are."

"Zack, those are gorgeous."

"Thank you. What about you?"

"I suppose only Savi knows this about me. I didn't celebrate any of the traditional holidays growing up. I've never had a birthday party or gone all out for Christmas."

"I understand your birthday, but why the others?"

"After I was born, the holidays were a day where our father was off work or home early. Resulting in a lazy, mean drunk sooner in the day. Savi was extremely careful when she spent money. She never knew when our father would go on a bender and not show up for work or get fired. As I got older, she tried to get me to celebrate holidays, but I refuse to go all out."

"I'm sorry, Scarlett. I didn't mean for this to turn sad."

"No way for you to know. The Morgans go over the top for Christmas. Sam took Savi to Paris to propose for her first gift. I may never make progress with my birthday, but I've been coming around slowly for the other holidays."

"Can you make a deal with me?"

"You can ask."

"I want a day to celebrate you but not on your birthday. You deserve a day. Hell, you deserve more than a day. Can we pick one?"

The depth of my feelings for him so soon make no sense. I suppose what they say about two souls meeting at the perfect time is true and he's mine. "What do you suggest?"

"November 24th."

Oh, Zachary. "The day we met. It's perfect."

"Thank you for sharing."

"You're welcome. Thank you for listening and not trying to push about my birthday too much."

"I never will. Other holidays I may nudge though. Arbor Day and Earth Day are two of my faves."

I laugh softly. "We should get some sleep. I'll see you tomorrow night. Good night, Zack."

"Sweet dreams, Scarlett."

CHAPTER SEVEN

ZACHARY

I hustle out the front door after little sleep. I make a quick stop for my standing order from the Perk before arriving at the precinct. This cup isn't going to be enough for the morning. I probably need an IV. Mom's episode last night wasn't long, but falling asleep afterward for me was taxing. Her brain is failing, and I understand she's confused. Each time she thinks I'm my father dredges pain up for me as well. It isn't intentional, but it hurts, nonetheless.

I check the assignments and note I'm on patrol with Davis today.

"Ready, man?" Davis asks as we head to the motor pool. He's about my height and equally, if not more, fit than I am. When Davis isn't with Tabi, he's at the gym.

"Yup, all set. You driving?"

The surprise on his face turns to glee as he takes the driver's seat. "Yes, I'm driving, Miss Daisy."

"Ha, ha, ha."

Davis pulls into traffic and starts our patrol for the day. "You good, man?"

"Yeah, didn't sleep well."

"What's her name?"

I shake my head. "It isn't a woman I'm dating." I almost said *the* woman I'm dating. "My mom is ill, and she moved in with me recently. She became disoriented last night, and I didn't sleep well afterward."

"Sorry, man. That's rough."

"It is. How's Tabi?" I ask to shift the focus away from me. Davis and Tabi have been friends with benefits for well over a year at this point.

"She's good. Slaying her goals at her new job."

"Good for her. Any plans to make it more of a dating thing?"

Davis gives me a sideways look. "Nah. What we have works for both of us. I have no intention of changing anything."

"Not a fan of commitment?"

"I'm not afraid of it. I don't want one at this point in my life. What about you?"

An image of Scarlett floats through my mind. "I started dating someone with potential recently. That's all you're getting out of me right now." *Forever potential, but I'm not sharing with Davis.*

"Fair enough."

I appreciate Davis not pushing for details. He's solid people. We take a call for an altercation near the playground between two moms. Calls like these make me wonder if the women are simply craving attention. According to dispatch, it's the third one in the last two weeks. After defusing the situation, we grab some lunch and escort a few VIPs to York Memorial. The closer to the end of shift I get, the giddier I become. There's only one reason— Scarlett.

When I arrive home, I shrug my jacket off and hang it at my door. "Hi, Mom. Hi, Gladys." They're sitting in the living room.

"How was your day, Saul?"

Schooling my reaction is getting increasingly difficult as the days wear on. "How was your day?" I opt not to add "Mom" again to avoid setting her off.

"It was okay. We watched the news and listened to music," she supplies.

"Good. I'm going to change. Gladys, a word first?" We step into the kitchen out of earshot. "How was she today?"

Gladys replies, "Overall, she had a good day. A few lapses over the entire day, but no prolonged issues."

"Happy to hear it. Has she eaten dinner?"

"Yes, she's set for dinner."

"I'll be right down." I hustle upstairs. As I pass my paintings, I beam with pride. I'm glad I told Scarlett. I've never shared that private part of myself with anyone I've dated before. It's telling she's the only woman I've ever let in so deeply. I refuse to allow the rapid pace to impact how I feel about her.

When I return downstairs, Scarlett is talking to my mom in the living room.

"Gladys mentioned you listened to some music today. What was your favorite song?"

"The Beach Boys song about the car." Mom starts humming. She's fairly on point. I join them in the living room.

"Hey, Scarlett. How are you?"

"I'm—"

Mom admonishes me without a second thought. "Your father and I taught you better than that. You kiss your wife hello."

Today I've been my dad and myself. Today we're married, tomorrow who knows. At least Scarlett's aware and willing to play along. I draw her against me and kiss her lightly on the lips. Then I whisper near her ear, "Hi, beautiful."

Goose bumps skate along her skin. "Hi." She pulls back. The look on her face screams our kiss wasn't enough. I agree with her, but it won't be more, especially with an audience. Our chemistry isn't fake. It's off the charts, and the heat is combustible. Tempering it is difficult. However, we're still in the shallow end, for now at least, but I'm looking forward to spending every evening with Scarlett, learning more about this amazing woman. Everything about her.

"Now you can ask about her day," Mom interjects.

My gaze remains focused on Scarlett. Shaking away the lust, I ask again, "How was your day?"

She looks between me and Mom, her hand still in mine. "Fun actually. I was on the pediatric floor today, and we had some special visitors. The kids were thrilled."

"How wonderful!" Mom adds. "Can you share who?"

"Unfortunately not. There was purposely no press for the event. Each year a group of local athletes come and hang out with the kids. They bring gear and spend time having fun with the patients. One patient has been present for the last three years. She was ecstatic to see her favorite player again."

I'm in awe of her. She's loyal and resolute. Scarlett is answering my mother but not compromising her promise to the players. I don't have to ask. I knew about the visit and escorted Marco Cappelli and a few of his teammates in a circuitous route to the hospital. Marco is a local guy who is an international superstar soccer player now. He lives in town but keeps a low profile. He's related to Luca somehow, if I recall correctly. Marco isn't the only celebrity who lives in town. Overall, the locals leave them alone. During the summer months, they stay away from tourist spots, though some of them live near the Nubble Lighthouse.

I was able to see Scarlett in her element today. If working with memory patients isn't her specialty of choice, working with kids would fit seamlessly. *Does she want a family?* During the visit was the first time I witnessed a man ogling and flirting with her. No, more than one man—rich, successful men—plural. Streaks of jealously coursed through me faster and stronger than ever before. I don't blame them. Scarlett is stunning on the outside. Yet it's the inside that draws me to her. She's kind, generous, and cares about others more than herself. It took resolve not to tuck her against me and claim her as mine. I didn't merely to keep our budding relationship private for now. However, my need to possess her publicly grows the more I learn about her.

Mom frowns but accepts Scarlett's nonanswer. "Has your husband told you about his athletic skills?"

Fear runs through me. We haven't discussed my days in youth sports at all. Hell, we haven't discussed our childhoods in any depth at all outside Savannah raising Scarlett.

"Not in any detail. Why don't you tell me while he cooks dinner and we get you settled for the night?" Scarlett kisses me high on my cheek and whispers, "Relax. We can handle this."

I hurriedly provide basic information to Scarlett. Only she can hear me. "I played soccer when I was young, then football and basketball through high school. I ran track in the spring to stay in shape."

Her eyes snap closed for a brief moment.

I wonder what thought flooded her mind. The ideas in mine are not appropriate for our current company. I want to explore her and learn ways to make her moan with pleasure, starting with my hands and mouth.

She opens her eyes and asks, "Were you any good?"

I bring my lips near the shell of her ear. "I'll let you be the judge after you hear what she has to say." I draw back and kiss her lightly before walking away. Once I reach the kitchen, I exhale slowly. Their conversation could go south quickly. I'm skeptical my mom can recall all the details of my high school football days. Hopefully I gave Scarlett enough information to fill in the gaps. Football was my sport of choice. The team was good for three of my four years during high school. We made it to the state tournament all three years and won it twice. Basketball and track were mostly for fun. I found I had an aptitude for running and placed in the state meets for four years.

After a brief trip down memory lane, I manage to prepare cheeseburgers and sweet potato fries for dinner. I set the food on the table and rejoin the ladies in Mom's room. "Scarlett, dinner is ready."

"Thanks. I'll be right there." She turns back to my mom and says, "I appreciate your insight."

"You're welcome, dear. Go eat. I'll be fine here," Mom replies.

I wait for Scarlett near the table and pull out her chair.

"Thank you."

"We should probably talk about our younger selves some more."

She agrees while inhaling a few fries. "I think Carol covered most of it—star offensive lineman, all state, all New England. I gather you were popular in high school." We make progress with our food while we talk.

I can't help but smirk. "I was. You must've been too."

She wrinkles her nose. "Not even a little bit. I only played tennis in high school, despite wishing I could be a cheerleader as well. Savi couldn't pull off the schedule with hers."

I cover her hand with mine. My childhood was out of a Norman Rockwell painting. Hers, not so much. Hearing the details makes my heart ache for her and her sister.

She looks from my hand to my face a few times before continuing. "Savi did the best she could. I didn't realize how much she gave up until she decided to move here."

I lift her hand to my lips and kiss the back. "You gave up things too."

"I suppose, but not as much as my sister."

"Maybe. Where is your dad now?"

Scarlett drops her head slightly. I lift her chin with our hands. "You don't have to share."

"It seems soon in our dating relationship, but you are my husband after all." She winks at me. "His choices molded Savi and me. When we moved here, he was in rehab for his alcohol abuse in New Jersey. He got out and, within eight months, fell off the wagon again. The last time I spoke with him, he was switching to an outpatient program so he could find a job."

"When was that?" I slide my chair closer and cup her face in one of my hands.

"About six months ago." She turns her face and presses a kiss to my palm, a silent thank you for listening.

The pain marring her face has me wrapping her up in my arms. "Scarlett."

"Yeah?" she mumbles against my chest, her hands snaking beneath my shirt. The warmth of her hands on my skin makes me pause.

"There isn't anything you could share that will make me run away from you."

The tension in her body decreases with each passing breath. She adds space between us. The angst is gone. Only unfiltered desire remains. Pouring out part of her tortured past doesn't decrease her need for us. I lower my mouth to hers and kiss her softly. In the sliver of space that forms when I pull back, she wets my lips with her tongue. *Holy hell!* I lift her off the chair and set her on the island. Scarlett hooks her ankles around my back. The heat of her core teases me. Her soft fingers glide up my back before she skims her fingernails down. Gripping the hem of my shirt, she tugs it overhead.

Her eyes widen, and she's speechless.

"What, gorgeous?"

"My imagination is an epic failure."

I feel my cheeks warm at the compliment. "What were you basing it on?"

She shakes her head slowly. "It doesn't matter. You're... damn fine!"

I grin at her and lift her scrub top over her head. Now it's my turn to verify the fictional images seared into my brain. "My imagination, however, is finely honed," I assure her. "Your perfection is patently unfair to other women."

Her fingernails cut into my skin at my words.

Scarlett may be taller than most women, but she possesses a perfect hourglass figure. Large breasts spill out of pink lace cups with a silk bow between them. Her olive skin is flawless. As I travel from the point of her lips down to the lace edge of her bra, I slip one strap down her arm and peel the lace forward. She lowers back onto one elbow as I suck her taut, rosy nipple into my mouth. Soft murmurs of pleasure fall from her pouty lips.

"Zack."

Moans of a different kind filter into my brain.

"Zack," Scarlett calls again.

"No! It can't be true!" Mom shouts from her room.

With speed I don't possess at this moment, Scarlett fixes her bra, tugs her shirt overhead, and is down the hall. Gripping the edge of the island, I attempt to sort through how I feel. Kissing a woman never felt like it does with Scarlett. It didn't with Kate, and we were together for five years. I grasp my shirt and tug it on before clearing the table. I briefly consider joining Scarlett, but I don't want to interfere. Call it a shortcoming or at least a perceived one, I'll leave handling my mother's care to the professionals.

Once I finish the dishes, I grab a water and take a seat on the couch. Scarlett finds me soon thereafter.

"Everything okay?"

"Yeah, she had some bad memories resurface about a football injury from our discussion earlier. Did you get hurt and miss part of your sophomore year?"

My face drops, and my stomach bottoms out, the urge to hurl bubbling up. "How does she remember my injury from more than a decade ago but can't remember my father is gone?"

Scarlett throws her arms around my neck, her fingers threading into my hair. Without a second thought, I guide her into my lap and hold her against me. Until her, I never had anyone who understood the conflicting feelings I have about my mother's condition. I never spoke to anyone either. The woman who raised me isn't there anymore, but she certainly looks the same.

"Will you tell me about her?"

She means my mom before her diagnosis. No one has ever cared enough to ask me about her before. Only about how hard it is to deal with today. Not true. I don't give anyone the opportunity to ask. "She was nothing short of amazing." My entire body tenses, and guilt seizes my throat. She's still alive. She shouldn't be spoken about in past tense. Yet… it is past tense.

Scarlett presses a kiss to my temple and murmurs, "Was is okay. Your mom, the person you're sharing about, isn't in the other room anymore."

In the brief time I've known her, Scarlett inexplicably has the right words to put my feelings about Mom's condition into perspective. All I can do is nod.

"Take your time. I'm here as long as you want."

Forever. I want forever. Logical, no, but her heart speaks to mine. I can't explain it. I take a few solid minutes to compose my thoughts. "She was the police chief's secretary from soon after I was born until she retired."

"Is her career the reason you're a cop?"

"No, but that's a story for a different time."

She meets my gaze, and I continue, "Despite working full time, she was the poster mom for everything—football booster, team dinners, basketball concession stand, trucking me to and from tournaments for basketball. She was present for each of my games—home and away. Our house was the place my teammates and friends knew they could get a hot meal and a parental ear with no judgment. Despite numerous offers, I opted against playing football in college. I studied criminology and psychology; then I attended the academy."

"You went away to college?"

"Yeah, I went to Northeastern. Boston is an amazing city."

"It is. So much history. What about Nadine?"

"She wasn't an athlete. Nadine has a creative mind. She was in the drama club and performed in every school production. Mom was there for her too. The hours Nadine put in before a production were equally as much but didn't allow for spectators. We never missed any of her performances."

Scarlett settles deeper into me, her lips grazing my neck. Little did I know her breath on my skin would spark a fire in my chest.

"You're creative like Nadine too."

Her words hit me square in the chest. No other woman has ever been able to make that statement. *Because you never shared yourself fully with any other woman.* I inwardly observe. "True, but my paintings are for me and no one else."

She lifts her head and gazes at me before saying, "You shared them with me."

"Before you, I never felt compelled to share all of me. Everything about you—about us—makes me feel and see things differently."

"Our connection is bone-deep and difficult to explain. Us, the dating us, not the fake married us. Although, being fake married did spark some honest conversation."

"Some, but not enough."

She shifts to face me squarely. "What do you want to know?"

"Everything. I want to know the precise location of each crack in your soul so I can protect it."

"That's going to take time—a lifetime even."

"It might. Considering you're already my wife, I think we'll have enough."

"We just might," she replies.

I shift with her in my arms into the corner of the couch. The silence falling around us isn't uncomfortable. It's filled with the promise of more. More of what a solid relationship is made of: trust, honesty, intimacy, and love.

CHAPTER EIGHT

SCARLETT

With classes, working at the hospital, and caring for Carol, the last few days have passed in a whirlwind. I hurry out the door to class later than normal. Luckily, Zack's townhouse is closer to school than my condo. I plop down in my seat and scan my texts.

Lia: Hey girl! Checking in. I miss you.

Me: Hey! Miss you too. I'm good.

Lia: Free for lunch?

Me: Sorry, having lunch with Zack. You can pop by.

Lia: Zack, huh?

Me: Yeah. I decided you were right.

Lia: Of course I was. See you Saturday

Me: See you then.

Choosing to date Zack came from more than Lia's astute observation, but either way, she was right. He has an innate quality that settles me. The contentment and warmth I feel with him, from him, is unique to him. From our recent talks, I've discovered he hasn't truly shared his emotions about his mom with anyone until he opened his heart to me. The significance of him choosing to divulge his innermost thoughts and feelings to me is equally as telling as me sharing with him. No one knows about my childhood or my mother, outside Savi and Lia. No one has ever asked.

I note the time and the tardiness of my professor.

Savi: Hey. How is the new job?

Me: Hey. It's a good fit.

The pain Zack is going through given Carol's diagnosis is difficult to watch. I've seen many family members go through it when I spent my rotation at the memory facility. My visceral reaction only happens for him. It strikes me hard—I care about him deeply already.

Savi: And the guy?

Me: He's great and will be coming to the gala with me.

Savi: Perfect! Let's set up a time to design gowns with Kelly soon.

Me: Sounds good. Love you.

Savi: Love you too.

I skip over to my emails and begin sifting through and swiping away the spam. There's one with my shift schedule for the hospital from Willa. I glance at it and note I have a day off next week. *Sweet!* Given the fifteen-minute rule for a teaching assistant has passed and we're nearing the thirty minutes for a professor, I pack up my things and head out the back of the lecture hall.

Me: Are you opposed to meeting somewhere other than campus?

Zack: No, what do you have in mind?

Me: My place? I'll grab sandwiches and meet you there.

Zack: That works.

Me: Any requests?

Zack: Surprise me.

I smile and make my way to the deli near home. I should know what my *husband* would want on his sandwich, but I'm guessing here. Armed with two subs, chips, and two different drinks, I park across from my condo beside Zack's car.

He's leaning against the door scanning his phone. "Hey, gorgeous," Zack greets me when he opens my door. On his day off, he looks hot. Disgustingly hot. He's wearing a dress shirt and dark jeans under a light jacket.

"Hi." I take his outstretched hand and slide to the rear door.

He draws me into his body and kisses me with consuming desire. Can't blame him, I feel it too. I'm trapped between Zack's hard body and my car, savoring his lips and mouth.

I fist his shirt and tug his lower lip between my teeth. "We should go inside," I manage.

He raises an eyebrow and retrieves our lunch and my school bag from the back seat. Once we're inside, he sets the bags on the island, and we hang our coats.

He pulls me flush against him and kisses me breathless. Each time our lips meet, I'm nothing more than a heroine in an old movie when the hero finally makes his move as the curtains close. "Are we alone?"

I twist in his arms to check the key bowl by the door and the coatrack. "Yes, I believe so."

"Which way to your room?"

"Not hungry?"

"You, now. Sandwiches, later."

I laugh. "There." I point over to the right, past the kitchen.

Zack wraps my thighs around his waist, his grip on my hips possessive and hard enough to leave no question how much he wants me, and walks around the island. While he moves, I work my way down his shirt opening an inch at a time. I hook my finger around the neckline of his undershirt and tug downward, so I can drag my tongue down his neck and mark his chest with kisses. His crisp, clean scent surrounds me.

After he sits on the edge of my bed, I grasp the sleeve of his shirt and unclasp the buttons. Hurriedly, I push the shirt down his arms and lift his tee overhead.

"Better?"

"Much. It's a sin to hide all of this from me."

"Is it now?"

"Uh-huh." I lean in and continue marking his skin as low as I can reach.

When I run out of space, he curls his arm around me and twists so he's hovering over me on the bed. "My turn, gorgeous." Without hesitation, he lifts my thin sweater overhead and casts it to the floor.

The warmth of his mouth on my skin as he travels south has me clenching my thighs together. Fortunately and unfortunately, the movement doesn't go unnoticed.

"Right here?" He presses another open-mouthed kiss to the crook of my neck. "Or here?" He draws his tongue down the sweet-smelling valley between my breasts again.

"Both," I rasp out. No one has ever asked me my preferences before. We're still mostly clothed, and I'm soaked with need. When I open my eyes, I note a puzzled look on his face. "What?"

He skims his finger along the lacy edge of my bralette. Prickles of awareness rise on my skin. "This is sexy as hell, but how does it come off?"

My lingerie choice for today is a navy lace bralette and matching bikini-cut panties. Giggling, I set my hand on his hard chest and push us to sitting. "Allow me." I cross my arms in front of me and bare my breasts to him. His magical hands mold to my mounds as he nips my taut, rosy peaks in turn.

I arch into him, silently begging for more. He obliges as I work the buckle of his jeans. Zack freezes the moment I slip my hand around his thick length.

Between pants, I ask, "Did I miss something?" A blinding red stop sign for instance.

He releases me from his mouth as his flecked hazel eyes meet mine. "No, you didn't."

The ability to read his thoughts would be helpful in this moment. Before I can overthink my actions more, I stroke him twice. His eyes snap closed, and he pushes out a harsh breath. I'm going to need more information… later. Instead of more words, he continues his quest to overwhelm me with spikes of need. Each caress of his tongue sliding down my body causes me to lose my grip on him.

I frown from the loss of him as I assist in wiggling out of my leggings, and he pushes his jeans to the floor. Zack continues upward from the tops of my feet to the point of my hip. Each lingering touch forces my spiraling need tighter in my belly. Gripping the sides of my panties at my hip, he tugs down toward my feet. After removing them, he hovers over me, skims his lips to mine and his fingers to my core. As he slips his finger between my folds, the friction only adds to the coil of pleasure compressing in my center.

"How long has it been since someone touched you?"

Given the pool between my thighs, his question makes sense. I consider offering an in-depth answer but opt for a simple one instead. "A man… over a year. Me… a few days." My response earns me a lifted eyebrow. "Have you looked in the mirror lately?"

A low growl emanates from Zack as he plunges two fingers into my heated center while sidling closer to me. He sets delicate kisses along my jaw before taking my mouth in earnest. My inner muscles contract around him. Waves of decadent pleasure course through me. When he adds a third digit and curls all of them, my body shudders and quakes in exquisite ecstasy. Self-induced orgasms never feel this good. A stark realization hits me as the pulses between my thighs diminish slowly. "I don't have any condoms," I admit, feeling defeated.

"Neither do I." His forehead meets mine.

"We should get some."

"We should and soon," he replies.

I reach between us and surround him in my hand, stroking him in time with his steady swirls on my swollen nub. The pressure builds within us separately, and we explode at once.

As our breathing slows, he asks, "Do you have a towel?"

"I'll get you one." Soon after, I return with a warm wet cloth.

"Thanks." He cleans up and moves to the edge of my bed. "What's on your mind, beautiful?"

"Why did you freeze?"

"Not used to you—to us—yet."

"Meaning?"

"I would prefer not to compare you to my ex, especially right now. You make me feel untethered, but in a good way. Does that make sense?"

"It does. You do the same for me. When I'm with you, I feel free of the restraints life has put on me, as if I could make a life for myself with my childhood baggage tucked in the attic."

"You can."

I cup his jaw and kiss him tenderly. With a quick glance at the clock, I hustle around my room and gather my Perk uniform for the final time.

"When do you need to leave?" he asks, tugging on his jeans.

I'm distracted by the slab of carved granite before me, despite my current time crunch and recent exploration of the same.

"Stop staring like that or you won't be on time for your last shift."

I tug my lower lip between my teeth. "What was your question? Oh… I need to leave here in thirty to be on time." I tug on my clothes, replacing my sweater with my Perk shirt.

"Go eat. I'll be right out," he instructs.

I steal a kiss to hopefully quelch my desire to climb him like a tree and slide back between my sheets, then hurry to the kitchen. "Do you want the turkey or Italian combo?" I ask aloud.

"Either is fine for me. I would prefer the salt and vinegar chips though. I saw them through the bag."

I'm about halfway done with my sandwich when Zack slides in beside me.

"Which iced tea do you prefer?" I point to the bottles.

"Both are fine, but I would choose the raspberry over the peach."

I grab the peach tea, finish my sandwich in record time, and hurry back to my room for a different jacket.

"I'll clean this up. Call me when you get home." He threads his hand into my hair and splays the other on my back. His kiss stops all rational thought and makes me melt into a puddle of mush. No consideration is given at this time for his magical fingers and the consuming orgasms he causes.

"I will. I'll see you tomorrow. Bye."

"Bye, gorgeous."

I slip out the door and skip to my car. Ideally, I won't be alone on shift today. I park in the lot behind the Perk just in time. After I toss my bag and keys in the locker, I meet Becca at the counter.

"Hey, Becca."

"Hi, Scarlett. I'm glad I didn't miss you. I'll be right back." She returns with a sparkly gift bag.

"We got you a little something to commemorate your time with us. We'll miss you."

I pluck the tissue paper and find a super cute coffee mug key chain in the bag. There's also a card signed by the entire staff, including Kelsey.

I hug Becca. "Thank you. This is perfect! The Perk was my first real job where I felt at home. Leaving for one in my field wasn't easy, but I can't do it all. I'll stop by once everything settles after the boards."

"You're welcome. I'm off. See you around, Scarlett."

I wave and start cleaning the tables. When I finish restocking the sugar and cream bar, Kelsey emerges from the kitchen.

"Hi, Kelsey. I didn't know you were here."

"I wasn't. I just got here. Val wasn't having a great morning. I wasn't able to finish what I needed to. Will took over. How is the new job?"

A memory of Zack hovering over me from earlier flickers through my mind. "It's good. My patient has Alzheimer's and is declining, but it's fulfilling." Sad to see Zack so wrought with pain though.

"How did you find the position?" Kelsey asks.

"My patient's son contacted Willa." As if I called him, Zack steps through the front door.

"Hey, Smithson," Kelsey states.

"Hi, Mrs. Ramirez."

"What can I get for you?" she asks.

"I'll take a large coffee, but I'm here to talk with Scarlett."

"I see." A pleased look crosses Kelsey's face. Either she talked to Willa or her husband about the job. Perhaps the look is about Zack and his visit during my shift.

"I'll get his coffee." I move behind the counter and start to pour. Zack and I exchange a few words without speaking while Kelsey looks on. I hand him his coffee, already prepared with cream and sugar. Is it odd for a barista to know a customer's order? No. Is it odd for me to know Zack's considering I don't work mornings? Yes, and Kelsey is wholly aware.

"Thanks." He reaches into his pocket and pulls out my phone. "You left this on the island."

I extend my hand toward him. The warmth of his skin on mine is welcome and makes me ache for more. Only when Kelsey knocks the napkins to the floor do I recall we aren't alone.

"It was great seeing you, Smithson."

"You too, Mrs. Ramirez."

However many years later, Kelsey stills smiles at her married name. After expeditiously collecting the napkins, she ducks into the kitchen.

"I didn't know Kelsey would be here tonight," Zack mumbles.

"Normally, she isn't. Are we a secret?"

"No. Hell, I wanted to claim you at the hospital when the soccer players were flirting with you."

My cheeks flame. None of the athletes were inappropriate, but two of them asked for my phone number. It was a welcome change to say I wasn't single, albeit newly taken. "I was trying my best to temper my looks in your direction."

"I caught them." His hand slides to the curve of my ass, away from any possible prying eyes. "I'll talk to you later." He presses a sweet kiss to my cheek before stalking to the door.

Immediately, my phone lights up with a text.

Zack: I would've kissed you more deeply if we didn't have an audience.

I turn and find Kelsey pretending to search for something behind the counter.

Me: I understand. This is going to require some sharing.

Zack: Share discretely please.

Me: I will. I'm as private as you are.

Zack: I know. Talk to you later, beautiful.

I take a few breaths and return behind the counter, prepared for the inquisition.

"Have you two been dating since he spilled coffee on you?" Kelsey asks.

"No, it's recent. We would appreciate your discretion."

"Of course." Her quick and measured response indicates discretion is limited to certain individuals. If I had to guess, the blue wives club, which includes Kelsey, Willa, and Maggie Washington, will know before my shift ends. Cap will know before morning if he doesn't already.

I shake my head and greet the customer who is eyeing the remaining pastries in the case. Kelsey slips back to her office as I take the customer's order. The rest of my shift passes at a measured pace. I close down the café and seek out Kelsey.

"Everything is closed up. Front door is locked, lights out," I inform her.

"Thanks, Scarlett. Here."

She rises from her chair and hands me an envelope. "Please don't be a stranger." Kelsey opens her arms to me, and I step into them.

"I won't. Thank you for understanding."

"No reason to thank me. You're ready to take on the real world. Truthfully, I was concerned when you first arrived."

I mutter, "Me too."

We laugh. A tad nostalgic, I turn in a circle in the kitchen before stepping outside. I slide into my car, take a settling breath, and drive home. After a long, hot shower, I scan my texts.

Zack: I got called in to cover the night shift. Lunch?

I frown, angry I missed his text while I was showering, but also because we won't be able to talk again tonight.

Me: Sure. I'm in pediatrics tomorrow. Lunch is around 12:30.

Zack: Meet you at the taco truck?

Me: It's a date. Good night, Zack.

Zack: Night, Scarlett.

The next one is from Lia.

Lia: I'm staying at Lily's tonight.

Me: Everything okay?

Lia: I'm good. I'm worried about Lily.

Me: Still rocky with Leo?

Lia: She thinks she's doing the right thing.

Me: For him maybe, but not for her heart.

Lia: Exactly. See you Saturday.

Me: See you then.

Lia's older sister, Lily, fell in love with her best friend Leo. In the recent past, his girlfriend, Danica, has basically given them an ultimatum. Lily and Leo can't spend time alone together, and Danica wants an engagement ring or she walks. Leo is torn. Lily has purposefully added distance between her and her lifelong best friend to protect her breaking heart. It's an awful situation, and I'm not sure what the right answer is. With this choice, Lily gets hurt the most.

I pad to the living room and lock the security locks and shut off the lights. Charger in hand, I return to my bedroom, unwrap my hair, and comb it out before falling into my bed. Sleep will be illusive given the tantalizing memories we created here earlier today.

CHAPTER NINE

ZACHARY

The past few weeks have been steady and predictable as far as the schedule. Gladys and Scarlett work together well. I look forward to getting off shift, which has never happened before. The sole reason—Scarlett.

Nearing the end of my shift today, I get a call from Willa.

"Hi, Zack. How are things going with Scarlett?"

"Fine, why do you ask?"

"I mean as your mom's caregiver. Is there something else I should know?"

Damn! I walked right into that! I surmise Willa is in Kelsey's circle of trust. "No, not at all. Scarlett is exceptional with my mother."

"Glad to hear it. I thought she would be given her aptitude with the memory patients here."

"I'm glad Cap suggested I call you." In many ways. Not only did my call to Willa provide my mother with excellent care but reconnected me with the one woman who stopped me in my tracks.

"Me too. I just wanted to check in. Bye, Zack."

"Thanks for the call, Willa." I hang up confused. Her call makes sense on some level, but why now? It's been weeks since Kelsey saw me and Scarlett together at the Perk. I shake off the weirdness and head home. The weekend is nearly here, and I'm looking forward to seeing my sister and her kids during their visit.

I hustle up my front steps and carry in a package addressed to me. I didn't order anything. The sender isn't obvious. I grab the box and head inside.

"Hi, Zack," my mother greets me cheerfully from the table.

My chest constricts, and my breathing hitches. Greetings like this one are what I miss the most. Not only has my mother been robbed but Nadine, me, and the kids as well. "Hi, Mom." I round the table and kiss her cheek. "How was your day?"

"Pretty good. We played Go Fish and watched *Hamilton.* It was amazing! Have you seen it?"

"I have actually. I agree, it was amazing. Hello, Gladys."

"Evening, Zack. I should be heading out, Carol. I'll see you in the morning," Gladys states.

"Good night, Gladys. Where is your wife? She should be home by now," Mom states.

Gladys pauses for my response, whether out of genuine concern or interest in how Scarlett and I are doing with the marriage charade. If only Gladys knew we're dating too.

I glance at the clock and dig into my brain to recall her schedule. She has class today. No reason for her to be late. As my concern ratchets up, the front door opens. Scarlett steps through it, bogged down and flustered. I hurry over to her and take most of the bags.

I set them on the island and retreat to her. Before speaking, I kiss her breathless. I would like to say it's for my mother and Gladys's benefit, but it would be a lie. When I pull away, I murmur, "Hi, beautiful. How was class?"

"Hey. Class was fine. I got hung up at the store."

Gladys approaches us. "Carol had a good day, Scarlett. We played cards and watched a movie. Have a nice night."

"You too," we reply in unison.

"What did you buy?"

Scarlett smiles. It's genuine and breathtakingly beautiful. "I wanted to bake, and you don't have the supplies." She kisses me again before joining Mom in the kitchen. "Hi, Carol. How was the movie?"

"Excellent. Have you seen it?"

"Gladys didn't mention the name."

"*Hamilton.*" Technically, it's a Broadway play, which was streamed to reach a broader audience during the pandemic.

"I've always wanted to. I never got around to it," Scarlett replies.

"You must. It's fabulous!" She turns and looks directly at me. "Son, take care of that soon."

"I will." This version of my mother is the one I remember and miss the most.

"Zack, could you join me in the living room for a minute? Please excuse us, Carol."

Carol nods and watches Scarlett extend her hand to me.

"Sure." I wonder what this is about. I dutifully thread my fingers with my wife's and follow her into the living room. The lines are blurry between dating and fake married. Is she taking my hand because she wants to or because Mom is watching? "Everything okay?"

Before speaking, she soothes the questions in my head with a tender and all-too-brief kiss. "Yes, do you think your mom would like to bake with us? She's clearly having a good day."

"She used to bake when I was young. I don't bake. I planned to watch you and taste test the results."

"Great! We'll see if your mom will let you only watch."

Her devious, sexy smile will be the end of me. The intriguing part is her smile is for my mother this time, not for me or herself. Not for something I did for her or an action that made her day easier. This is all for my mother. Scarlett is beyond what I could ask for to care for my mom. If I'm being honest, for me too. "That's playing dirty."

She winks at me. "Maybe so." Scarlett saunters away with a spring in her step given she may be able to one-up me in the next few minutes. She's going to keep me on my toes for years to come. *Years?* I let my words settle and realize the notion of Scarlett never moving out doesn't terrify me. The thought warms me and provides hope I can capture the same type of love my parents had.

When I return to the kitchen, my woman and my mom are sorting through the bags Scarlett brought. Nothing about claiming Scarlett for real scares me, and I'm looking forward to sharing my feelings with her.

"Did you buy the whole store?" I ask.

"Of course not, babe. You… we didn't have any good cookie sheets or parchment paper."

The term of endearment is one thing, the almost slipup is another. Yet my mother is smiling and assisting Scarlett in gathering the ingredients. Flour, sugar, butter, eggs, and chocolate chips litter the island.

"Are you going to help, Zack?" Mom asks.

I scowl at Scarlett though I'm not truly upset. I'll immerse myself in this wonderful evening with my mother and the woman I'm rapidly falling for.

She smirks at me. "I didn't say a word."

"How can I help?" I wash my hands, slide beside Scarlett, and wait for instruction.

"You need to learn so you can teach your sons," Mom reminds. "When are we thinking of having a baby or two or four?"

Trial by fire it is. Our married future is on the discussion board today. "We haven't decided when to start our family yet." My reply is vague enough.

Mom has other ideas. She questions my wife too. "You want one, right, Scarlett?"

I pin my gaze to my unflustered, steadfast, raven-haired beauty.

"Yes, I want a family. I need to pass my boards first."

"I can work with starting next year," Mom determines.

A resonating sadness trickles into my heart. She may not be here then. As if my *wife* knew my brain would immediately calculate the likelihood of her meeting our children or at a minimum remembering them, Scarlett tucks herself against me. I press a kiss to the top of her head and take a breath. "Mom, she didn't stay that."

"I know. I know. An old lady can hope."

Scarlett assists my mom in measuring and verifies each ingredient until the batter is complete. It isn't lost on me that the first batch of cookies made in my home is by Mom and my girlfriend/fake wife. Can I call her my girlfriend? I inwardly shake my head.

After the first batch is in, Mom takes a seat at the table. "I don't recall baking being so exhausting."

"Would you like to turn in, Carol?" Scarlett asks.

"Not yet, dear. I need to taste test the first batch."

"What was I thinking?" Scarlett scoffs.

Mom laughs, and Scarlett continues cleaning the island. She joins me at the sink to add more dishes.

"I'm sorry about her questions," I murmur near her earlobe.

Her body reacts to the light caress of my breath on her skin every single time. "Don't be. I knew the lines would be blurry when I agreed to marry you within these walls. I appreciate your vague answer to Carol, but I want to know the true answer when we can talk."

"You would?" My tone comes out surprised.

"Don't you?"

The sheer idea she could be in our dating relationship as deeply as I am so soon sends emotions pulsing through me, feelings and sensations I've never experienced before her.

The timer buzzes.

I surround her wrist with my hand and cup her face before she turns away. "Yes, more than I should for as long as I've known you." I brush my lips across hers. "We'll talk more soon."

She nods, kisses me again, and slips the first batch out of the oven. Scarlett moves the cookies to the cooling rack. I didn't have a cooling rack before today. With the next batch ready for the oven, Scarlett plates one cookie for Mom and two on a second plate.

"Whenever you're ready, Carol, but it's still hot." Scarlett takes a seat across from her.

I move behind her and set my hands on her shoulders. Goose bumps bubble against my heated palm. As she looks up at me, the desire in her stare is impossible to miss. I lean down and kiss her lightly.

A contented sigh from across the table blankets our melded lips. Her happiness and stability are the reason for this charade, right? A charade that feels more real each passing day. I resist shaking my head. Instead, I pull away ever so slowly to savor the vanilla of Scarlett's lotion teasing my nose.

"Delicious, this cookie is perfect," Mom exclaims. "Zack, could you gct me a small glass of milk?"

I return to the kitchen. Soon after I rejoin her with the drink, the timer sounds again. Scarlett repeats the process of moving the fresh cookies to the rack and scooping a new set onto the pan.

Once she sets the timer, Mom announces, "I'm ready to turn in, Scarlett."

"Okay." Scarlett turns to me. "Charming, when the timer expires, could you pull the pan out and set it on the stovetop. I'll finish when Carol is set."

Charming? No one has ever called me that before. "I've got it."

"Good night, son."

"Night, Mom." Alone with my thoughts right now is not a good place for me to be. Overall, this evening has been nothing short of idyllic. Mom remembered who I am, and the woman I can see myself with far into the future is willing to pretend we're more than we are. We fake it well. Almost too well. Yet the mere fact she wants to know if, when, and how many children I may desire in the future is telling. Scarlett and I may be on the same page regarding the long-term potential of our sham marriage. I could wrap may head around waking up with her nestled against me each morning. The timer pulls me out of my thoughts—ideas and plans for my future that require deeper examination and discussion with Scarlett.

I set the pan on the stovetop and successfully move nine of the cookies to the cooling rack. My attempt to discard the evidence of my failure with the other three is thwarted by soft laughter. Caught red-handed as I slide the remnants of one cookie into the trash.

"That's hot," she states while leaning against the island.

I arch an eyebrow in question.

"Trying to learn a new skill in the kitchen. No reason to hide the fact you're human, Zachary. I already know."

"What else do you know?"

"You're an exceptional man who puts his family ahead of himself, including me—fake or not. Only Savi has ever done the same. You know what you want, but you're willing to wait for the right time. I would be lucky to call you mine outside of these walls."

I toss the oven mitt onto the counter and eliminate the space between us. "Is that what you want?"

"You. I want you."

"My life is messy."

"So is mine. You haven't seen it yet. I hope you never have the displeasure of meeting my father."

I crush my mouth to hers and cement my agreement with her request. Our relationship is just beginning. The future will sort itself out between our families and our careers. Knowing Scarlett will be beside me calms me and excites me at the same time.

Breathless, she adds space between our lips. "Any chance you were able to go shopping today?"

I frown at her.

"Yeah, me either."

I pretend to make a sharp move to the front door. "I'll be back in twenty minutes."

She laughs and drops her head against my chest. "No, tomorrow or the next day is fine. We don't have to rush."

The last thing I want is to push off making Scarlett scream with pleasure. However, the mere fact my mother lives here adds a level of discomfort I'm not sure I want to unpack. We aren't two teenagers sneaking around. We're grown adults. You would think that would be enough for me to get past the weird factor. It's not. "Did you send me a package?"

"It's here already?"

"Yeah, it came today. Can I open it?"

"Yes. It's a gift."

I let my hands drift down her curves as I step away to locate the box. I tear into the box like a kid on Christmas who still believes in Santa Claus. There are four elegant lights that match the décor of my home. Before I ask what they're for, I catch a glimpse of the invoice: artwork display lights. She truly sees me. All of me, not the mess my life is these days. "These are…." My words catch in my throat. "Will you come with me?"

"Anywhere."

I take her hand in mine, kiss the back of it, and lead her downstairs. Half of the basement is a gym, but the secluded partitioned part is a studio. I haven't been down here in quite some time. The landscapes along the stairway are a mere drop into the depth of my personal catalog. I lead her inside my private sanctuary.

"May I?" she points to the canvases stacked along the wall.

I drop my chin only enough to acquiesce to her request. Thoughtfully and slowly, she pulls each canvas forward before moving from one stack to the next. I know which one she pauses on the longest. It's a landscape of sorts. The painting is a depiction of one of the few recurring childhood memories I have with my father. The lake and small cabin where he took me fishing is about a two-hour ride from here. The canvas is split into four sections, one for each season. There is a man and a boy on the dock that straddles summer and fall. However, the boy—me—is painted in full color while the man—my father—is blurry.

"This is extraordinary. You painted this after your father died in the fall." It was a statement, not a question. "It's heartbreaking and poignant."

I slide my arms around her from behind. "Thank you. It shouldn't surprise me you see the depth of the painting like you see all of me."

"You do the same for me. Perhaps pretending to be married pushed our relationship faster, but no one has ever chosen me for me... until I met you." She turns in my arms and conveys her words with our lips. We dance upstairs, check the locks, peek in on Mom, and fall into my bed... together. As much as I would like to explore each inch of Scarlett's skin, I don't. I tuck her, clad in only skimpy shorts and a tank top, against me and allow sleep to overtake me. Despite the normalcy of my mother's countenance, the sadness of knowing it may be the last one I ever experience takes its toll. The sole benefit of today is Scarlett was able to see the woman I remember—the meddling but loving mother I miss the most.

CHAPTER TEN

SCARLETT

Cocooned in Zack's arms is the only way I want to wake up. The warmth of his hard body protecting me from everything outside these walls and within my brain is intoxicating. Our alarms blare and fight for supremacy.

He groans when I reach to silence my alarm.

"I agree, but we need to move."

"I don't like it. Releasing the peace of our tiny bubble right now is not what I want."

I turn and take in his sleepy face and mussed hair. *Sweet mercy!* I catalogue the dusting of freckles on his nose and press a light kiss to his lips. "Me either, but we need to."

Begrudgingly, he loosens his hold on me. I pad into the guest room and get ready for the day. I opt for scrubs with Marvel characters on them. The kids love the fun scrubs. It's a great conversation starter too if they don't feel like talking.

We're enjoying a cup of coffee when Gladys arrives. "Morning. How was her evening?"

I give Gladys a rundown of our evening activities. "Good for Carol. Have a great day, kids."

We laugh and make our way into the attached garage. Zack escorts me to my car and kisses me goodbye. "I'll see you tonight. I forgot to ask yesterday. Will you be able to come early to meet Nadine and the kids tomorrow?"

"Sure. We'll figure out a time tonight."

He steals another quick kiss and closes the car door. Before I know it, I'm parking at the hospital. Willa parks in the spot right next to me.

"Morning, Willa."

"Hi, Scarlett. How is your patient?"

"She had a great day yesterday. It was nice to meet the real her, despite it being brief. It was nice to see her son relax around her a bit as well."

Willa's face lights up. "Zack is a great guy. Caring for a parent with her disease is difficult, especially without training."

Not only is Kelsey talking Zack up, but Willa too. The confirmation is nice, but I don't need it. "It's a horrid disease that robs all parties of meaningful connection. Thankfully, Zack got a reprieve last night. I should head in. Have a good day, Willa."

"You too, Scarlett."

Her words keep rolling around in my head. I report to Judith in pediatrics and greet my first patient. Julianna has been here for quite some time. Her cancer isn't responding to treatment. She was the patient lucky, or unlucky, to be here for the last three visits with the athletes. Her chart indicates her cancer has spread, and she and her family have declined further treatment. My heart constricts. I can't imagine making such a choice for my child. Yet three years of treatment is a long time. I check her vitals as gently as possible, hoping to avoid waking her. Once I successfully complete my check-in, I slip out of her room and move through my next three patients. Two are here for routine tonsillectomies, and the third was in a car accident yesterday but will be discharged after lunch.

I grab my phone and wander down to the cafeteria for food. The moment I sit in my seat, I hear codes for my patient. I chuck my food and rush upstairs. I know it makes no difference, but I rapidly push the elevator button, hoping to make it in time.

I rush to her room and take her hand in mine. The others on staff are already deep into the code. Wails from her parents echo behind me. Within a few minutes, Julianna is gone. After the team clears out, I give her parents some time alone.

I step into the lounge and exhale sharply. I didn't meet her until last month. I've been her nurse a few times since then. Despite the short time I knew her, it hurts to lose a patient, especially a child. After a few deep breaths to compose myself, I continue through the rest of my day. After my shift, I check my texts before I pull out of the hospital lot.

Lia: Hey girl! Will I see you tomorrow before my shift?

Me: I should be there bright and early.

Lia: Perfect! My shift is at one. Miss you, bestie!

Me: Miss you too!

The next text is from Zack.

Zack: Have a great lunch break, gorgeous. See you at home.

Home. It's the perfect way to describe him. He feels like home for me. It doesn't matter if we're at his townhouse or my condo. I'm happy and content wherever he is. During the drive, I attempt to shake off my crappy day.

Little do I know, it's going to get worse. As I park and enter the house, Carol is screaming about Saul and him missing some event with Zack and Kate. I jettison my bag and jacket and attempt to assist Gladys.

Who's Kate? "How long?"

"It's been over an hour," Gladys replies.

Poor Carol. Her brain is betraying her more rapidly each day.

"Who are you?" Carol interjects into her wails.

"I'm Scarlett. I'm your caregiver overnight."

"He's cheating on Kate with you!" *Kate must be Zack's ex.*

"No, Zack and I are a couple."

I don't miss the joy on Gladys's face at my last statement, regardless of the circumstances. A bit of relief floods my body when I realize Zack isn't home yet. Ideally, we can calm Carol before he gets here. He can't hide the pain washing over him when Carol calls him Saul. It breaks my heart a little more each time. Choosing to honor his mother's wishes of in-home care is taking a toll on Zack too.

"Wait, you got married at the beach." Carol pauses.

I know better than to interrupt or correct. We never corrected her incorrect recollections of our relationship. Zack and I simply go along with her. Her breathing is regulating, and her movements are slowing.

"You wore a bright white dress to match your complexion. Off-white on olive skin is no good."

I nod, hoping she'll continue. Gladys discreetly checks her pulse, and I count her breaths to calculate the decrease. Close to normal.

"Why does your badge say Clemons and not Smithson?"

Crap! Think quick. "I haven't gotten my new one yet. The hospital is slow."

"Okay. Zack's wife should have his name."

"Don't worry, I do." *Maybe, hopefully, someday in the future.*

Her vitals have slowed to normal range.

"Do you want to change or turn in, Carol?" Gladys inquires in a soft tone.

"I'm tired. Sleep is a good idea."

"Would you like anything first?" I ask.

"No, thank you. Good night, Gladys. Scarlett," Carol states and snuggles under the covers of her bed.

I click the rails in place and slip out of her room.

Gladys is tugging on her coat.

"Thank you for staying. Was that her only lapse today?"

Gladys hangs her head. "No, the others were not remotely as severe though. None of them took more than a few minutes to get her unconfused."

"Have a good night, Gladys."

"There's a good chance she will wake during the night."

"I'll be ready."

Gladys exits the front door. I peek in on Carol again and then head to the kitchen. I search the fridge for something to cook. I'm starving since I skipped lunch. After filling the sink with water and submerging the chicken to assist in thawing, I tug off my scrub top, twist my hair into a messy topknot, and start my personalized music station on my phone. I note a smiley face text from Lia but nothing else. After locating the rest of the ingredients, I get to work.

As I near the end of preparing dinner, Zack crosses the threshold. Normally, he heads straight upstairs. Tonight he doesn't. His face is withdrawn and sad. I step into his embrace. A kiss to my forehead and then an apologetic one to my lips.

"I'm sorry for being so late. A coworker's little sister died around lunch. He was in no position to go home alone. I intended to text you, but things went from chill to worse and then calmed a bit. I left him at his parents', nursing a beer on the couch."

"I don't mean to add to the crappiness of today, but I lost a patient, and your mom had a moderately long episode. Gladys was handling it when I got here."

The timer sounds, so I kiss him softly and pull away.

"How long?" he asks.

"Why don't you go change, and we can talk over dinner?"

He acquiesces and leaves the kitchen. I set the table, plate the food, and pour drinks in the time it takes him to store his weapon and change into shorts and a tee.

Zack pulls out my chair and waits for me to sit before speaking again. "You don't have to cook for me."

"I know. I want too. I didn't get to eat my lunch. My code was during... *oh no!* Was her name Julianna?"

His lips pull into a thin, firm line. "Yes."

I cover his free hand with mine. "She was my patient."

"I'm sorry, Scarlett."

"Me too. Before you ask again, your mom's episode lasted nearly two hours."

"What was the trigger this time?"

I scrunch my face, preferring not to bring up this topic now. "Us—sort of. Who is Kate?"

His fork pauses midair. He catches my gaze again before setting it down. "She's my ex. We were together for about five years near the end of high school and the first two years of college. Mom believes we grew apart and broke up. The reality is Kate elected to spend a semester abroad. We decided the time apart would be good for us to see if we were meant to be together long-term. She met someone during her first week in London and broke up with me. What did Mom say about Kate?"

I relay the information Gladys provided and let him filter through it before speaking again. "You know as well as I do, the timeline in her head is skewed. She doesn't recall the gap between then and now."

The anguish, guilt, and blame on his face is agonizing to watch.

"Don't worry about me. I can handle waiting for answers. I'm not naïve. I know you dated before we met, like I did." Not a lot and certainly not smartly, at least for me.

He takes both of my hands in his. "It would take herculean effort for me to not worry about you. I care about you. Our current situation is twisted given we're dating and married in here." He motions around his home. "It doesn't diminish how I feel about you."

I press a kiss to our joined hands. "I care about you too."

"I'm sorry if she made you feel uncomfortable."

"Stop. None of this is your fault. Your mom, as well as you and your sister, received a crappy hand. We met at a time when Carol is at her most vulnerable. All I can promise is to talk to you when she says something about you or your life that, as your *wife*, I should already know, but don't yet."

"Thank you."

"Of course."

We finish our meal in silence and curl up on the couch to watch an episode or two. At some point, we both fall asleep. Who knows when? The only indication is the notification mocking us on the screen—"Would you like to continue watching?"—near three in the morning when Carol wakes and calls for Saul. Leaving the blissful warmth of Zack's body is torture.

I make my way to Carol's room. "Who are you?" After a long pause, "You're the floozy Zack is cheating with."

Unfortunately, Zack hears her words as he approaches her room.

I bite the inside of my cheek to keep my emotions in check. I care about him, and the pain her words cause is gut-twisting. While we both know she doesn't mean them, nor does she know what she's saying, it's still disrespectful to Zack—and me.

Despite knowing better, he addresses Carol's statement, "Mom, this is Scarlett, my wife. Kate and I are no longer together. We haven't been for years. Kate is married to a man she met in England during college. Aside from those facts, I would never disrespect my marriage by cheating."

"No, no, no. That can't be right. Her badge doesn't have your name!" Carol exclaims. She looks for my badge, but I already put it in my purse.

As calmly as I can muster, I remind her, "Carol, we talked about this earlier. My new badge isn't ready yet."

She ponders my words and then asks for Nadine. "Where is my daughter? She'll tell me the truth."

Zack scrubs his hand down his face. "Mom, this is our home. Nadine doesn't live here. She's coming to visit tomorrow though."

Undiluted facts should provide calm for Carol, at least they have in the past. I set my fingers on her wrist to take her pulse. She doesn't pull her hand away. That's a good sign.

"Is that no-good Trevor coming too?" Carol asks. Perhaps she's more perceptive than Zack and Nadine give her credit for.

"I don't think so," Zack replies.

"Good." Her response is emphatic and clear. She turns her face toward me. "I'm fine now, Scarlett. Still prettier than the movie actress."

"You're right. Your heart rate seems to have normalized. Thank you, Carol. Do you need anything?"

"Another blanket would be nice," she requests.

"I'll get it," Zack offers.

"Such a good son," Carol murmurs.

He's a good son and so many other things. I would pay a significant amount of money to soothe the pain he feels each day dealing with Carol's disease. We haven't known each other long, but experience has taught me the toll is heavy and unyielding.

Zack returns with a fluffy blanket and spreads it over Carol. "Good night, Mom."

"Night, son."

I check her pulse again and find it has regulated. I verify the rails are up and ask, "Do you need anything else, Carol?"

"No, I'm better now," she assures me.

I'm not convinced.

"Good night," she adds.

I make my way to the kitchen. Tension envelopes the muscles of his shoulders, each sculpted rope of sinew clearly defined. His hands grip the lip of the sink as his head hangs heavy. I slide my hands around his toned abs and set my head against his back. With each passing breath, his body relaxes a fraction. When his shoulders sag to their normal position, he turns and ensconces me in his arms.

"It isn't your job to take care of me too," he mumbles against my hair.

I add only enough space between us to see his reaction when I reply, "I want to. Plus, I would be a crappy wife if I didn't."

If I wasn't watching him, I would've missed the half smile curve at the corners of his mouth and almost as quickly disappear.

"You should try to get some sleep," he suggests.

"What about you?"

"I'm too fraught with tension and anger to sleep now. It's too early for me to go running, though no one would bother me. I'm going to punch the heavy bag downstairs for a bit."

"Do you want company?" I offer.

"No, but thank you." He leads me upstairs and tucks me into his bed… alone. With sneakers and socks in hand, he slips out the door. As much as I know he shouldn't be alone, I know better than to push. He'll share when he's ready. I allow the crisp scent of Zack to surround me and let sleep claim me for a little while.

CHAPTER ELEVEN

ZACHARY

I lace up my shoes and tug on the gloves.

Punch.

How did Nadine handle this for so long on her own?

Punch, cross, jab.

It has only been a few months, and I'm drained.

Punch, cross, kick.

Is Mom the reason Trevor left? Truthfully, I don't want to know if it was something between Nadine and Trevor. Nope, my younger-brother brain can't handle such information. It's a topic Nadine and I don't discuss in detail. Never have, never will.

Punch, punch, cross, cross.

No, Scarlett is not Trevor. She's everything I ever wanted for myself: smart, kind, loving, patient, and sexy as fuck.

Kick, roundhouse, punch, cross.

Frustrated the boxing isn't working, I take a seat on the weight bench. Maybe me taking over for Nadine was a fool's choice. *No, you both promised to keep her home as long as possible.* Should I call her and cancel her visit? *No, can't do that. You told Mom she was coming tomorrow—today.* A pointed conversation with

Nadine and Mom's doctors may be necessary. So far her episodes are manageable. What happens when they aren't? Sleep is necessary to function, especially in our lines of work. Perhaps I should let Scarlett out of her contract. The lack of sleep can't be easy for her with classes and her boards this summer. Although this is the second time we've been up for a prolonged period because of Mom instead of choosing to watch the next round of hijinks Josh Lyman and Sam Seaborn concoct.

What about you? I ask myself. Truthfully, I haven't been studying as much as I should be, but that isn't Mom's fault. It's my choice to spend my extra time with Scarlett instead of focusing on my exam. It needs to be addressed, although mine is after Scarlett's.

I glance at the clock and realize I've been stewing in my thoughts for too long. I guzzle some water and trudge upstairs. I peek in on Mom to verify she's still resting before climbing the next staircase. When I cross the threshold, I note my bed is empty and made. I never make my bed. *This woman.* I shake my head and find Scarlett in the guest room.

"Better?" she asks.

"Not really, but less stressed for now."

She steps closer to me and almost sets her hand on my chest but refrains given my sweat-stained shirt. Her fingers recoil because she's freshly showered and dressed. "Progress is good. What are your plans for today?"

"Don't have any other than ordering groceries and studying."

"Okay. Want some coffee?"

"I'll make it when I come down." I lean forward and skim a sweet kiss on her lips.

"Okay, I'll come back early, say three?"

"Scarlett, why is the conversation strained?"

She exhales. Clearly, she was thinking the same thing. "Will you come over when you can before your sister is set to arrive?"

"Yes. I want as much time with you as I can have. However, we need to set some ground rules going forward so we can study appropriately and date."

She wrinkles her nose, a quirk I love about her. After a moment, her face lights up, and she kisses me again. "Deal."

I shower, dress, and head downstairs as Gladys is arriving. She's an astute woman. She takes one look at me and says, "You need to leave and relax somewhere before your sister arrives."

She's absolutely right. "Yes, ma'am."

We step into the kitchen, and Scarlett hands me a hot cup of coffee. I don't miss the knowing smile on Gladys's face. She seems to be a true matchmaker at heart.

"How many times was she up last night?"

"Once after two. Same trigger as earlier in the day. Zack provided factual information to straighten out some of her disconnections," Scarlett answers.

"Did she balk at you?" Gladys turns back to me.

"No, actually she didn't. She listened and then calmed after I shared the truth—mostly—as it is today."

"Still thinks you two are married?"

"Yeah," I reply.

"At least her vision has you living happily ever after like she did."

I never considered it that way. "Thanks, Gladys."

"Drink up and get out of here. Both of you."

A confused expression crosses Scarlett's face.

Gladys saves me. "He needs a break too. He's leaving as soon as he's done with his coffee." She points at the mug in my hand. "I don't care where you relax but promise me you will before your family arrives."

"I will."

"Scarlett," Carol calls from her room.

"I meant what I said, young man," Gladys reiterates and disappears down the hall.

"I should go," Scarlett mutters and washes her mug.

I trap her against the sink and press one kiss to the curve of her neck. "I'll be over within the hour."

She turns in my arms. "Okay." She frowns.

"What, beautiful?"

"Why don't we go together? I'll be back here to meet your family and work tonight anyway?"

"Brilliant. Give me ten minutes. I'll meet you in the garage." A quick peck and I'm off to grab my stuff. I manage a quick goodbye and slip downstairs. I open the passenger door for Scarlett and hurry around the car.

"Want to talk now about our schedule?"

I pull out of my complex toward her condo. "Sure. We need to dedicate some time, at least five days, to studying and at least one night to dating only."

"I can work with that. Lunches don't decrease the one night, though."

"Agreed. However, it needs to start tonight."

She raises a curious eyebrow in my direction. "Why?"

"We both need some sleep first. Then we can start our new plan."

I can see the wheels turning in her beautiful mind. "I'll try my best. I'm not great at napping."

I park and hustle around the front of the car to open her door. I extend my hand to her and pull her against me. A promising kiss later, I follow her up to her condo. Noting Lia's keys in the bowl, she raises her index finger to her lips, threads her fingers with mine, and leads me to her bedroom.

"Can we try to rest for a little while?" I request.

"I'll give it a shot. What time is Nadine arriving?" She toes off her shoes, shimmies out of her jeans, and sheds her open-back top.

The sight of her nearly naked makes my mouth as dry as a desert. "Some time in the afternoon," I manage. Following suit, I strip down to my boxer briefs and climb into her bed from the other side. I adjust myself when her back is turned. Now isn't the time, considering I asked to take a nap. She sidles against me, throws her leg over mine, and sets a hand in the middle of my chest, her head nestled against my shoulder. I tug her closer and close my eyes. Hours later, I wake and find her still beside me, but she's reading.

"Hi, sleepyhead." Her sweet voice warms me.

"What time is it?"

"Slightly past noon. When is the last time you slept soundly?"

I press a kiss to her forearm and consider her question. A pit forms in my stomach.

Clearly, she noticed. "I won't judge you, Zachary."

The way she says my name affects me differently than any other woman. She's also better at reading me than anyone else. "I know. It was before Mom moved in. Terrible but honest."

"Did you not trust Gladys?"

"No, that isn't it. I didn't always assist Gladys, but I was up during her awake times at night. Occasionally, I didn't get back to sleep at all."

"You're welcome here to sleep anytime, even if I'm not here, but please warn Lia."

I laugh. "Thanks. I'll consider it. We should eat something and then head back."

"Sounds good. I heard Lia's alarm about an hour ago. She should be functioning by now."

We get dressed and step out of her bedroom.

"Hey, Scar. Smithson," Lia states in a cheerful tone.

"Hi, Lia," we reply in unison.

"What time did you get here?"

"Seven-ish. You were sound asleep," Scarlett responds.

I search their fridge, pull out the fixing for sandwiches, and get to work. Fifteen minutes later, the three of us nosh on toasty, perfectly crafted subs with chips.

"Do you have a brother, Smithson?" Lia asks.

"No, sorry, Lia."

She shrugs and finishes eating. "I have a shift tonight, and then I'm staying at Lily's."

"Still not any better, huh?" Scarlett asks.

"Nothing has changed, but tonight is their standing movie night, which Danica nixed. I don't want her to be alone."

"You're sweet, Lia."

"It's what little sisters are for," she replies and leaves to dress for work.

"Ready to go?" I ask.

Scarlett lifts her shoulder but says nothing.

"What's wrong, gorgeous?" I surround her with my arms.

"Nervous, I guess."

"Nadine only wants me to be happy. You make me happier than I've ever been."

"Pinkie promise?"

I lean back and hook my pinkie between us. She curls hers around mine. "Pinkie promise."

We pull into the garage right before two.

Gladys is settling Mom into the chair in the living room.

"Hi, Mom. Hi, Gladys," I say, standing beside my mom.

"You're back. You look better," Gladys acknowledges.

"I took your sage advice."

Gladys looks past me to Scarlett for confirmation.

She replies, "He slept the entire time."

"Good. He needed it."

She's right. I did. Sharing with Scarlett was helpful too. As I'm about to prepare Mom, the doorbell sounds. I hustle to the door and step outside onto the stoop.

"Hi, guys." I give my sister, niece, and nephew a crash course in the status of my relationship with Scarlett. I'd meant to call them earlier today but slept instead. I assured them we would explain in more depth later.

The kids whoosh past me and hug my mom at once. Sheer joy materializes on her face. That's a good sign.

"What's with the bags, sis?" I take the bags from Nadine's hands.

"We're going to crash here tonight to spend extra time with Mom, also to give you a break."

"You don't have to do that," I reply, though I'm ecstatic I'll be able to take Scarlett on a real date.

"I do. You came when I needed help. Let me do it for you."

I throw my arm over her shoulders. "Thanks. More accurately, I need good sleep."

Nadine laughs. "It doesn't change when you're a single parent, but I understand completely." We join the kids, and my sister greets our mom.

After they hug, I introduce Scarlett to Nadine but choose my words carefully. Beside my woman, I thread our fingers together. "Nadine, you remember Scarlett. Babe, my older sister. It seems you've reacquainted yourself with these two." The kids are fawning over my mom.

I see the nerves all over Scarlett's face. "Nice to see you again. How was your drive?"

A smile cracks on Nadine's face. "Well, you are equally as stunning today as the last time I saw you. The drive was smooth."

"Thank you." The awkwardness seems to fade, and we visit in the living room.

"Gladys, could you join me in the kitchen?" I ask.

"Sure."

We meet near the edge of the island. "Any chance you spoke to Nadine about me?"

A look of feigned surprise appears on Gladys's face. "Who me? No."

I don't often put my elders on the spot, but in this case, I make an exception. I just stare at her until she relents.

"You needed a break."

"I appreciate you taking care of me. It isn't your job."

"I don't mind. Until Scarlett, you needed some looking after. You have to take care of yourself too."

"Why don't you take off the rest of the day? The three of us can handle things here."

"Please don't wait so long to ask for help next time."

"I don't recall asking for help this time," I reply with a wink.

Gladys drops her head. "I'll see you in the morning." She bids Mom a good night and heads home early.

"What do you think about a few rowdy games of Go Fish?" I suggest.

"Grandma will school us, Uncle Zack," Tallie states.

"She might, but it'll still be fun."

"I'm in," Tanner jumps into the game.

"Me too," Nadine and Scarlett say at once.

"Mom?" I wait for her to look in my direction.

"Yes, let's play cards."

We settle around the kitchen table, and Nadine shuffles. The trash talking between the kids takes less than two hands. While Nadine admonishes them, Mom is grinning from ear to ear.

"They sound like you two so many years ago," Mom croons.

"I'm not old!" I exclaim.

"No, but Mom is," Tanner mutters under his breath.

"Tanner Jackson!" Nadine shouts.

"Wow, Mom. It was a joke. You are older than Uncle Zack."

The good old-fashioned ribbing ends when Nadine crushes everyone at the table.

"You guys play with Grandma. We're going to figure out dinner," Nadine states.

Nadine, Scarlett, and I retreat to the living room again.

"Why don't you two take off after you give me the number of the best pizza place around?" Nadine suggests.

Surprise graces Scarlett's face. "I'm sorry, what?"

"Gladys and I cooked up a date night for you two. I'm staying here, and you two are leaving. Zack needs a break, and you need a night off."

I lean over and press a kiss to Nadine's cheek. "You're the best sister ever!"

"Only one you've got." She glances over her shoulder. "I won't let what happened to my marriage happen to yours."

Silence hangs between the three of us for a solid minute. "He left because of Mom?"

"We aren't talking about my issues in depth right now. Mom was about half of the problem. I wasn't focused on my marriage at all, and he went elsewhere."

"I have no good words for him."

"He isn't completely to blame for the breakdown. However, he is for how things are working or not working now. Enough about me. You two need to go."

"Woody's is the best pizza, and they deliver." I scribble the number on a piece of paper and rush upstairs to pack. When I make it back downstairs, Scarlett and Nadine are chatting quietly in the living room.

"I will. I promise," Scarlett states.

"Do I want to know?" I ask.

"Don't you worry. Scarlett and I have you under control," Nadine replies.

I haul Scarlett against me and lower my lips to her earlobe. "We'll see about that, gorgeous." Goose bumps rise on her skin, and if I had to bet, she's clenching her thighs too. I release her.

"Go, have fun. Mom's next appointment is in a month."

I hug Nadine, say a quick goodbye to the kids and Mom, thread my hand with Scarlett's, and usher her out the door.

"My place, and then we figure out dinner?" Scarlett suggests.

I kiss her hard as I realize we'll be alone outside of my townhouse. Desire plummets southward—not that I don't desire Scarlett all the time—knowing I will have time to savor each inch of her incredible body without the worry of interruption. "Yes." I close her car door after another kiss and follow her home.

CHAPTER TWELVE

SCARLETT

Excited doesn't begin to explain my emotions right now. True, I did tell Zack dates weren't necessary, and I meant it. However, the impromptu ability to spend time alone together is unexpected but appreciated.

We hustle to my condo. The moment the door is open, he sets his bag on the floor and cocoons me in his arms.

After a round of scintillating kisses, which only make me yearn for more, I ask, "Shouldn't we eat dinner first?"

"I would prefer to strip off your clothes and taste every inch of your luscious curves first."

"As long as I get to do the same," I request.

The surprise on his face dissipates as quickly as it appears. I lift his shirt overhead, work his buckle loose, and slip my hands around his rock-hard length.

"Scarlett…." His voice comes out coarse and raspy.

I ignore the sexy undertone of my name and continue marking a path with my teeth and mouth along his chest and abs. His muscular thighs tense when I push his jeans and boxer briefs to the floor and kneel before him.

"You don't—"

Instead of answering with words, I drag my tongue along the front side of his shaft, lick the precum off the tip, and take him into my mouth. With each pump, his voice sounds more strangled.

"Scarlett, I need you to—"

I cut off his thoughts by looking up at him. His eyes are stormy, and it only adds to his appeal. The moment his shaft hits the back of my throat again, he pulls away, reaches down, and lifts me from the floor.

"I will not allow you to make me come first. Not today, maybe not ever."

Ever?

He drags his thumb over my swollen lips and leads me to my bedroom. With a slow, sensual pace, he removes my clothes, tasting and savoring each area of exposed skin. He guides me to the edge of my bed and kneels before me. Prickles of need sting my skin as he unclasps my bra and casts it aside. His fingers brush lightly over the swell of my breasts.

"Zachary…." His name comes out more like a whimper, and he's barely touching me. He coaxes sensations and emotions from me like no other man. When he said each inch, he meant every last one. He lavishes attention to both breasts, twisting, biting, and sucking before travelling across my abdomen and back again. Hooking the sides of my panties, he draws them to the floor. Before he has a chance, I spread my legs and bare myself to him.

He's momentarily silent. "You are trouble, aren't you?"

"Only for you. Only with you."

Each open-mouthed kiss he places along my inner thighs brings him closer to my sopping center. The first swipe of his tongue shoots spirals of pleasure through me. Clearly, my previous experiences were epically dismal. I'm at his mercy, and it's been no more than a minute. He delves his tongue into my heated core while expertly pinching and teasing my magical button. Not only are his hands magic, but his tongue is too. The spiral tightens with his steady, deliberate strokes.

"Holy hell!" My release crests, and my core clenches with decadent sensations stronger than ever before. Before the ripples of my orgasm cease, I claw and pull until he is hovering over me. "I need you now."

He shakes his head. I twist beneath him and pull a strip of condoms from the bedside drawer. Other than a raised eyebrow, he doesn't address the sheer number or how they appeared in my night table. I borrowed them from Lia. I tear one off, push up to my elbows, and roll it down his shaft. Zack takes my mouth in a blistering kiss and aligns himself with me. With slow precision, he pushes forward, burying himself as my muscles ripple and stretch to accommodate him. I draw him inexplicably deeper when I hook my leg over his hip.

A low hiss falls from his lips as he opens his eyes to look down at me. Words aren't necessary. Each emotion he's feeling and processing is painted on his gorgeous face. He pulls back and thrusts forward. Every penetrating movement sears us into one. Spikes of need radiate from me and pulse around him. His heart is pounding beneath my hand as he lengthens, filling me more.

"We feel…."

The pressure from his thumb on my nub careens me over the edge. Zack splintering in pleasure is the most exquisite sight I've ever seen. He lowers to his forearms and kisses me breathless.

I'm not ashamed to admit I've had more than a few partners. It's how I learned aggression would get me what I needed or at least bring me closer to it. Zack has tilted my opinion on its axis. Every other man was more focused on himself rather than the two of us. On the other hand, Zack is zeroed in on me to his own detriment, which won't work for me.

"What crazy ideas are floating in your dirty mind, beautiful?"

"Not crazy, not dirty either. Not this time. Observations mostly."

"Care to share?"

I settle my thoughts a bit before speaking. "We haven't really talked about it, but in my dating history, none of the guys were like you here." I motion to the bedroom. "It was always about them getting off. I realized it shaped how aggressive I am in the bedroom."

"Idiots."

I giggle softly. "I will readily admit, what just transpired is nowhere near anything before. Given that… I'm asking for a little more give and I'll offer the same."

"That's all?"

I scrunch my nose. "Ye—"

He cuts me off with a feverish kiss, one that tells me I could ask him for a star, and he would find a way to get it for me. "I realize we're new and skipped a lot of the getting-to-know-one-another stuff given our fake titles and all, but a true partnership is what I want for us. We'll find the right balance in the bedroom and outside of it."

"Sounds perfect. We should get some food before the kitchen closes. Have you eaten at the Inn on the Blues?"

"Not recently. Do you have a menu?" he replies.

I roll my eyes. Of course I have a menu for the restaurant downstairs from my condo. "What girl doesn't have a stack of local menus in her kitchen?"

He laughs and moves off the bed.

"It's wrong to be that hot from every angle!"

"Have you looked in the mirror lately?" he replies.

I feel the heat creep into my cheeks. He returns to the side of the bed after pulling on only his shorts and kisses me again. "Where are the menus?"

"Middle drawer of the island. I'll be right out." I throw on leggings sans panties, a tee, and a running hoodie. Running isn't my thing, but it fits well and is a great color.

"I'll take the small Caesar salad and the steak tips," he shares.

"Got it." I call and place our order. "We have about thirty minutes. Let's set up outside while we wait. You might want some more clothes though."

"You want me to cover up?" There's a devilish twinkle in his eye.

"Hell no! I mean, I don't want to share the view with anyone. Also, it's breezy on the deck."

"A tad possessive of my abs?"

"Not only your abs. All of you."

He hauls me flush against his body and kisses me slowly. "Good, I feel the same about you." He releases me and tugs on a shirt before we step outside to set up for dinner.

I tug the pillows out of the storage bin and set them on the rattan furniture.

"The view is amazing," he says, leaning against the railing. "A similar view was on my wish list when I bought my townhouse. Nothing was available at the time."

My condo is directly across the street from the beach. Someday I'll need a new place to live, and the hefty price tag that comes with a view like this one and a bigger place will be astronomical. "The view sold me on this place. I'm going to miss it when I have to move."

"Why would you move?"

"At some point, I would like to live with my husband and children instead of Lia. She's great, but I'm not looking for a wife." I grin at him.

"We never did finish our conversation about kids. You mentioned you wanted a family but not how large." He looks at me expectantly.

I don't want to scare him off. Not sure I can, but... "I want at least two children. However, I'm leaning toward more after meeting the Morgans."

"You thought that might scare me?"

I shrug. "Maybe a little."

"Not even a little. You forget I know the Cappellis well and there are five of them. The bond they have is extraordinary. I would love for my kids to have the same." He presses a kiss to my temple and moves away from the railing. "Let's get our food."

Much to my dismay, though required, we take a break from our conversation to go pick up our dinner. It takes literally five minutes for us to walk downstairs, check out, grab drinks, and return to the porch. I devour my salad and then my lobster mac and cheese. Zack takes his time with his steak tips though. Once I'm through, I curl into the corner of the couch and listen to the waves. It's faint, but I can hear it. It's much harder during the tourist season. He hauls me into his arms once he finishes eating.

"Please thank Gladys and your sister profusely when you talk to them next," I mumble against his neck.

"I will. What do you say to a movie or an episode?"

"Episode works." We clean up and watch an episode of our show snuggled in my bed with the French doors open. Midway through the second one, I slip beneath the covers and kiss my way from the top of his foot to the juncture of his jaw. He squirms when I drag the flat of my tongue along the V cut at his hips. At least this time it appears Zack is willing to let me be in control.

"Relinquishing control is killing you, isn't it?"

"Not yet, but I'm nearing the end of my patience."

"We shall see." I lower my lips to his, and our tongues dance and twist until we're panting. Leaning over, I grab the strip of condoms, tear one off, and set it beside me. I shimmy down a bit and intend to nip and kiss my way back to his toes. When I reach his navel, he hooks underneath my arms, hauls me up, and rolls the two of us over. I'm trapped beneath my carved specimen of the male species. I revel in the power of him for a solid minute before I devise a plan to retake control.

A grin materializes on his face when he whispers, "It won't be easy."

"I'll figure it out, charming." The fact we're still learning one another is my best weapon right now. I snake my hands along his flanks before encircling his shaft with one hand and skimming my fingernails down along the inside of his thigh. The instant his eyes snap closed, I hook my leg around his knee and flip us back over.

"That's dirty, sweetheart."

"Is it?" I sheathe his length, notch him at my entrance, and take him deep in one downward plunge.

Once the sheer bliss of being nestled between my legs again sets in, he adds, "You're a vixen. You're giving me two options: try to control you in the bedroom and fail or unequivocal surrender. Correct?"

I rise and impale myself on him again before replying, "You can try, or you can come along for the ride." I hinge forward, changing the angle of my hips and grind against him. The additional friction on my clit is heavenly.

"Option two sounds like so much more fun," he forces out before meeting me in the middle.

"It is. That falls into the little more give I asked for earlier. Unequivocal surrender… sometimes."

"I can work with it."

"Glad to hear it. Like I'm willing to attempt to let you be in control too."

"Would my control allow for restraints?" His question comes out soft, testing what my boundaries are.

"I'm not opposed to trying anything once."

"Noted, gorgeous." The tension in his body increases exponentially. His fingers bruise the curve of my hips as we chase ecstasy together. "Let go with me, baby."

Arousal floods my core, my muscles clench around him, and the waves of my climax crest at the same time he explodes. I collapse against his chest. His hands slide up and down my back in opposite directions. Once our breathing is back to normal, I attempt to move.

"Give me a few more minutes," he murmurs against my skin.

In my sated state, I'll give him anything he asks for, including my whole heart. *I'm falling in love with him.* Soon thereafter, we clean up in the bathroom and strip my bed. I start the laundry while Zack remakes my bed.

"Want to finish the episode I interrupted?"

"No, I want to sleep with you in my arms until morning."

I nod and join him in my bed.

Despite our good intentions of sleeping, which we both desperately need, we spend hours exploring every dip and curve on one another. For each kiss or nip from me, Zack offers the same. The taste of us on my tongue, coupled with the pleasure zipping between us, engraves onto my soul.

His alarm wakes me way too early. He slips out of bed as silently as he can. I catch his gaze. More accurately, he catches me ogling him. He winks at me and says, "Stay there, gorgeous. You can sleep a bit longer."

I shake my head. "I'll make you some coffee and lunch."

He glares at me. "I can handle it." He finishes dressing and sits on the edge of the bed. "Have a great day. I'll see you tonight."

"You too. Be safe."

My words make him hesitate for the slightest of moments, so slight that I almost missed it, and he's beside me. "Always." His kiss reaches from my lips to my toes before settling into my heart.

Thankfully, I'm able to grab some extra sleep. I stumble into the kitchen near nine and find Lia doing laundry.

"Hey, girl. How is Lily holding up?"

Lia shrugs. "I'm not sure. She went to Boston for work to avoid the whole night."

"Why didn't you come home?"

"I didn't know until I was deeply ensconced in her Dunne's ice cream stash and my book."

"Did you know you could get pints of Dunne's and bring it home?"

"Duh! How's it going with Zack?"

I attempt to hide the smile the mere mention of his name causes, but I fail spectacularly. "Good—well, great. I care about him, Lia. I may be falling for him. I know it's soon, but we feel different." It's more than "may," but I'm not ready to let Lia in on all my feelings yet. I want to make sure first. It isn't something I can take back.

"Ohhhh. Yay! I'm so happy for you!"

"Thanks, Lia. What are your plans for today?"

"Laundry, studying, and sleep. You?"

"Studying until work."

We settle into our respective study space, me at the island and Lia sprawled out on the ottoman and couch, and get to work. The only interruption is a text notification near lunch.

Savi: Hey, sis. When are you and Zack free to have lunch with us?

Me: Hey. I'll ask him to check his schedule. Kiss the kiddos for me.

Savi: Sounds good. I will. Love you.

Me: Love ya too.

I text Zack to remind myself about lunch and crack the books for a few more hours before I shower and head over to work.

CHAPTER THIRTEEN

ZACHARY

I push through the precinct doors and stand in line for roll call. The good news is I have desk duty today. Thankfully, it won't be taxing. Spending the majority of yesterday ravishing Scarlett and allowing her the same courtesy was decadent and unmatched. It was worth it, but I should have taken advantage of the time to sleep well.

Once Cap finishes, Greyson elbows me. "You look exhausted."

"I am." The lack of sleep is a completely acceptable trade-off.

"What's her name?"

"Dude, again with the lack of respect. Not only are you disrespecting me but my woman too."

"So you're admitting there is a woman."

I consider avoiding his question, but I don't. The idea of making our fake marriage real doesn't terrify me, nor does sharing we're dating. "Yes, there is and, no, I won't tell you who she is."

"Why not?" Greyson almost whines.

"You don't need to know. Eventually, I'm sure you will meet her." I would prefer to keep Scarlett to myself if possible. I know it isn't realistic, but my stunning woman is perfection in a curvy package. "I respect her and myself too much to gossip about our relationship. You should consider it yourself." I walk away. I give Greyson until the end of the day before he spills the little bit of news he learned and I have a flood of inquiries about my woman. At lunch I check my messages and reach out to Nadine.

> *Scarlett: Hey! Please remind me about lunch with Savi and Sam.*
>
> *Me: Okay. See you later.*

The call connects with my sister. "Hey, sis!"

"Hey."

"Thank you again for forcing us to leave."

"You're welcome. I remember the strain, especially the lack of sleep. I mean, I slept, just not well or enough. It wasn't the only issue in my marriage, but it certainly pushed us over the top."

"I understand. Given your subterfuge with Gladys, has she updated you on Mom's status?"

"She has, but I would appreciate your perspective."

I drop my head. "She's on a roller coaster, Nadi. One day she has a good day, up and about playing cards with Gladys and watching *Hamilton*, and the next...."

Nadine fills in the rest. "She doesn't know your name or where she is."

"Yeah, exactly. It's awful."

"I'm not sure if it's worse for her or for us."

I reply, "I would say it's about even or slightly worse for us."

"I agree. I wasn't a fan of moving her in with you, but it was necessary. That isn't a slight."

"I know. You feel like you failed her by having to choose your family over her. I get it." The guilt Nadine carries is too heavy for the choices she was forced to make. I know we made the right decision moving Mom in with me.

"Exactly."

"We'll see what her doctor recommends, but I'm not sure I can handle moving her yet."

"I get it, more than you know." Nadine pauses and then switches topics. "On a completely different note, Scarlett is—"

"Everything I need and ever desired for myself."

"I was going to say perfect, but your words are better. I love her for you, Zack."

"Thanks."

"Balancing yourself, Scarlett, and Mom isn't going to be easy. Please ask for help next time well before you're overwrought and exhausted."

"I will."

I field one inquiry all day but patch through numerous calls despite the fact it's Sunday. When I arrive home, Scarlett is already there, and Gladys is gone.

"Hi, Mom," I say as I step into the kitchen and find my woman and my mom cooking. "Hi, babe." I kiss Scarlett lightly. "What's going on here?"

"I wanted to help cook," Mom explains. "Scarlett suggested we make your favorite dish for dinner. It's almost done."

I never told Scarlett my favorite meal. "Sounds perfect. I'm going to change. I'll be right back." When I return, they are plating dinner. By the looks of it, Scarlett either guessed properly or Mom told her. My favorite childhood meal is homemade macaroni and cheese with three varieties of cheese. I'm secretly hoping for the former.

I pull out Mom's chair, then Scarlett's, and take a seat. "This looks amazing!"

"Of course it is! Your wife slaved in the kitchen," Mom informs me.

Scarlett stifles a chuckle but watches me until I take my first bite. *It's scrumptious.* "Well done, sweetheart." I lean over and kiss her.

"Hey, I helped," Mom interjects.

We laugh and enjoy the rest of dinner. I don't need Scarlett to share Gladys's report for the day. Mom had a good one.

"Son, can you handle the dishes while Scarlett helps me turn in?"

"Absolutely." I clean the kitchen in about the same time it takes for Scarlett to assist Mom. "How was the rest of your morning? Did you sleep in?"

She wrinkles her nose. "I tried to, but I'm no longer a fan of sleeping alone."

"I like waking up with you tucked against me too."

"Good, I plan on using your comfy bed instead of the guest bed."

"I see. Are you going to steal half of my closet too?" I see thoughts and ideas spin in her mind.

"Not yet."

I'm completely on board with her sentiments. I don't know exactly how our future will play out. As long as Scarlett is beside me, I can handle anything. Well, at least I hope I can study without her innocently distracting me while she does the same. "Time to study?"

"Yes, no wiggling out of it for either of us."

"Fine."

"First, my sister wants to have lunch with us soon. When is your next weekend day off?"

"I have Saturday off in two weeks. Work for you?"

"Sure. I'll text her right now."

While she texts her sister, I grab drinks and my books. We spend the next few hours studying before falling into bed. Near one, a loud thud startles us awake.

I'm on my feet and partially dressed when I hear Mom's voice echo up the stairs. "Scarlett."

Scarlett is halfway downstairs.

I tug on some clothes and follow her. My mother is lying on the floor at the foot of her bed. She's wearing pajamas, a sock on one foot and a flip-flop on the other. Scarlett is examining her from head to toe.

"Carol, what day is it?"

"It's the weekend. Sunday, I think."

"Good. Can you wiggle your toes for me?"

Mom does.

"Can you squeeze my hand?"

Mom complies.

"Carol, can you sit up slowly?"

"Yes." Mom sets her hands on the hardwood and pushes up to sitting with Scarlett's help.

Scarlett's tone is soft and calm when she asks, "Where were you trying to go?"

"Home. This is your home with Zack. I don't belong here."

"Right now, you live here," Scarlett reminds her.

"No. My address is 18… 1882 Gerrard Lane."

Scarlett drops her head. I don't recall telling her my childhood address, but Gerrard Lane isn't correct.

"Let's get you back into bed, Carol," Scarlett suggests.

"No, I want to go home."

I join them on the floor and face my mother. "Mom, this is your home now." Maybe we were wrong moving her here. Perhaps I should've moved into our childhood home instead of her moving to Nadine's first. No matter what we choose, this disease continues to steal my mother away.

"No, this is your home." Mom's tone is adamant and steadfast.

"It is, but it's your home too. You sold the house."

"Why would I do that?"

Anguish flows through me. I glance over at Scarlett who nods slightly. It's plausible my words will send my mother into a full-blown episode. "You sold the house after Dad died. Then you lived with Nadine for a little while, and now you live here."

With tenderness and sadness, Mom whispers, "My Saul is gone?"

"Yes."

A wave of unmistakable grief passes over my mother. She pushes to her feet. With assistance from Scarlett, she resettles into her bed and tugs the covers to her chin.

"Good night," she dismisses us.

We leave her tucked in her bed. The turmoil she must be feeling is unfathomable, her soul-crushing grief renewed. The moment we're in the living room and obscured from Mom's view—although she's likely not focused on us anymore—I hold Scarlett flush against me. Her heart beating against my chest soothes me more than I could possibly explain. After an indeterminate amount of time, I add some space between us. "How did you know that wasn't my address?"

"It's the address of the Tanner family from *Full House.* She presses a kiss to my lips and sets her head against my shoulder, her breath teasing the crook of my neck. "You should go get some sleep."

I press a kiss to the top of her head. "Not alone."

"I need to stay down here for a bit longer to make sure she's okay. Go. I'll be up in a little while."

I shake my head defiantly, settle onto the couch, and open my arms to her. "I'm staying with you."

"As much as I want to feel your arms around me, you need good sleep, Zachary."

"I appreciate your desire to take care of me, but it's either okay sleep here with you or crappy sleep upstairs wishing you were beside me." Note to self: Scarlett melts into a puddle of mush when confronted with pure, unadulterated honesty.

She staggers her legs around mine and lowers herself on top of me. I tug the cozy blanket from the back of the couch over both of us and chase the last few hours of sleep before work.

Before six, I hear the faint tones of the alarm. The next thing I hear is my name as someone nudges me.

"Zack, Scarlett, you're both going to be late."

I peel my eyes open and see Gladys beside us. It takes a second longer to realize it's already six in the morning. "Thanks, Gladys."

She nods and leaves.

"Scarlett, we need to get up."

"No, I want to stay here with you," she mumbles against my chest.

"It's past six, sweetheart," I inform her.

The moment she processes my words, she's sitting on her heels over my leg. "We never set an alarm down here."

"No, we didn't. We have to go."

She leans down and skims a kiss across my lips before hustling upstairs. Fifteen minutes and a flurry of activity later, we hurry downstairs to start our day. Despite it not being her job, Gladys has brewed a pot of coffee and set two muffins on paper towels on the island.

"Thank you, Gladys."

"Merely a small thing I can do to assist you two lovebirds."

Curious phrasing, but today I'll take it. We hustle to work after a quick kiss. I barely make it to roll call on time this morning. As expected, Cap summons me.

"How is your mother?"

I close my eyes briefly. "Deteriorating, Cap. For lack of a better term, she tried to escape last night. She was trying to go home."

"She lives with you, right?"

"Yeah, she wanted to go back to my childhood home and see my dad."

"How terrible. I'm sorry," he offers.

"Me too. What can I do for you?"

"I have assigned you two shifts with the detective division next week. Please check the schedule, dress code, and report as required."

"Thanks, Cap."

"You're welcome. On a more personal note, Kelsey asked how Scarlett is doing."

I can't prevent the smile the mere mention of her name causes. "She's great with my mom."

Cap pauses. Not what he was truly asking. Clearly, Kelsey shared about our Perk discussion and phone delivery. "We're doing well. Schedule is a tad tricky, but we're working with the time we have. Our schedules will loosen up a bit when she graduates and passes her boards."

"Glad to hear it. I shall report to my wife only positive comments."

I laugh. "Much appreciated." What is everyone's sudden interest in my dating life? I shake off the thought and start my patrol for the day.

The day passes smoothly. On the way home, I pick up some flowers for Scarlett and a plant for Mom's room. I pass Gladys on my way into my complex and wave.

"Hey, honey, I'm home."

"Shhhh!"

I lower my voice and repeat myself. "Hey, honey. I'm home." I hand her the huge bouquet of flowers. I chose them for the colors. I have no idea what variety of flowers are included, but given her reaction, I chose well.

"Thank you. These are beautiful. How did you know my favorite flower?"

A small grin curls at the edge of my mouth. "I got lucky."

She beckons me closer with her finger. "We both did." Her lips are soft against mine.

I lift her onto the island and settle between her thighs. "Yes, we did." Scarlett makes me believe a love and marriage like my parents had is possible for me—for us. I lose myself in her scent and the taste of her on my tongue until the timer pulls me from my delicious thoughts. The sheer notion of taking Scarlett on this island makes me harden instantly. Then my brain reminds me of our reality, I'm aroused, and I won't do anything about it, not here. "You had time to cook?"

She presses a kiss to the tip of my nose. Every inch of her luscious body brushes against me until she reaches the floor. She pulls the pan from the oven and turns everything off. It's only then do I notice the table is already set too. "How was your shift?"

"I was in pediatrics. Nothing serious today. Took care of a few long-terms and discharged three siblings who were treated for smoke inhalation." Long-terms are patients who return frequently due to their diseases or stay for long periods of time for the same reason. "What about you?"

"I was on patrol. It was uneventful, which is preferrable. I almost forgot, Cap set me up with two shifts with the detective division next week."

"That's exciting! I'm so happy for you."

All I can do is smile at her. This woman genuinely wants me to reach the goals I set for myself. I can't say the same for any other woman I've dated in the past. I want the same for her.

"How is the studying coming along? Can you get the sour cream, salsa, and drinks?"

I comply and pull out her chair.

"Thanks."

Apparently I'm starving. I take a few bites before complimenting her. "This is delish!"

She smiles and continues digging into the chicken burritos she made.

"To answer your question, I'm moving through the material at a good pace. What about you?"

"Right now I spend half of my time on my classes and the rest on the review sheets for the boards."

I polish off the rest of my food and steal a bite from her plate.

"Steal my food again and I'll stab you with my fork."

"Damn!" Surprise is evident on my face.

"There's more on the stove."

"Not a fan of sharing?"

She winks at me. "Generally, I don't mind, but my tacos from lunch were gross."

"Fair enough." I refill my plate and ask, "How many more weeks of school?"

"Five more weeks of classes and then exams for two weeks. Then I have two months to prep for the boards and find a job."

"Have you decided which specialty you want to pursue?"

She frowns. "I'm waffling between pediatrics and memory care."

"Is there a way to have both?" I doubt it, but I ask anyway.

"Not really. Unless I choose pediatrics for my day job and continue to work with patients like your mom in the overnight hours."

Then she won't be here anymore. Fake married in these walls within a week of knowing one another is a bit unorthodox, but I'm not willing to let her go. I compose myself before asking, "Is that what you want? Two jobs."

"No, not at all."

I exhale sharply as quietly as I can muster. The relief that courses through me is immense. "Is there a way for you to decide other than how you are right now?"

"Not really." The distress of making the wrong decision is weighing on her.

"You're stressed about choosing?" I lift her hand to my lips and kiss the back.

"Yeah, I am. I don't want to choose wrong." The tension in her frame increases tenfold.

"I'm here to listen whenever you want to talk. However, have you considered talking to Willa, or do you have a guidance counselor for nursing school?"

She grins at my terms.

"Maybe she has a solution you haven't thought of, or she can create a position for you? I don't know. For example, you're a nurse at the hospital and float between the units whether over the course of a week or whatever she needs."

Scarlett pushes back in her chair, stands, and throws her arms around me. "Thank you. I didn't think of that as an option. I do have a semester-end review and meeting with Willa and the program director."

"Anytime. As much as I don't want to remind you, we need to study."

She drops her head and heads to sets up our study area. A few hours of work later, we turn in for the night.

CHAPTER FOURTEEN

SCARLETT

Unfortunately for me, Carol's restlessness continues. She was up twice last night. I was able to slip out of bed and handle the second time without waking Zack. My shift today will require copious amounts of coffee. Zack is working with the detective division today. His pinstripe suit is perfectly tailored to his body. The total package is mouthwatering. Yet the sleeves rolled to his elbows to stay clean, leaving his forearms exposed, is insanely hot. The ideas floating through my mind right now are delicious and worth trying, but…

"Scarlett."

I hear my name in the recesses of my brain.

Zack slides his arm around my waist and lifts my gaze with two fingers under my chin. "Are you okay? What are you thinking about?"

I glance around us and crook my finger, beckoning him closer. I answer a hairsbreadth away from his soft lips. "Future-detective Smithson's work clothes, especially the exposed forearms, causes all kinds of reactions." His tux for the gala may make me combust.

"If I were to dip my hand into your sexy lace panties, would I find you soaked for me?"

Yes, absolutely yes! "Without question."

"It's too bad I can't verify right now." His voice sounds strangled, which is additionally arousing.

"Yes, it is."

He sets my entire body on fire with a fierce kiss that reaches from my lips to my toes. "Go change. I'll finish the coffee and breakfast."

I hurry upstairs and change as he demanded. I needed to anyway. Seriously, I need to control my responses to him. Mentally, I slap myself. No, I don't. I need to purchase more panties though. I push my sexy thoughts away and return to the kitchen.

"Better?" His question is laced with interest and a dash of squashed desire.

"I'll survive."

"Me too, gorgeous."

We greet Gladys, and I give her a rundown of last night's care before we make our way to work. The only benefit is my meeting with Willa is scheduled for three, so I'll be off the floor a bit earlier than normal today. I walk into the hospital, and Stacey immediately sends me upstairs to pediatrics. Since my talk with Zack last night, I'm not any closer to choosing. After putting my bag and phone in my locker, I greet the other nurses and get to work.

Keegan is back with complications from his treatment. "Hi, Nurse Scarlett."

"Hi, Keegan. How are you feeling today?"

"Much better. I think my mom overreacted this time."

I check his vitals and reply, "Moms are usually right."

"I know. It's better for her if I'm home. It's easier for her to work and take care of me at the same time."

"She's doing her job."

Keegan glances over at his mom. She's in a conference call from the looks of it. Her job must entail working with people from other countries. It's early in a typical American workday. "Those clients are in France and Italy. It's the afternoon there."

"You're looking good to me. I'll see if we can get you home today."

"Thank you."

I exit the room and make a few notes before opening my next file. The name makes my stomach fall to my toes. Benjamin Ramirez. He was admitted about two hours ago with unexplained weakness, pale skin, and overall crankiness, which is normal for a toddler. The other symptoms, not so much. I knock on the door and enter. "Morning, William. Kelsey. How's he doing? How are you doing?"

"Morning, Scarlett. They're still working on it. We're fine," Kelsey answers.

"Hey, little guy."

"Hi. Who dis?" he asks.

Cap answers, "Do you remember Scarlett from Mommy's work?"

Ben says my name he's used to, "Let?"

"Hey, Ben. Don't worry, it's a new place to see me." I check his vitals, the IV line, and make notes. His pallor is better. I raise my hand in front of him for a high five. He complies with good strength. For extra confirmation, I slip my finger into his hand. His grip is decent. "Do you need anything?"

"No, we're fine," Kelsey replies.

"I'll be back when his test results post."

"Thank you," Cap replies.

"You're welcome. We'll figure out what's going on with your little guy."

Cap nods, and I slip out of the room. I immediately contact food services and request two parent breakfast trays for them. I notate his chart and move on to my next patient.

"Hi, Mariah." Mariah is back for another ulcer on her leg.

"Hi, Nurse Scarlett." I check out her leg and her vitals. The infection is worse this time.

"You must be Dad. Pleasure to meet you." The man standing near the window turns to face me. His stature would be imposing if his weariness wasn't evident.

"Morning. I'm James. I take it you've cared for Mariah before."

"Yes, sir. The last time she was here. You were catching up on your sleep. It seems hospital sleep isn't your friend."

He smiles. "No, it isn't."

I nod. "Looks like you need some stronger meds this time."

"No worries, I've got this!" Mariah announces.

"Yes, you do!" I smile, elbow bump her, and leave the room. I take a seat at the nurses' station, makes notes, and refresh my screen for Ben's test results. I know it's as effective as repeatedly pushing the up or down button on an elevator, but it's all I can do right now.

Nearly two hours later, Ben's results come through. I inform his doctor and make my way to his room.

"Let, you're back," Ben greets me. It wasn't quite that clear, but I understood him.

"I am. How are you feeling?"

Kelsey smiles, and Cap acknowledges my presence in the room.

"Better." He nods tightly to show emphasis.

"Good." I turn toward Cap and Kelsey. "His test results are back. Are either of you anemic?"

"No," Cap replies.

"I was as a young child, but nothing past age six," Kelsey offers.

"The doctor ran a host of tests to check the levels in his body. All were normal except his hemoglobin level. The doctor tested him for a condition called thalassemia. It's an inherited blood disorder caused when the body doesn't make enough of a protein called hemoglobin. It's a treatable condition. His appears to be minor and may only require additional folic acid and monitoring as he gets older."

Palpable relief passes between them. "Thank you, Scarlett, for the information and the breakfast. It wasn't necessary."

I could tell they needed coffee and food. Being in a hospital is stressful. Add on top of that it's their child, it was the least I could do to make them more comfortable. "You're welcome. Dr. Bronson will be in to discuss more treatment specifics with you. Then I'll see how soon I can get you on your way home."

"Thank you," Kelsey replies.

I leave the room and let out a slow breath. Given my need to decide on a specialty, caring for Ben hit a bit differently today. Regardless of the age of my patients, you never want to lose any. The likelihood of losing patients in a memory-care placement is inevitable. Whereas with pediatrics, it's not as high. Ben's case may be the tipping point for me. It wasn't serious as far as his diagnosis. At the end of the day, he'll be going home, much like Keegan and Mariah in a few days.

In the locker room, I grab my phone and check my messages.

Zack: Any chance you can meet me?

The message was sent two minutes ago.

Me: Where?

Zack: Outside the ER.

Me: On my way.

Zack: I'm waiting.

I can't stop the smile on my face. I don't need more attention than any other woman. Zack seems to find the right balance. Somehow, he knew I needed to see him today. It hasn't been an especially difficult day as far as types of patients, only how they affected me.

I step outside and look to the right.

From my left, I hear, "Hi, beautiful."

I turn my gaze left, and there he is with tacos and a coffee. He truly gets me; plus he knows I was up most of the night. "Hi." I stare at him for a beat before asking, "How opposed are you to me kissing you right now?"

"Not opposed at all."

"You realize there are cameras and the entire staff could see."

"I'm fully aware and ready to handle our relationship being known publicly. You?"

Instead of answering, I set one hand on his chest and cup his jaw with the other. "I can handle anything with you." I kiss him hard. I don't know how long we're kissing, but it sounds like we have an audience. I hear two voices calling from behind us. They pull me back to true reality, not the reality with only Zack and me, which is preferrable. I add some space between us and set my head on his chest. I don't acknowledge his coworkers yet, but ask, "How many?"

"Two, Hagen and Greyson," Zack responds and presses a kiss to my head.

I turn to face our inquisitors tucked into Zack's side.

"How long has this been going on?" Hagen asks.

"Long enough," Zack replies. I'm sure he doesn't intend on sharing the whole fake married aspect of our relationship. The fewer people who know about our charade, the better.

"No wonder you refused to share her phone number. You were pursuing her yourself. What about the other smoke show?"

When was this? Who is he talking about?

"You're an idiot, Greyson. Essie is married to my mom's nurse's son, something you would notice if you were paying attention."

The longer we chat with his coworkers, the more hospital staff surreptitiously take a walk or stroll outside for air. The most notable from the emergency room is Carly. Not to cast aspersions, but Carly is a known gossip. She's cute, blonde, and bubbly but not annoyingly so. I give her until the end of shift before the entire hospital and PD know about Zack and me.

"Scarlett. Officer Smithson," she greets us both.

Before I can acknowledge her, I get paged to Ben's room. "I need to go. Thank you for lunch." I kiss him quickly, then grab the bag and my coffee. I won't be able to eat slowly or enjoy them, but the sentiment is appreciated. I never experienced it before, but I'm a fan of someone, more specifically a smoking-hot, protective, creative man, taking care of me.

"You're welcome," he replies as I walk away.

It's impossible to miss the hoots and hollers from his coworkers. You would think their questions in my presence would've been enough. I inhale the tacos, put my phone in my locker, and gulp down my coffee before stepping into Ben's room.

"Let, Let!"

Dr. Bronson pauses, then continues follow-up instructions with Cap and Kelsey.

"Hi, Ben. Ready to go home?"

"Yes."

I softly explain to him what I'm going to do to get him home. I take my time removing the IV and letting him choose a Band-Aid. He selects a Paw Patrol bandage with Everest on it over the Spiderman with the slimmest hint of hesitation. I clean him up and tug on clean clothes laid out on the bed.

He stands and throws his arms around my neck. "Thank you."

"Anytime, buddy." I hope there isn't a next time, but I'm glad he's comfortable with his visit. When he completes his chat, Dr. Bronson leaves the room.

"Thank you, Scarlett." Kelsey draws me into a hug while I'm still holding Ben.

"Momma, squeeze too tight."

We all laugh, and Ben shifts into Kelsey's arms. "Please say hello to Zack for us," Kelsey requests.

"I will. Let's stroll on out of here." I escort them to the exit through the emergency room.

Carly catches me when I make my way back inside. "So how long have you and Smithson been an item?"

I glance around us and guide her into a small alcove. "Look, Zack and I both prefer to keep the details of our relationship private. It's been long enough that we're both comfortable with other people knowing we're together. Those details are what I choose to share at this time."

"I understand and respect your boundaries."

"Thank you, and I appreciate your discretion with the little information I shared."

"Have a nice afternoon, Scarlett. Don't forget your meeting with Willa in thirty minutes."

"Thanks, Carly." It isn't odd for Carly to know the schedule. She's second-in-command in the emergency room and has access to all the schedules to pull as necessary for major traumas and staffing shortages from other floors.

I return to the nurses' station and check the boards. Keegan is ready to go home. I grab his chart and spring him and his mom. When I return from escorting them out, I rapidly finish my charts for the day and head to my meeting with Willa and Ms. Swanson.

"Come in, Scarlett," Willa calls as I'm about to knock on her office door.

"Afternoon. Hello, Ms. Swanson."

"Hello, Miss Clemons."

So formal.

"As you know, this meeting is required for your nursing program to graduate. Your classwork and field work here are exemplary. You're to be commended for your dedication both here and in the classroom," Willa opens the meeting.

"Thank you."

"Miss Clemons, I echo the sentiments Mrs. Cappelli has stated. You're on the verge of finishing first in your class. It's an amazing accomplishment."

Wow! I knew I was close to Jenna, but in the lead, no way. "I appreciate it. Thank you, Ms. Swanson."

"Given your grades and stellar work here, you have met your requirements to graduate and apply for the board exam in July. Have you given any thought to which specialty, if any, you wish to pursue? Are you planning on staying local?"

Ms. Swanson's ringtone prevents me from answering immediately. "My apologies. I need to take this. I'll see you tomorrow, Willa. Congratulations, Miss Clemons."

I wait until Willa's office door closes before replying, "I hope to stay local. As far as the specialty, I'm still caught between two. There's no way to make both work at the same time without working two jobs. Frankly, I don't want to do that after graduating."

"I understand. If I can pry, what two are you deciding between?"

"I'm torn between memory care and pediatrics. After today, I'm leaning toward the latter. Caring for Carol is rewarding and frustrating at the same time." Not only because of my growing feelings for Zack. "Staying with memory care will put me in contact with more patients in end-of-life situations. I'm not confident I can handle the emotional ramifications for my entire career."

Willa takes a few moments before responding. "I understand. You are correct. Those specialties don't cross, you can't do both without two jobs. You have plenty of time in your career to shift over to the patient base you don't select initially. I hope my advice helps. We have openings on both floors. I highly encourage you to apply for one of them."

"I hadn't considered simply holding off as an option." It makes the decision so much easier.

"You mentioned Carol. How is that going?"

A wave of sadness passes through me, a little for Carol but mostly for Zack. "She's deteriorating. Carol is well into stage five. It's heartbreaking for her family. Her agitation increases, as do her restless nights."

"How long do they plan to keep her at home?"

"As long as possible. They have an appointment on Thursday with her team."

"How is Zack?"

I pause to carefully select my words. "He's dealing as best he can and attempting to maintain his own life."

"Does that include his relationship with you?"

"That was fast," I blurt.

Willa raises an eyebrow in question. "What do you mean?"

"He stopped by today to bring me lunch and coffee because I was up with Carol twice last night. Not only did Hagen and Greyson see us together, so did Carly."

Understanding crosses her face. "I was asking because I think you two are a good match. I didn't know he was here today. However, the entire staff here and in our first responder community will know soon if Carly does."

"Yeah, we know."

Willa laughs. "Here are the applications for both floors. They're due in three weeks. Both positions would afford you time off after the end of the semester to study. You could begin working provisionally once school ends per diem if you wish."

"Thank you. I'll give it some thought and talk with my sister." *And Zack.* It should terrify me to get his input, but it doesn't, not even a little.

"Have a nice evening, Scarlett."

"You too." With a spring in my step, I make my way to my car. As if lunch, coffee, and announcing our couple status to the hospital isn't enough, there's a card and a rose on my car. I've never felt about a man the way I do about Zack, and I'm never letting him go.

CHAPTER FIFTEEN

ZACHARY

Today's appointment is necessary, but I'm dreading it. I step out of the shower and catch Scarlett's silhouette through the ajar door. Waking up beside her has become a life goal. The trick is going to be how to balance my life and caring for my mother.

"I feel you staring," she says as she tugs on her leggings.

I push the door open more. "You're gorgeous and mine. I have permission, don't I?"

She saunters closer, and I tug her against me. "You do, but we need to choose our timing better."

"I know. I don't like it, but I know. What time are you done with class today?" I press a kiss to her lips and reluctantly release her.

"I should be home by noon. What time is Carol's appointment?"

"Ten. Can I stop by when we're done?"

She pauses fixing her shirt. "You're always welcome." We finish dressing and are enjoying our coffee when Gladys arrives for work.

"Morning, lovebirds."

I'm still not sure why she uses the term when Mom can't hear her. Yes, we're dating, but…. "Morning."

Scarlett runs down Mom's night for Gladys and puts her mug in the dishwasher before grabbing a water and a muffin. "I gotta go. Text me when you're finished."

"I will."

She presses a light kiss to my lips and bounds toward the front door.

"You two are perfect together," Gladys states.

She isn't wrong. "Maybe."

Luckily, I'm saved by Mom waking for the day to avoid continuing this conversation with Gladys. I know Scarlett is the one for me; I simply want to share my feelings with her first.

After dressing and breakfast for Mom, we take two cars to her appointment. Nadine pulls into a spot a few rows behind us about the same time.

"Morning, Mom," she greets our mother first. "Gladys. Zack."

"Sis."

"Morning, Nadine," Gladys replies.

Mom says nothing.

We make our way to the office and check in. We're only in the waiting room for a few minutes before they take Mom back for new scans. She requested Gladys accompany her for the scans instead of Nadine this time. Nadine obliged.

"How was she last night?"

"Same as since we last talked. Her episodes are increasing in frequency—day and night. None have been major though."

"Do you think our current plan is adequate?"

"Other than not getting enough sleep, Scarlett handles her episodes well. Mom heeds her."

"I know we promised her, but what if her team thinks she needs to be moved to a facility?"

I drop my head in my hands. Despite the difficulty of having my mother in my home, I don't want to renege on our agreement. "Let's see what her doctors say after her scan."

"Okay."

"How are the kids? Any progress with Trevor?"

My sister frowns. "The kids are fine. They've adjusted to Trevor not acting like their father anymore."

"Jackass."

She shrugs. "He asked to come home. Apparently, things aren't working out with Kellie."

"How do you feel about that? Do you want him back?"

Nadine stews on my question for a bit longer than I expect.

"You don't have to answer."

"It isn't that. I never thought I would be here. Divorced with two kids. I wanted what our parents had. The naïve part of me believed Trevor was the guy. To answer your question, no, I don't want him back. I don't care if Kellie, whom I've never met, throws him onto the street. He isn't coming back to live with us."

"Good for you."

"What about you and your *wife*?" My sister uses air quotes as if I'm unaware that Scarlett isn't actually my legally wedded wife.

A huge smile grows on my face. "I'm falling for her hard. It's impossible for me not to see her as my wife for real in the future."

"I'm happy for you, Zack. Scarlett is wonderful with Mom, and she makes you smile brighter than any woman before her, though there weren't many. The true test though is does she know all of you?"

"Thanks. If you're asking does she know I paint, she does." I was wholly honest when I said I never shared my paintings with any other woman. It's telling I shared with her, especially if Nadine sees it as well.

"Has she seen more than the ones along the staircase?"

"Yes. She actually gifted me display lights for those four."

Nadine smiles over at me. "Hold on to her, Zack. She sees every facet of you. You've never let any woman in as deep as her."

"I plan to." It's terrifying and blissful at the same time.

Dr. Brown calls us into his office. "Zack and Nadine, please have a seat."

He has bad news. I should've expected it.

"Your mother's scan revealed increased plaques on her brain. Her condition is nearing stage six. I strongly recommend moving her to an inpatient facility."

My heart aches in my chest. I knew the day would come when Nadine and I needed to make this choice, but I'm not ready.

"How fast will her limitations increase?" Nadine asks.

"It's hard to say. I suggest making the calls to put her on facility waiting lists immediately if you haven't already."

"Thank you, Doctor," I mumble, thoughts and worries pinging around in my head. Interestingly, one of them is Scarlett and the fact she gave up working at the Perk to work for us.

"You're welcome. Feel free to take a few minutes to talk in here before you leave." Dr. Brown closes the door behind him.

"What do you think?" I ask my sister.

"It truly isn't up to me. It's up to Gladys, Scarlett, and you. The burden is on the three of you. We can have a serious conversation with each of them and then decide. How do you feel about it?"

"I think we need to talk to Gladys and Scarlett, but also put Mom on the waiting lists too."

"Are you sure about that?"

"No, not at all, but it isn't about me. I can't imagine a bed will become available this week. It'll likely take weeks."

"So we're agreeing to put her on local waiting lists and go with Gladys and Scarlett's opinion as to whether they can handle her care at your townhouse?"

"Yes."

"Okay. This sucks, Zack."

"Yup, it does. So very much." It's devasting and heart-wrenching to make this choice. I never wanted this responsibility. I'm sure Nadine didn't either.

"Any chance Scarlett is available to talk now?" Nadine asks.

I would much prefer to spend the afternoon twisting the sheets in Scarlett's bedroom with ocean air washing over us. I glance at my watch. "She should be arriving home any minute now."

"Can you invite her to meet us at your place for lunch or out if you prefer? We can talk to Gladys after settling Mom in the car."

"Out. Any preferences?"

"No. You decide."

I pull out my phone and text Scarlett.

Me: Can you meet me and Nadine for lunch?

Scarlett: That bad?

Me: Possibly.

Scarlett: Sure. Where?

Me: The gazebo on Short Sands in about an hour.

Scarlett: I'll be there. xoxo.

I inform Nadine. "She'll meet us for lunch."

We join Gladys and Mom in the waiting room. Once Mom settles in the car, Gladys turns to us. "It isn't good news," she suggests.

"The plaques are more evident. Dr. Brown feels it's time to move her to an inpatient facility or, at a minimum, on wait lists. We want your opinion and Scarlett's as well," I share with Gladys.

"Overall, her condition has deteriorated rapidly in the last five months. Her episodes are still manageable, although they are increasing in frequency. I would agree with Dr. Brown as far as the waiting lists. I wouldn't say she needs to be moved tomorrow, but starting the process is a smart plan."

"Thank you for your candor. We are meeting with Scarlett for lunch. We'll keep you informed of our decision," Nadine answers Gladys.

"Thank you. I'll see you later, Zack. Bye, Nadine." She drives away with Mom and heads home.

"Where are we going for lunch?"

"I'm going to grab sandwiches at the deli near Short Sands. We're meeting at the gazebo," I inform my sister.

"That works. I'll take a—"

"Italian combo with salt and vinegar chips and a peach iced tea. Don't worry, I remember." I place the order and drive to pick it up. After I park, I take a moment to absorb the salty breeze and calming sounds of the waves. When I arrive at the beach, Nadine and Scarlett are chatting like they're old friends.

"Don't let me interrupt," I say as I approach them.

"Not at all. Nadine was sharing some embarrassing stories about you from childhood." Scarlett rises and kisses me hello. Too short a kiss in my opinion, but I respect we aren't alone. I don't miss the glee on Nadine's face either.

"Not the falling through the ice story," I whine.

"The one and only," Nadine replies.

"Not right, sis. Not right. What if I share the comb, chocolate sauce, and peanut butter story?"

Nadine freezes and shakes her head. It would serve her right. "Fine, no more childhood stories unless you share them first. Fair?"

"Fair." I empty the contents of the bags onto the table and distribute everything. Scarlett's eyes light up when she realizes I've been paying attention. I noticed she would've preferred the turkey, salt and vinegar chips, and the raspberry tea when we ate at her condo, though she willingly gave me the chips and the tea because I requested them.

"Thanks." She squeezes her hand on my thigh beneath the table.

"You're welcome."

We eat in silence for a few minutes before discussing Mom's appointment. About halfway through, Nadine shares Dr. Brown's findings with Scarlett.

"You want my opinion?" Scarlett asks.

"Both you and Gladys's," I reply.

"Her condition is worsening. I know it isn't easy to hear, but it's the truth. Dr. Brown's advice is wise. The two of you can always hold off if a bed becomes available before you're ready or feel it's unnecessary. As far as my opinion, I can manage her increased symptoms until you"—she motions between Nadine and me—"feel it's time for her to be placed. I know it isn't an easy decision. Your focus needs to be on Carol and where she'll be safest, not necessarily where you two promised she would be or what you want."

Honest but tough words from Scarlett, though it'll cost her job. Nadine fails to mask her reaction. I gather she expected Scarlett to advocate for Mom to stay home as long as possible to keep her job. I never doubted for one second Scarlett would put Mom above herself. It's me who feels responsible for taking her income away. Clearly, Scarlett doesn't blame me at all. I'm an imbecile for failing to see she would put her patient above herself before now.

"Thank you, Scarlett. We appreciate your insight. We're leaning toward putting Mom on the waiting lists for local facilities."

"If I may suggest one you should avoid unless it's the last resort," she says.

"Any insight you have would be appreciated," Nadine adds.

"I would avoid Pine Glen in Wells. Two of my classmates' parents recently took over, and they're having issues with staff turnover and are unable to provide a safe patient to staff ratio," Scarlett shares.

"Understood. We're grateful for you giving up your time off and your input, Scarlett."

"You're welcome." We finish our lunch, and Nadine takes off to get home before her kids.

The sunlight and the ocean breeze accentuate Scarlett's already stunning features. She mesmerizes me. "Do you have things to do before work tonight?"

"No, I planned to spend my free time with you when you were finished with Carol's appointment. Do you want to talk more?"

"Yes. No. Maybe. Hashing out my mom's care plan isn't how I was planning to spend time with you. Come on, I want to show you something." We dump our trash and stroll with our fingers threaded together down the beach.

"I'll go anywhere with you, but where are we going?"

She can bring a smile to my face regardless of the tenor of my day. We are almost to our destination.

"When I was about ten, I found this cavern tucked in the rocks along the edge of Short Sands beach. We haven't reached the true beginning of tourist season, so it's likely empty right now, like much of the sand."

"Wow, this is beautiful!" she says, surveying the rock formations. "How deep is it?"

We explore the cavern slowly and then meander our way back to her condo. I drop my keys in the bowl near the door and toe off my shoes.

"Do you want to talk more or just be?"

"Both, but mostly just be with you." Before I get distracted or we get too caught up in talking or each other, I set an alarm on my phone for five. We lay on the balcony couch. Scarlett tucks against me, her head on my chest, the ends of her hair tickling my forearm gripping her rib cage. For a while, neither of us speak.

"What didn't you share when Nadine was with us?" she asks softly. She can read me better than anyone ever has. I have no chance of hiding anything from her, not that I want or plan to.

"I feel like I'm failing."

She shifts back and lifts her eyes to meet mine. "At what?"

"All of it—work, studying, caring for Mom, courting you."

"You aren't failing at any of it."

I have no words to respond. Thankfully, she isn't done.

"First, if you were failing at work, Cap wouldn't have recommended you for the exam and the open spot in the detective division."

She has a point.

"If I'm impacting your studying, we can do it separately."

"No, the last thing I want is less time with you." My words come out harsher than I plan them to be. Not less true, but… I refuse to give up the cobbled together time we have. Exactly like we are now. I'm not focused on Scarlett. I'm worried about me, about my life.

She pushes off my chest to sit up. The glimpse of her purple lace bra isn't helping me focus on our discussion either. Straddling my leg, the warmth of her briefly short-circuits my brain. I look skyward to recenter my focus.

"As far as caring for your mom, what else do you think you should be doing?" She's putting me on the spot.

"I don't know. Should I be visiting with her right now? Knowing she might not know who I am or the devastating choice to play along when she believes I'm my father. Faking that hurts deeply. She doesn't remember me, her son, but the love she shared with my father she recalls more frequently. The more sacrificial and poignant part is I want that type of love, but I want her to remember her relationship with me too."

"Zachary, look at me."

Slowly, I turn and lower my gaze to her face.

"In here"—she points to my head—"you know that isn't true. In here"—she places her hand over my heart—"it hurts like hell because the mother you know is increasingly slipping away each day. Balancing each aspect of your life with her care isn't an easy task. You already knew that to be true when you took over for Nadine."

"I wasn't prepared for the heart-splitting pain her failing brain would cause."

Her hand slides up from my chest to cup my face, the warmth of her hands spreading through me like wildfire. "No one ever is, regardless of the amount of reading, self-proclaimed preparedness, and actual preparation. Family members, especially those who choose to be caregivers, always need a reminder. Alzheimer's is a debilitating and degenerative disease that ravages not only the patient but her family as well. Choosing to accept Dr. Brown's recommendation doesn't make you or Nadine horrible children. It makes you human, compassionate, and willing to recognize her care is beyond your capabilities regardless of any promise you may have made to your mom before she reached her current stage."

My eyelids flutter closed as I compose my thoughts. Before I open them to look at her again, I begin to speak, "No one has ever succinctly wrapped the impact of Mom's diagnosis and how I feel better than you."

"I meant I would listen, Zack, and I always will. As far as your mistaken belief that you're somehow failing me, I assure you, you aren't. I also meant when I said I don't need to be wined and dined. No man has ever made an effort to show me they care more than you. You leave flowers and notes for me to find. Hell, you're the only man who learned how I take my coffee, what sandwich and chips I prefer, and willingly allows me to steal your bed without complaint. Did our relationship start off oddly? Sure. Does it mean we are skipping around in the learning-about-one-another aspect? Also yes. Are you failing as my boyfriend? No, not at all."

I love that title. I want to keep "husband" as well—someday. "The chaos of my life is a lot right now. I care about you, and I refuse to allow it to ruin what we're building." I more than care about her. I can't imagine my future without her.

"It won't. I care about you too. No matter how long we're in your self-described chaos, we're in it together." She lowers her mouth to mine and kisses me slowly, leaving no question in my mind her words are honest.

I wrestle control of our kiss from her and travel as low as her V-neck tee will allow. I lift her tee overhead and slide the strap of her bra to her elbow. I guide her to standing and rise to my feet. With each step backward, we lose an article of clothing. After verifying her door is locked, I move behind her at the edge of her bed. I drag my hands up the back of her thighs and spear her core. She rides my hand until her inner walls are pulsing around my fingers.

So far she hasn't attempted to retake control. Being with Scarlett is different and mind-blowing each time. I guide her to the middle of the bed and turn her to face me. I hover over her, holding her wrists above her head with one hand. With the other, I wrap her leg around my hip and plunge into her tight, soaked center in one movement. We feel better than ever before.

"Sweet mercy!" falls from her lips.

"Is that a good thing?"

She draws me deeper with her other leg wrapped around me. "Yes. Oh my… yes!"

With each thrust, Scarlett meets me with equal, deliberate strokes. Every time with her is increasingly earth-shattering. Watching her fall into bliss—raptured bliss we create together—

is the most exquisite sight I've ever seen. Her fingernails bite into my hand, and we tumble over the edge at the same time.

I collapse on top of her and release her wrists. Her hands slide over my shoulders and settle on either side of my waist. Almost immediately, I realize my mistake and tense. We didn't use protection. I didn't protect us.

"Breathe, Zack. I have an IUD."

I exhale sharply and look down at her.

"I want a family one day, but today or anytime in the next year or two isn't when I want to start trying."

"Same, though I'm a little older than you." The trill of my alarm sounds from somewhere on the floor.

"Is that what I think it is?"

"Unfortunately, yes." I kiss her deeply, withdraw, and shut off the alarm.

"I'll be out in five minutes. Then I need to pack my books, and we can cook at your place."

"That works." I watch my gorgeous woman walk into her bathroom. No woman ever believed in me like she does. Scarlett is confident I can handle all aspects of my life right now. While the seeds of self-doubt will always be present, I'm going to trust her and her words. Keeping those in mind, I'll make the best decisions I can for each part of my life and handle the repercussions, if there are any, with her beside me.

CHAPTER SIXTEEN

SCARLETT

Bright sunlight draws a strip on the ceiling above the window. As much as I don't want to, I leave the warmth of Zack's embrace to head home before dress shopping. I wash up and take a seat on the edge of his bed.

"Baby, I need to go. I'll meet you at Morgan's at one."

"Stay with me," he grumbles, barely awake.

I'll admit, sleepy Zack is hot as hell, but still second to future detective Zack. "I can't today. I have an appointment for my gala dress."

"Fine. I'll see you later."

At first I'm not sure if he's upset or not. The last week or so with Carol has been anything but smooth. She wakes almost nightly but is easily coaxed back to bed. Zack and Nadine have put her on a few local waiting lists. Most indicated it would be at least a month before an opening. "Did you forget?"

"No," he grumbles. "I don't want you to leave so soon."

"Either way, we would be getting out of bed to greet Gladys. This way, I can give her the report and you can stay in bed a bit longer."

He smiles with his eyes still clamped shut. "I love the way you think, beautiful. I'll meet you there."

I kiss his soft, full lips, which most women would kill for, and attempt to move away.

He hauls me back into his arms. "That was nice, but it won't do for the next six hours." Zack kisses me with a newfound possessiveness I love. There's no question he's mine and not worried about meeting Savi the slightest bit.

"Better?"

"For now." He kisses my forehead and releases me.

I make a cup of coffee and wait for Gladys to arrive.

"Morning, Scarlett," she greets me.

"Morning. Overall, her night was okay. She woke twice but never left her bed. We talked for a bit, and she fell back to sleep."

"Thank you. Have a great time with your sister."

"Thanks. Bye, Gladys."

I head home. When I turn from depositing my keys in the bowl, I find Lia sound asleep with a cute guy on the couch. The television is playing cartoons. I smile inwardly when I recall finding Savi and Sam in the same position early in their relationship. I tiptoe past them and slip into my room. I consider going back to sleep for a little while, but sleeping alone has lost all its luster. I don't need to sprawl out in my queen-size bed. Snug in Zack's muscled arms is the only place I sleep well. I dump my books on my bed, grab a study guide, and review for the next hour or so.

Freshly showered, I step into the living room and note both Lia and her overnight guest are gone. I walk toward So Elegant to meet Savi at ten. As I round the corner, I find Lia strolling back toward home with goodies from the Perk.

"Morning, roomie."

"Morning, Scar. This is for you." Lia hands me a scone and a coffee. "I appreciate you sneaking in."

"No problem. Was the cute guy your classmate?"

A look of disappointment appears on Lia's face. "Yeah."

"You need to talk about it?"

Lia shakes her head. "Nothing to talk about. He isn't looking to date anyone right now."

"Sorry, Lia."

"Me too. Have fun dress shopping. Will you be back before lunch?"

"Not sure. Are you working this afternoon?"

"Tonight until close."

I hug her. "Thanks for breakfast. I'll see you in the morning."

We walk our separate ways. I take a heavy sip of my latte and tuck my scone away for later. Savi rounds the corner to the shop at the same time I arrive.

"Yay! I miss seeing you so much!" As usual, my sister looks perfect in casual clothes. She did before earning enough for designer labels.

"Hi, Savi." I absorb the sisterly love in her hug. She presses the doorbell, and we're greeted by Billie, Savi's sister-in-law.

"Savannah and Scarlett, nice to see you. Come in." She offers us goodies from the Perk, but I decline.

"No thanks, Billie." Savi and Billie hug, and I take a seat.

"Let me get Kelly for you. She's in the back." Kelly Barnett is a sought-after couture dress designer. When she applied for a job costuming for movies, she met her husband on her first costuming job. Not only did she launch a new avenue for her career, but they live happily ever after with two kids and a dog.

"Morning, ladies. Nice to see you both again. I have a room set up for each of you. Savannah on the left. Scarlett on the right."

I reluctantly set down the remainder of my latte and step into the dressing room beside Savi. I scan the dresses and select one without trying it on. I save it for last, knowing it'll be perfect. I tug on a mermaid dress in royal blue and step outside. Savi is beside me, also wearing a royal blue dress, but hers dips low in the back and has a halter-style neck.

"I like it, Savi, but it's missing something."

"I agree. I don't like that one on you."

"On to the next," I state and turn with flair back into the dressing room.

Billie and Kelly laugh. I try on the remaining dresses and nix them all. I circle back to the one that caught my eye when I first stepped behind the curtain. It's aubergine silk with ribbons of material crisscrossing my back. The gorgeous dress fits to the waist, offers a modest amount of cleavage with a slightly flared full skirt, a thigh-high slit, and the only accessory every girl wants—pockets.

When I step out from behind the curtain, all talking ceases.

Savi breaks the silence. "Wow, Scar. That's stunning."

"Kelly, you have seriously outdone yourself with the design," Billie offers.

"Thanks. I love it. I chose it first but wanted to make sure."

Kelly approaches with her alteration kit and asks, "Is anything pulling or tight? Is the hem where you want it?"

"It fits as if I gave you my measurements and you designed it for me."

Kelly smiles.

"More like there's a man in your life who makes you feel complete and comfortable with yourself exactly as you are," Billie adds.

She's absolutely correct. "He does."

A chorus of "awwwws" surrounds me.

"Welcome to the club, Scarlett," Savi states.

I shake my head. "Nothing is official. We're still new. However, everything feels different with him."

"You mean rock-your-world different or outside of the bedroom?" Billie asks.

I blush, knowing my sister is part of this conversation. Then when I think more about it, I own the heat Zack puts in my heart and body. Savi isn't naïve. She took me to get on birth control when I was sixteen. "Both actually," I reply.

"Even better," Kelly adds. "Do you need shoes?"

"No, I have my eye on a pair that will cost me a fortune but will be perfect."

"Are they in my closet?" Savi asks.

We all laugh.

"You have a pair, but I want my own."

Savi smiles. "You're welcome to borrow them and hold off on buying your own."

"Thanks, Savi. I'll think about it. You should go with the emerald strapless."

"It's my first choice too."

Kelly asks Savi the same questions she asked me. After she rings us out, we schedule a time for us to pick them up before the gala. "Thank you so much for stopping in."

"Only place to find the perfect dress is here," Savi reminds her.

"Thank you," Kelly graciously accepts the praise she rightfully deserves.

We say our goodbyes and exit the store.

"I'll see you in a little over an hour for lunch. I'm going to change and have Zack pick me up."

"I wanted to say without our guys present, you look settled, Scar."

"I am for the most part."

"Is it about Zack?" Savi asks.

"No, not at all. If I could have conjured up a man perfect for me, it would be him. I'm torn between two specialties. I need to decide in the next two weeks. I'm leaning one way but not fully committed. I don't like being in flux."

"I know," Savi confirms. We stop near Savi's car, and she hugs me tightly. "I'll see you in a little bit."

"Promise me you won't go all big sister/mom on Zack."

"I'll do my best to be chill."

I laugh and shake my head.

Me: Can you pick me up instead of meeting me there?

Zack: Of course. Done shopping already?

Me: I knew the moment I tried it on.

Zack: Have a pic?

Me: No, you're going to have to wait. It'll be worth it.

Zack: Fine. I'll be there in about thirty minutes.

Me: See you soon.

I hurry upstairs and change into nicer clothes for lunch. Exactly twenty-nine minutes later, Zack is knocking on my door.

I throw it open and greet him properly with a kiss that should tide us over through lunch.

"Hi to you too! Should I leave and come back to experience more kisses like that?"

I playfully slap his upper arm. "No, you can't. We can kiss more before we leave, but you can't mess up my makeup."

"You're equally if not more gorgeous without it."

My heart explodes into a million tiny shards. He truly believes his words. Before I can form an appropriate response, he devours my mouth, obliterating all thoughts other than him. Each kiss ratchets up the heat between us, and the restraint required to avoid ripping off his dress shirt is immeasurable. Content we'll be able to make it through lunch without pawing at one another, I slowly break our kiss.

"Time already?" Zack whines.

"Yes, unfortunately." I loop my arm through my purse and link our hands together.

As we walk to his car, Zack asks, "Remind me again about your sister and her husband."

"Savi was Sam's assistant. Over the course of a year, they fell in love, she earned partner, and they moved here." We cross the street, and Zack opens the passenger door for me.

"Scarlett."

I hear my name but can't make out the speaker nor can I place the voice.

"Scarlett." The closer he gets, the more into focus he becomes.

My throat closes up, and I find it hard to breathe. I grip Zack's forearm to prop myself up.

He traps me behind the door of his car. "Who is that?" Strong waves of tension and protection roll off Zack.

I have no doubt he won't let me out from behind this door unless I ask and he's completely confident the speaker isn't going to hurt me. Protective Zack is hot as hell. "My father." He looks thinner but, otherwise, the only other thing of note is the gold band on his left ring finger. The woman and young boy trailing twenty yards behind him appear to be approaching with more caution. I tap out a text to Savi and wait for a response.

Me: Dad showed up. We were getting in the car to meet you.

My father speaks again. "Scarlett, are you going to introduce me to your boyfriend?"

I inhale deeply and address my father. "What are you doing here? How did you find me?" My phone vibrates in my hand. I glance down at the preview.

Savi: We're on our way.

Thankfully, it won't take long for Savi to get here.

"I came to visit you for your birthday. It's in a few days. I wanted to introduce you to my wife and your brother," he replies.

I know damn well when my birthday is. If my *father* knew me at all, he would know I don't celebrate my birthday. Never have, never plan to. Zack lowers one hand and threads his fingers into mine. "You didn't answer my question. How did you find me?"

"I remembered the coffee shop and got lucky."

"Brother?" The kid appears to be approximately ten years old. The woman... his wife is the antithesis of my mother in every way. From stories Savi shared and the pictures I've seen, my mother was vibrant and made everyone around her smile. Savi has displayed a picture of my mom in every home we shared. It's on the credenza in her office at home. Our mom is smiling at something out of the frame. It's the image I have of her in my head. His new wife is blonde, thin, and a plain Jane.

"Stephen is your half-brother," my father corrects me.

I tighten my grip on Zack's hand. Savi parks behind the car and tears open the door and rushes up to us. Sam rounds the car and stands beside her. Either Savi briefed him on the way or they've met. The more likely scenario is Sam had an extensive background check completed before he pulled our father out of the clutches of a mafia-connected loan shark. Sam paid off my father's debt to save Savi near the beginning of their relationship. I know Sam well enough to know he won't interfere with our father unless he threatens Savi or me. Sam will have to go through Zack first—literally—if my father threatens me.

"Look, Linda, you get to meet both daughters," my father addresses his wife.

She smiles but doesn't speak.

"We had an agreement," Savi shouts.

My father's tone is harsh when he replies, "No, you made demands and I heeded them until now. I don't need your permission to see my daughter, Savannah."

Savi's foot is tapping on the pavement, and her hands are clenching and unclenching in fists. "Permission, no, but you agreed to let her thrive here, to let her find her way," Savi reminds him.

"Maybe so, but her birthday is in a few days, and I wanted to share my good news. Linda and I got married, and you have a brother."

"How dare—"

I appreciate Savi putting herself between me and our father, but it isn't necessary anymore. "Savi. Savi," I call her.

She turns to face me.

"Perhaps this isn't the place to have this conversation. You and I both know he isn't going to leave until he says what he needs to."

Zack wraps our entwined hands around my back and tucks me into his side.

"What do you suggest?" Savi asks.

"What about the café near the amusement park? They have private outdoor seating."

"Fine by me." Savi turns to our father. "Why don't you meet us at the café down the street and we can talk?"

"Thank you, Savannah," my father replies.

"Don't thank me. Thank Scarlett. She's choosing not to send you packing without hearing you out first." Savi turns on her heels and gets back into her car.

I wait until our unwanted guests wander back to their car before releasing the tension wracking my body. Zack turns me against his chest, and his other arm collapses around me.

"I take it he doesn't show up often," Zack opines.

"Never. Despite what he said, I know he heeded Savi until he didn't have a choice. There's more besides his new wife, my brother, and my birthday."

"You have an idea?"

"Yeah, he's either in debt again and needs money or he's fallen off the wagon. I won't help him again. Twice was enough."

He kisses the top of my head. "You are more incredible than I could possibly fathom."

"Thank you, but the strength comes from choosing wrong and being let down before."

We make our way to the café and join Savi and Sam at a table.

"Savi and Sam, this is Zack. Zack, my sister and her husband, Sam."

"Pleasure to officially meet you both." Zack extends his hand to them, which they graciously take.

"We've met before?" Sam asks.

"We met on your very first day in York Beach," Zack shares.

"He spilled coffee on Scar at the Perk," Savi informs her husband. After nearly ten minutes pass, she mutters, "I feel like I'm waiting to be executed."

"This is literally two blocks away." The moment the words leave my mouth, my father, his new wife, and my little brother round the corner. From the look on her face, I get the feeling Linda isn't too pleased with the situation.

"Thank you for waiting and agreeing to hear me out," my father mumbles as he takes a seat across from us. "There are two reasons for my visit. First, I wanted you to meet Linda and your brother, Stephen. Despite how it looks, I didn't know about Stephen until three months ago. He's ten years old and lives with Linda in New Jersey."

"Stevie, these are your older sisters, Savannah and Scarlett."

"Hi, nice to meet you." Lucky for Stevie, he looks like Linda. He's blond, rail thin, and has dark-rimmed glasses.

"Hello," Savi and I say in unison. "The second reason?" Savi asks.

"Scarlett's birthday, of course," he replies.

"You truly don't listen, do you?" Savi grumbles.

I set my hand on her forearm. "I've got this, Savi." I take a deep breath and compose my thoughts before addressing my father. "I don't celebrate my birthday. I never have. Not once in my entire life."

Linda looks shell-shocked. Clearly, my father didn't share all his missteps during my childhood with his new wife.

"If you were a better caretaker when I was younger, you would know it's painful for me to celebrate knowing Mom isn't here. Painful for me to be happy on the same day she died. Difficult to avoid blaming myself for her death. Hell, you would know if you tried to get to know me now."

Zack's arm tightens around me, and he flips his other hand in his lap. I curl my hand around his.

"I don't know what to say." Arthur Clemons speechless, that's a first.

"What's the true reason you're here?" Savi asks. Her skepticism is warranted, given our history with our father.

"I understand your reluctance to believe I've changed. I failed both of you as a father. Now, I have a second chance with Linda and Stevie. Should I have called first? Yes, but I doubt you would be willing to meet with me if I had. There's no ulterior motive this time. I'm working my programs for alcohol and gambling. I found a respectable job. I've truly made progress, and I thought you two would like to meet me sober and meet your brother."

He may have a point there.

The look on Savi's face is utter shock. "How long will you be here?"

Our father attempts to speak but fails more than once.

Linda sets her hand over his and answers, "We'll be here until Friday. Stevie is on spring break. We're staying at a hotel in Portsmouth. The local ones were booked. Perhaps we can set up a time to get together?"

I look over at Savi and agree without words.

"Why don't you give me your number, and we can set up a lunch?" Savi asks.

Linda produces a pen from her purse and scribbles her number on a napkin. "Thank you. I understand our showing up was abrupt and disruptive. I look forward to getting to know both of you better. Pleasure to meet you, gentlemen. Have a good day, ladies."

"You as well" is all I can produce as a reply.

Silence falls over the table until Linda speaks again. "Arthur, Stevie, let's go."

Without another word or indication how he's feeling, our father rises from his chair and follows his new wife and son toward their car.

Zack leans in and whispers, "What can I do for you right now?"

I turn away from Savi and Sam so only he can hear me and Savi can't read my lips. It's a skill she honed while mothering me. She eavesdropped on all my conversations without discreetly lifting the receiver in the other room. "I don't need anything. I can handle my father and everything else the world throws at me with you beside me." I press a kiss high on his jaw.

"I feel the same way about you."

Zack and I stay in our own little private, wordless bubble until Savi clears her throat. "So, Zack, welcome to our crazy family."

Zack laughs, and Sam shakes his head. "Thanks, I think."

"As much as I would like to talk about our father and his apparently newfound stability and sobriety, I need to get ready for work. I don't know what your schedule looks like, but the only day I'm free for lunch is Thursday," I share.

"We can probably make that work too," Savi replies. She rises and opens her arms to me. "This isn't what I had in mind for our meet-the-boyfriend lunch."

I laugh. "Me either."

Savi whispers, "He's good for you. I like him."

"Me too, Savi. Me too." I release her and smile.

The guys shake hands, and we walk back to my condo. We're about halfway there before Zack utters a word. He lifts our linked hands to his lips and kisses the back of mine. "Truly, how are you?"

"It felt good to put him in his place, to get some of my pent-up feelings out. However, he does appear to have made strides in the last six months. I'm willing to meet him for lunch and take small steps from there. Afterward, I need to focus on finishing school, choosing a specialty, and kicking the boards' ass."

"I'm insanely proud of you for becoming who you are on your own, Scarlett."

"I had a lot of tough love from Savi, but I am too." I key open the door to my condo, and we step inside.

"Why don't you grab what you need and meet me at the house? I'll pick up some food to cook for dinner."

"Okay."

He winks at me. "Any requests?"

"No, whatever you choose will be fine." I slide my arms around him and kiss him lightly.

Thirty minutes later, I head to work with decisions to make for my professional future, my personal life, and a mountain of studying with a tiny amount of sleep.

CHAPTER SEVENTEEN

ZACHARY

Since our impromptu meet-the-parent lunch with her father, Scarlett has thrown herself more into her studies. I'm not sure if he was the catalyst or the fact her birthday is today. Since we met, I considered ways to celebrate her on her birthday without it being in bold, colorful lettering. After her statements to her father, I dialed back my plans a bit. The morning was chaotic because we were up a few times last night with Mom. I barely got an appropriate kiss goodbye. I promised not to push her, and I won't. I switched assignments with Hagen to make sure I was home as early as possible. For whatever reason, the citizens of York Beach were not visiting the precinct today. I'm grateful.

"Hi, Gladys," I greet her when I arrive home.

"You're home early," Gladys observes.

I purposefully didn't share about Scarlett's birthday today to respect her wishes. "Got lucky today. How did it go here?"

Gladys's face falls. "Today was moderately difficult. She spent most of the day calling for your father. Her nap didn't calm her mind."

"How long has she been sleeping?"

"About thirty minutes. I'm not sure she'll make it all night, Zack."

"No problem. We can handle it," I reply.

Gladys raises an eyebrow. "We?"

I shake my head. "I'm mostly a bystander. I get up at least the first time Mom does. I owe it to her to be better."

"Her—Carol? Or her—Scarlett?" Gladys inquires.

"My mom," I answer honestly. The garage door opens as we wrap up our conversation. "I'll share with Scarlett. Have a good night, Gladys."

"You too." She waves to Scarlett on her way out.

I draw her into my arms and kiss her breathless. "Hi, gorgeous. How were your classes?"

"Boring, but I'll take it. I'm almost done. One more week of class, one week of exams, and then graduation. How bad was Carol's day?"

"Gladys used the words moderately difficult. She's been sleeping for about thirty minutes."

"What was the trigger today?"

A deep sadness fills my chest. "My dad."

"I know it hurts, but perhaps it would be easier for you to look at it as if she remembers him because it was who led her to be happiest. Her marriage gave her you, Nadine, and her grandchildren."

Her words render me mute. I always saw her seeing me as my father as a bad thing, like my mother didn't remember me at all. Looking at her attachments from Scarlett's perspective gives it an entirely new outlook. All I can do is tighten my hold on her and breath her in. Once I settle my heart rate and thoughts, I pull back. "Why don't you change while I start dinner?"

"What are we having?"

"Spaghetti with meatballs and cheesy garlic bread." I don't miss the look of delight and confusion appearing and disappearing as quickly on her face.

"Okay. I'll be right back." With a quick kiss, she bounds upstairs.

When I finish pulling out the ingredients and pour two glasses of wine, she rejoins me in the kitchen. My woman is gorgeous regardless of her clothing choices. However, my Scarlett, everyday Scarlett with no makeup, hair tied away from her face, wearing skintight leggings and a threadbare tee is my absolute favorite. "How can I help?"

"Can you sit there with this glass of Riesling and let me cook for you?" This is only a small push. I won't push back if she fights me.

She takes a seat and a heavy sip of the wine.

"Thank you."

She nods. "How was your day?"

The pasta water is boiling, and the meatballs are cooking. Before answering, I add the pasta and slide the bread into the oven. "It was slow. Only two concerned citizens stopped in today. I was able to study some while manning the desk."

"That's good. You have another six weeks or so, right?"

"Yeah." I catch her gaze, round the island, and kiss her like I'll never get enough. I never will. Scarlett makes me slow down and appreciate the little things in life, knowing at any time, it could change and will never be the same.

"Zack?" My name comes out in a pant.

Water is overflowing from the pasta pot. Sizzling sounds filter into my brain. "Yes, beautiful?"

"The water."

"Huh?"

She pushes off the stool. Ignoring the friction of her body sliding down mine is impossible. She moves to the stove and lowers the temperature of the pasta pot. I surround her with my arms from behind, my rock-hard length settled between her cheeks. The sigh falling from her lips stirs my already-at-attention shaft more. I kiss her temple. "Thanks. Back to your seat please."

She hesitantly obliges. I finish cooking with no more mishaps. We take a seat at the table and dig in.

"This is amazing!" she exclaims after the first bite hits her tongue.

"It's only pasta."

She sets down her fork. "No, it's not. Did you talk to Savi?"

I wrinkle my brow in confusion. "About dinner? No. Why?"

"You chose my favorite comfort food for tonight on your own?"

Well done, Zack. "It happens to be mine too."

"Cheesy bread too?"

"Especially the cheesy bread."

"Thank you." She covers my hands with hers.

"You're welcome."

"Zachary, I don't mean only for the pasta. It's hands down amazing, but I mean for not pushing, for respecting my request."

I love you. Yet I can't bring myself to say it to her. If I do, she'll know she possesses the ability to crush me into a billion miniscule pieces. I need to accept she won't before telling her. Exactly like I won't crush her either. "Scarlett, I've never met anyone like you. I wasn't expecting you and how we would change me. I understand why you don't want to have balloons and streamers today. I will go out of my way to make you happy." I almost add "for the rest of my life" but don't. I swipe the single tear falling down her cheek with the pad of my thumb.

"I'll do the same for you."

The air around us is heavy and thick with unspoken words. It's in the way we look at each other, but neither of us can voice it. I'll spend every day for the rest of my life making Scarlett's dream come true. The trick is going to be making myself believe I deserve her and won't screw it up.

While we clean up, I ask, "Do you need to study?"

"No, I'm taking tonight off. Do you?"

"No, I got enough done during shift. What do you want to do?"

She taps her index finger on her lips. It's sexy as hell, and she doesn't realize it. "Will you watch a few episodes with me?"

"Yes. Can we watch upstairs?"

A sly smile curls at the corner of her lips. "Sure." She peeks in on Mom as she passes before climbing the stairs.

Each day we skirt the rules I set in my mind for Scarlett's working hours. It's bad enough she sleeps secure in my arms. I'm torn between doing the right thing and doing what will propel us forward as a couple. Limbo sucks. The torment in my mind doesn't help either. I'm a grown man, and I feel guilty considering making love to my girlfriend in my own home. My heart and mind tumble my thoughts around for a few solid minutes. I push them away and focus on snuggling with my woman on the worst day of her life. One that repeats each year.

My only hope is my mom sleeps past midnight so it isn't officially her birthday anymore.

She strips down to her panties and a camisole. After setting her clothes on the dressing bench, she slips beneath the covers. That simple act dampens every sex-filled idea in my mind. She makes sure her clothes are ready to throw on at a moment's notice. I tug my shirt overhead and join her. Propped up on pillows, I drop my arm around her and tuck her against my side. She presses her lips to my chest and sets her head down before starting the next episode.

Halfway through the second episode, Scarlett snores softly. I smile, slip the remote from her hand, and stop the stream. I tug the blanket up to cover her and let my eyes drift closed. Right after five in the morning, I wake up cold. I slide my arm out and note Scarlett isn't in bed anymore. I hate she moved out of my arms and I didn't wake.

I tug on a shirt and pad halfway down the staircase. My paintings with the newly installed display lights catch my eye. She sees me. Why can't I bring myself to admit it to her?

"Thank you," I hear my mother softly say.

"You're welcome. Do you need anything else?" Scarlett asks.

"No, I'm fine."

I hear the telltale sound of coffee brewing. My beautiful woman isn't coming back to bed today. I tiptoe back upstairs and consider going for a run. Instead, I hurry through the shower so Scarlett will have time before she leaves. As I step out of the shower, I hear Gladys arrive early.

Scarlett steps into view as I survey my closet for an appropriate shirt and tie. She wraps her arms around my waist and sets her head between my shoulder blades. "Thank you." She kisses my damp skin and releases me.

"You're welcome. Go, the water is fresh and crazy hot like you prefer."

She winks at me and tugs off her clothes without completely closing the bathroom door, leaving the nip of her waist and the curve of her ass on full display for the briefest of moments. I adjust myself and head downstairs. Scarlett is a lifetime of sinful temptation. Unfortunately, I don't have time to worship her properly right now.

"Morning, Mom. Hi, Gladys," I greet them as I step into the kitchen.

"Morning," Gladys replies.

Mom looks up from her breakfast but says nothing. I prepare two cups of coffee and a to-go breakfast for both of us. Scarlett skips into the kitchen a few minutes later.

"Ready?"

"Yes. Bye, Gladys. Bye, Carol. See you tonight."

Gladys sends us on our way.

I kiss her deeply beside her car. "I'm sorry I can't go to lunch today."

"Don't be. Savi and I can handle it. Have a great day with the detectives."

"You know I would prefer to be with you, right?"

"Yes, and I want you there too, but he barged into our day without as much as a call or heads-up. True, we probably would've ignored him, but still."

I smile, steal another kiss, and open her door. I'm rooted in place until she pulls away. I drive to the precinct and head to my soon-to-be new home. I hope.

CHAPTER EIGHTEEN

SCARLETT

Yesterday was the best birthday I've ever had. The fact I set my phone on silent was helpful. Though the truth is, there's only one reason: Zack. I could never adequately explain how much it meant for him to truly hear me when I said I don't celebrate and resist the urge to force me to do it anyway. It made me love him more. *Love?* Without question or reservation, I've fallen for Zack. Now, I need to share my feelings with him. Easier said than done. I'm scared. The examples I have of a solid marriage are recent, none with longevity. I think about it more, and I realize I do in fact have an example of a stable, long-term marriage—Mr. and Mrs. Cappelli. Not Lia's brother and Willa, but Lia's parents. Before I reconsider, I text Lia.

Me: Any chance your parents are home?

Lia: I'm on my way there now. Join me.

For a brief second, I consider attending my last seminar, which is an extra review.

Me: I'm on my way.

I hope the Cappellis don't think I'm off my rocker. Throwing the shifter into park, I reconsider but then decide asking questions won't hurt. Lia throws open the front door and waves me inside.

"You good?" she asks as I climb to the front porch.

"Yes and no. I'm freaking out."

"About school or choosing a floor or something else?"

No reason to hide where I'm stuck. Lia is my bestie. "Zack."

"Well, Mama is the right person to soothe your soul and offer solid advice about love. Come in." Lia ushers me inside.

"Oh, Scarlett! Wonderful to see you." Mama Cappelli throws her arms around me.

Containing the tears is harder than I anticipated.

All it takes is one look at me for her to go full mama bear. "What is the term you young people use these days? Spill it? Pour it out? Tell me what's on your mind, young lady."

I laugh. There's no way Mama Cappelli watches *Sweet Magnolias* to know "pour it out" is actually a thing. She shoves a plate of muffins in front of Lia and me. Lia selects one, and we pick at it together.

"I need some advice. I met a guy."

Lia jumps in, "Mama, she's talking about Smithson."

I glare at my bestie, but I don't miss the smile on Mama Cappelli's face.

"Smithson is a good man. Rough situation with his dad passing and his mother's illness. It takes a toll on a family. I'm sorry, please continue. I gather you already know those details."

I dip my chin. "He makes me feel things I've never felt before. It's terrifying and exciting all at once."

"Ah, young love. How does he feel about you?"

"I think we're both stuck in the afraid-to-admit-our-feelings stage. He takes care of me when he doesn't have to, he pays attention, and, most importantly, he listens when I share or request something. He follows through when he says he will and refrains when he says he will. Yet he's holding back; I'm not sure why though. My parents weren't married long before she died. The rest of my couple examples are less than ten years. You and Papa Cappelli are the only example I have of a long, stable marriage. What does a lifelong commitment and building a life require?"

"What about me?" Papa Cappelli joins us in the kitchen.

"Hey, Papa. We're spilling secrets about love and marriage," Lia informs him.

"Morning," I greet him.

"All this beauty in my kitchen is always welcome. You're too young, *fiore*."

"We aren't talking about me, Papa, but I strongly disagree. You and Mama were already married at my age."

"She speaks the truth, *amore mio,*" Mama Cappelli reminds him.

"Yes, she does. They both have time though," Papa Cappelli replies.

"They do, but one should never be afraid to express their feelings. It's the only way to move forward. Luca never gave up on Willa, and we're gaining another grandchild."

I look between them, and all I see is love. They are disagreeing about the right course for me, and yet they respect one another and their opinions. It's what I want, a partnership, and Zack gives it to me. The bigger question is, do I wait or tell him now?

"To answer your question, a relationship with longevity takes honest communication, respect, humility, and a healthy dose of amazing sex," Mama Cappelli shares.

"Mama! Ohmigod!" Lia shouts with a pained look on her face.

"*Fiore,* there are five of you. Do you seriously think we're celibate?"

"No, Papa! But still… now after forty-plus years of marriage… gross!"

I can't contain my laughter anymore. My heart is full and settled. I wish I could get to Zack right now. It'll have to wait, but Mama Cappelli is right. I need to tell him and soon.

"Not to cut this short, but don't you have a lunch meeting with your dad in an hour at Morgan's?" Lia asks.

"I do. Thank you both for your advice. I appreciate your insight."

"The two of you should join us for family dinner when things settle down with his mom," Mama Cappelli suggests.

"Thank you. We will." I round the island and hug them both.

"We're here for you anytime, Scarlett."

I push down the brewing tears. Mama Cappelli is the best. I always wonder if my mother would be like her if she were still here. I take a deep breath and settle myself. The what-ifs get me from time to time. Now isn't the time to dwell though. Lia follows me to the front door.

"I'm so glad I found you when I moved here." I hug her tightly as well.

"Me too. Good luck."

"Thanks. I'll see you on Saturday morning." I hurry to my car, significantly lighter than I was before I arrived. I pull into Morgan's lot right on time, and the hostess escorts me to our table. Only Savannah has arrived so far.

"Hey. How are you?"

"Good. You?"

Savi lifts an eyebrow in question. "Outside of this lunch, my family is amazing. What's up with you? You're different since I last saw you."

"I sorted through some relationship and work stuff in the last few days. Plus, Mama Cappelli's muffins can heal nearly anything."

Savi smiles. "Good for you. You decided on a specialty?"

I nod, but before I can answer, the rest of our party arrives.

Linda and Stevie grab a seat, but our father pauses with his hands on the back of his chair.

"Arthur, sit," Linda instructs. He says nothing but takes a seat. I don't know my father sober, nor as a married man.

"Thank you for coming," he acknowledges us.

"You're welcome," I reply.

Savi greets him with a curt nod.

Our server takes our drink order and leaves.

"So… Stevie, you're ten. Fifth grade, right?" I break the ice.

Delight crosses his face. I gather he thought we would ignore him. "Yes, fifth grade."

"What is your favorite subject?" Savi asks.

"English, actually. I think it's because my mom always forces me to read extra pages each day."

I laugh along with Savi and Linda.

Once we order our meals, Linda co-opts the conversation. She inquires about Savi and me in the interest of getting to know us better. Her questions will also share information with our father, who is listening intently. Both of us respond to her questions vaguely. As we eat, our father asks a question here or there, but his wife and Stevie are fueling the conversation.

Baby steps, and I'm fine with them. Linda is neutral as far as I'm concerned.

"Do I have any nieces or nephews?" Stevie asks. Smart kid. The question makes sense given his age.

As Savi is about to answer him, August Morgan chooses this precise moment to stop by our table and introduce himself to our guests. I'm confident Sam made Auggie aware of this meal and requested his brother check on Savi. Little does Auggie know he may have saved his sister-in-law from divulging more than she's ready to share.

Savi does in fact wiggle out of answering the question as our server drops our check and our father moves to leave.

"Arthur," Linda directs with a pointed tone.

Our father turns back. "Savannah and Scarlett, thank you for coming. I appreciate it more than you know. I don't deserve your accommodation. I wouldn't dare ask for your forgiveness for how profoundly I failed you as a father. However, I would like to move forward slowly to get to know you now as adults."

Shock ripples through me.

"Perhaps we can come back up for a visit this summer. In the meantime, I would like to talk to you both more frequently," he concludes.

"Linda has our numbers. I can handle more calls," Savi replies.

"Me too," I add.

"Thank you. I'll call soon." With that, our father walks away from the table.

Linda looks between the two of us. "It has been a pleasure meeting the two of you. Despite his failure to ask enough questions, your father is trying. All the progress he shared with you is completely accurate. He's working on himself, and I appreciate you both taking time to open the lines of communication with him going forward."

"You as well," Savi replies. "It was great to meet you, Stevie. To answer your question, which was cut off, you have one niece and one nephew. Maybe you can meet them the next time you visit."

Joy lights up our little brother's face. "Really?"

"Yes, really."

Stevie throws his arms around Savi and thanks her. Then he hugs me too. "I always wanted more siblings."

Linda smiles and follows her son out to the lobby.

"You good?" Savi asks.

"Surprisingly, yes," I reply. "I'm glad Linda was here to guide the conversation."

"Me too. She seems like she's good for him. I believe her when she shared about Dad's sobriety."

I hug Savi, and we make our way to the exit.

"How did it go?" Auggie approaches from the kitchen. Despite being the owner, he prefers to assist his head chef.

Savi laughs. "Not terrible, Auggie. I'll call Sam off for you as soon as I get to my car."

"No worries, Savannah. He isn't asking. I am," Auggie replies. He understands quite a bit about estranged parents, given his childhood.

"We're good. Thanks."

"You're welcome." He hugs us both before we leave.

I take a few settling breaths as we reach our cars. "Love you, Savi. I'll see you and the kiddos soon."

"Love you too, Scar. Kick ass on your finals."

"Oh, I will!" I plan to secure the valedictorian spot if it kills me. It might if I don't sleep in the next week.

Savi laughs and drives away. I check my phone.

Zack: I wish I could be there with you.

Zack: See you when you get home.

Me: I understand. I'll be there in a little while. xoxo.

I smile and make my way to my condo. I pack up my books, clean clothes, and my completed application for work tomorrow. The countdown is on. I have two exams next week and then graduation.

I hurry to work and greet Gladys. "Hi, Gladys. Carol."

"Hello. How was lunch with your dad?" Gladys asks.

I don't recall sharing with Gladys. Either way, I shrug it off. "It was awkward at first but necessary. We made some progress. The scars he left behind are deep and will require healing. Baby steps."

"Good for you. Carol had an okay day. Minimal issues with lapses of memory, but she stumbled in the bathroom."

"Understood. Has she eaten yet?"

"Yes, she's eaten."

Gladys leaves, and I assist Carol in settling in for the night. Then, I start making dinner. I'm about halfway through preparing when I get a text from Zack.

Zack: I'm going to be late.

I have so much I want to share with him, but it isn't his fault he's going to be late. Also, he needs to make a great impression. When he nails the exam, he will earn the promotion. I sigh and respond.

Me: No problem.

I finish dinner, eat some while I wash the dishes, and make a plate for him. After another check on Carol, I grab my books and study for my upcoming exam. After a few hours, I turn in. Near midnight, I wake in an empty bed and tend to Carol. Easing her back to sleep doesn't take long. Thirsty, I head into the kitchen and find Zack's dinner plate is washed. Where is he? As quietly as I can, I open the basement door and descend halfway. Light shines beneath his studio door. My desire to let him paint subdues my urge to share my day as well as to see what he's painting. When he's ready, he'll share with me. As far as I can recall, he hasn't painted anything since I started working with Carol. I turn on my heel and retreat to bed.

CHAPTER NINETEEN

SCARLETT

The dean of nursing stands before the crowd. "I would like to introduce the valedictorian of the one hundredth class of our school, Scarlett Mae Clemons."

I'm not sure who is cheering harder, Savi or Zack. The pages with my speech vibrate in my hands as I take my spot at the podium. To calm myself, I find Zack in the crowd. With the knowing gaze and a devilish grin, he pushes me to deliver my speech. "I overcame a rough childhood to get here. It took grit, gumption, determination, and lots of tough love from my sister." The crowd laughs, and Savi drops her head. I finish my speech and find the entire audience on their feet. Public speaking is never something I care to do again, but I'm glad I earned this speech.

The dean approaches the dais and distributes the diplomas. As I cross the stage, I know moving here was the best choice for me. When the ceremony ends, I weave my way through the crowd, accept flowers, then jump into Zack's open arms. Savi, Sam, the kids, and Lia are smiling wide.

"I'm so proud of you, beautiful," Zack whispers and places a kiss high on my cheek.

The only approval I ever sought was Savi's. The sheer notion someone outside of my sister is proud of me matters more than he knows. "Thank you, charming." I hug everyone more than once. I'm grateful the ceremony is during the day and Gladys agreed to stay with Carol until we get home.

Savi is planning a graduation and board exam bash for the end of the summer. After another round of congratulatory kisses, hugs, and photos, we make our way outside. Zack rounds his car after closing my door. He threads his fingers into mine as he pulls out of the parking lot. I'm more focused on how far I've come and how much more I need to do than where he's driving.

"Zack, this isn't the way home." I was looking at his profile, not our route.

He slays me with a gorgeous grin. "I know. We aren't going home yet."

"Because?"

Before he responds, he pulls onto a gravel, nondescript driveway.

Glancing up, I see we're at a restaurant near the water. The views are picturesque. Not to mention, the colorful Adirondack chairs near the shoreline near a firepit look inviting.

"You graduated as the valedictorian of your nursing school. We're celebrating tonight. Just the two of us."

"I have to relieve Gladys."

"You don't. I arranged for Nadine to spend the night to care for Mom. The kids are spending the weekend with Trevor's parents. You worked so hard going to class or work, studying, working with Mom, and not sleeping enough. You deserve to celebrate this milestone properly and tonight, not in a few months."

"You don't need to do this for me."

He turns to face me more fully. "I want to, Scarlett. I listened, and I heard you. More importantly, I believe you. You deserve this and so much more. Someday I'll be able to give it you. For now, I'll work with the occasional times I can plan. Please let me."

The sadness in the word "someday" is heartbreaking. Carol's disease has essentially forced Zack—at least in his mind—to forgo chasing what he wants for himself. I'm not sure there's a way to make him believe he's enough exactly as he is in the very moment.

"No one has ever truly listened and wanted the real me. You aren't giving yourself enough credit either. I assure you, without our dinner this evening, you aren't failing me in any way." I narrow the space between us and kiss him softly.

"Thank you, gorgeous. Shall we celebrate?"

"Yes, we shall."

He laughs softly and leads me into the romantic restaurant. We place our order, and the server walks away.

"How are you feeling about finishing?" he asks, our hands linked between us on the table.

"Ecstatic and terrified at the same time."

"What do you mean?"

I can't contain my smile. He truly listens. "I'm glad school is over, but I still have the boards to pull off. I'm over-the-top excited about working with the kids on the pediatric floor. I need to pass the boards, and then I'll be the real thing. What about you?"

He laughs and lifts my hand to his lips. "You are the real thing."

"You know what I meant."

"What about me? I look forward to the shifts with the detective division. Working cases is where I always wanted to be. Helping solve a case is an amazing feeling. I can't wait to start a case from the beginning though."

Our server approaches with our salads and discreetly walks away after setting them down. We chat more over our delicious meal and decide to take dessert to go.

"Can we sit?" I motion to the chairs and the fire blazing between them.

"Anything you want, beautiful."

You. I want you every, single day. We take a seat in the colorful chairs. The waves lap against the shore in a soothing rhythm. "Zack, I—"

His phone trills with an incoming call. He answers only after he checks the name. "Yeah, Nadine."

I scoop the bag with dessert from the ground, link my free hand with his, and make our way to his car.

"I'm so sorry." Frustration and concern mar his chiseled jawline. The pain and sadness in his eyes is difficult to watch.

"Stop, this isn't your fault."

He mutters something I can't make out.

"Could you repeat that?"

My gorgeous but in pain man grips the nape of his neck and looks at me. "I don't deserve you."

Oh my heart. I grab his forearm as tightly as I can and stop him from walking. "Zachary, look at me."

He turns his gaze to me.

"Nothing about you is undeserving. If anything, it's the other way around." I'm not prepared for the next words to pass his lips.

"I can't do this right now. I don't have one full day.... There isn't enough time for me to demonstrate how amazing you are and the impact you've made in my life." He throws open the door but says nothing more.

I drop my head and sit in the passenger seat. My stomach is churning and not with the butterflies Zack's words usually cause. "Where are we going?"

"I'm taking you to your condo and then meeting Nadine at the hospital."

"You don't want me to come with you?" The words catch in my throat.

"I need to handle this with my sister."

The remainder of the ride passes with abject silence. I don't have a grasp on the English language or my emotions to string together a group of coherent words anyway. Zack pulls up to the curb, and I'm out the door before he can move to open it. Not once do I look back as he pulls away. *What the hell happened?* I barely make it into my condo before the tears plummet down my cheeks.

How did tonight go so wrong? I was on the cusp of spilling my feelings to Zack, and now… I'm all alone, his mother—my patient—is in crisis, and he's broken into a million pieces. It doesn't take me exceptionally long to consider going to the hospital on my own. However, he clearly asked for space to deal with Carol's health with only Nadine. After a pint of Dunne's ice cream, I toss and turn all night long, wishing I could stand beside Zack and support him.

The notification on my phone wakes me at three in the morning.

Zack: They're keeping Mom for observation. You don't need
*   to come in to work tonight.*

Me: Can you come over after work?

Zack: I need some time to figure out my life.

Me: Alone?

Zack: Yes.

Despite feeling all cried out, copious tears fall in rapid succession. I drop my phone on the bed and let the pain take over. Hours later, I hear Lia rustling around in the kitchen and then a light knock on my door.

"What are you doing here?" she whispers as she sits on the edge of my bed.

"I think Zack broke up with me." But he didn't fire me.

Shock appears on Lia's face. I hand her my phone, and she scans my texts. "I don't understand."

"You and me both."

"I thought things were good with you two, solid good."

"So did I. We were having dinner to celebrate, and Nadine called about Carol. The next thing I know, he's dropping me off here, and now he wants time. I'm so confused. I was about to spill my feelings out loud, Lia, and now this."

Lia throws her arms around me and commiserates with me. She makes us brunch and then leaves to get ready for work. I drag myself over and plop down on the couch.

"Do you want me to stay home?" Lia offers.

"No, nothing really you can do except sit with me. Thank you though."

"You would do the same for me."

She's right. I would. I mope around for a few hours and climb back into bed. Holy hell, my heart hurts. How am I going to work for him if he won't speak to me? What if he's done? I wallow some more and let sleep overtake me again.

Near noon the following day, I text Gladys.

Me: Is Carol home?

Gladys: Yes. Didn't Zack call you?

Me: No.

Gladys: Okay. I'll see you later.

Me: I'll be there.

Near five, I pack my bag and the first book for the board review and make my way to work.

"Hi, Carol. Gladys." I maintain a cheerful tone. Zack isn't home yet.

"Hello." Carol's response is barely audible.

"How are you feeling, Carol?"

She drops her head but says nothing in reply.

"How was her day overall, Gladys?"

"She's still tired from the hospital."

"Okay. Thank you."

"What about you?" Gladys asks.

"What about me? He decided to handle it alone; it wasn't my choice."

Realization crosses her face, confirmation of Zack's choice to shut me out. "I see. Have a good night, Scarlett."

"You too, Gladys."

I join Carol in the living room for the news and then assist her to bed. Afterward, I grab my bag and set it on the guest bed while willing my tears away. Before I think better of it, I move my stuff out of Zack's room and into the upstairs bathroom. I crack open my review book and study. Near ten, I crawl in the stuffy, uncomfortable guest bed and attempt to sleep. Carol wakes at one, and I spend nearly an hour talking with her.

"You're such a nice young woman, Scarlett. Take care of my son for me. He needs someone strong like you."

Her words pierce my chest like countless daggers. "Thank you, Carol." If only Zack still wanted to be mine. As if Carol's words weren't enough on their own, Zack overheard them as he passed by her door, and he chose to keep walking. I decide to put him on the spot. After verifying Carol is set, I follow him to the kitchen.

CHAPTER TWENTY

ZACHARY

"Are you going to talk to me or ignore me?" Her anguish squeezes my battered soul.

I'm rooted in my spot facing the sink. My shoulders are slumped, and my back is tight with tension. "I don't know what to say. For once, I was choosing me, choosing my life. You deserve better than to have your celebratory dinner interrupted. You deserve my undivided attention, and I can't give it to you."

"You feel guilty because you weren't sitting at home when your mother needed medical assistance?"

"Yes. I failed her. I wasn't here."

"You trusted your sister, her other child, to handle it. She did. Now Carol is back here. Her disease isn't easy, Zachary."

My head drops, and my chest tightens when she uses my full name. "She's my responsibility."

"You have done more than necessary to keep your promise to Carol. What about what you need?"

"What I need doesn't matter."

"Did we matter? Did I matter?"

I can't bring myself to turn around and look at her. I'm a coward. "More than you know. I can't bring you in any deeper. I'll talk to Willa about replacing you."

"Why? I didn't do anything wrong, Zack. Carol is my patient, and I don't quit on my patients."

Now we're back to Zack. "You deserve more than this." I swivel to face her.

"I decide what I deserve, not you. I need you. I wanted a future with you. Clearly, I misread our connection and time together. I mistakenly thought I meant something to you."

Wanted? Past tense. A few tears roll over the balls of her cheeks. When I take too long to respond, Scarlett trudges upstairs and closes the guest room door behind her.

The urge to destroy something cascades through my body. I storm downstairs and tug on my boxing gloves. It may be the wee hours of the morning, but I continuously punch the heavy bag until my arms feel like Jell-O. My patrol shift today isn't going to be a treat. I let sleep claim me for a short while on the mat in the basement. I suppose some sleep is better than none.

I feel a hard nudge to my hip.

"Zack, get up," Gladys commands, standing over me.

"What time is it?" I lift my wrist in front of my face and scowl.

"Time for you to get moving, young man. You pay me to care for your mother, not you."

Damn! "Yes, ma'am." I scramble to my feet and hustle to the precinct. The fact I didn't see Scarlett this morning is a double-edged sword. My heart aches, not only because I want to see her but because I hurt her deeply… again. I hurry to the motor pool and hop in the passenger seat with Davis.

"You look like hell, man," Davis offers as his first words of the day.

I glare at him. "Thanks." My reply is short and sarcastic.

Davis shakes his head and pulls into traffic. "How can you look so terrible? You have a smokin' hot girlfriend, and you're riding with me."

"At least half of that is true."

"Dude, you didn't? How did you screw it up?"

"Honestly, I don't know how to unfuck the situation I got myself into. I shut her out when my mother needed to go to the hospital and then again when she tried to talk to me. To top it off, it was the day of her graduation."

"For the first time since I met you, you were happy—truly, visibly happy. I may not be a relationship expert, but you'ren idiot!"

There's no response. He's absolutely right, and I know it. The bigger question is, can I fix it? "Yeah, I know. I didn't know how to handle it all." I can't share about the detective exam with Davis, but the exam is something else I need to wiggle out of before I head home tonight.

"Like I said, I'm a relationship novice—hell, I'm barely a rookie—but groveling and lots of it will be necessary given how severely you seem to believe you royally screwed up," Davis assures me.

I cross my arms over my chest and let his words twirl around in my head before acknowledging him with a clipped nod. The rest of our shift passes with limited conversation and no calls.

Davis pulls into the motor pool and offers a final bit of unsolicited advice. "The sooner you start begging for forgiveness, the easier it'll be for you to win her back."

"Thanks, Davis." With my bag in hand, I knock on Cap's door.

He lifts his head. "Come in, Smithson. You look like hell."

I shrug and set the bag of books on his desk.

"What's in there?"

I close his office door and take a seat. "The books you gave me to study. I can't take the exam. My mother is failing."

"I see. Given your win last week, I'm surprised by this development."

I successfully connected two pieces of a case, leading to the arrest of a person of interest. I let my shoulders drop further. "I want to take the exam. However, I can't put in the adequate amount of time necessary to do it properly."

He steeples his fingers. "I thought things were going well with Scarlett caring for your mother."

The mere mention of her name sends my body reeling into despair once again, not that I could forget her or how perfectly we fit. Without a doubt, my feelings are etched on my face.

Cap is perceptive. "You screwed up your relationship too?"

"In epic fashion."

"I won't allow you to cast this opportunity aside. Take a break from studying for the next week. Scarlett was Kelsey's employee and an acquaintance of mine. Romantic partnerships—all relationships—require honest communication and trust. I'm guessing you screwed up in the communication department. If she'll hear you out, talk to her. Share how you screwed up, and then beg for forgiveness."

"I'll see what I can do, Cap."

"I don't usually insert myself into the personal lives of my subordinates. However, given the improvement in your demeanor, you and Scarlett are good for one another. Good luck."

I leave his office, my mind spinning and my heart aching. There's no denying his insight. Scarlett is everything I want. How to win her back is a different story. With newfound gusto, I rush out to my car. As I drive home, the giddiness of knowing she'll be there slowly returns, though it's later than usual. The good news is Mom will likely already be turned in when I arrive.

The same giddiness bottoms out the second I reach my kitchen and find the note on the island.

Zack,

I've installed a monitor in Carol's room. I'll be in the guest room and will keep to myself until you find my replacement. Scarlett.

I scrub my hands down my face. Zack, not Zachary. *Fuck!* Getting her back is going to take immeasurable effort and backup. Before I think better of it, I text the only person who can help me climb out of the crater I dug.

Me: I screwed up.

Lia: Big. Huge.

Me: I know. How do I fix it?

Lia: At the risk of breaking bestie code, you need to beg and do it well.

Me: I will.

Lia: If you're successful, then you'll answer to me for hurting her deeply.

Me: Understood.

Lia: Good luck, Zack. You need it.

I warm some leftovers and start to create a plan. Taking Lia's advice, I send Scarlett a text.

> *Me: There aren't appropriate words for me to explain how sorry I am.*

When I don't get an immediate response, anger seeps in more. Scarlett is the most exceptional woman I've ever had the pleasure of spilling coffee on. I refuse to lose her because I'm terrified of my feelings. I don't get far into planning when I'm called back in to work.

Reluctantly. I knock on the guest room door. When she doesn't answer, I try the knob. It's locked. Is she locking me out or herself in? If that isn't an ice pick deep into my heart. I send a text message to make sure she's aware I left.

> *Me: I have to go back to work.*

> *Scarlett: Okay.*

As I hustle back out the door, I mull over her lack of response to my first message and her response to the second one. She's rightfully angry with me. I hurt her due to my own stupidity and shaky grasp on how she makes me feel. I've never felt whole before. I did with her for a brief moment in time. The gaping dark hole replacing the sense of completeness is unbearable. The mere fact she responded to my second message sets her above every other woman I've ever met. Despite her anger toward me, she intends to fulfill her promise to care for my mother. I'm a goddamn fool for shutting her out.

I compartmentalize my emotions as I head to the scene. I park a block away when I arrive. A fire at a strip mall on the outskirts of town is being extinguished by the fire department. As I approach, I note four companies responded.

"Hey, Madden, Collings. Where's command?" I ask as they adjust the clamp on the hydrant. Both are with station ten.

Madden speaks up first. "Hey, Smithson, command is set up on the south side of the parking lot."

"Appreciated." I hustle to the command center and wait until Cap is free.

"Follow me," Cap instructs. "I apologize for not being clear. You're assigned to Detective Jones for this call. Two victims were pulled from the novelty store. It appears to be a murder-suicide, the owner and his wife. The fire started in an attempt to cover it up."

"Thanks, Cap." I appreciate him not giving up on me despite my request for the same. The words I didn't say, I'm sure he heard anyway. Throughout the night, I work with Detective Jones and his team to gather evidence and process it properly.

I don't make it home until ten the following morning. Scarlett is long gone. I greet my mother, who is listening to some music, and then find Gladys washing dishes.

"How was the overnight?" Gladys asks.

I can barely contain my excitement. "Exactly what I want for my career. Well, the work, not the overnight part."

"Good for you. Now fix what you broke with Scarlett." Gladys is squarely on team Scarlett. I don't blame her.

I'm stunned. "I plan to. I only need to get her to talk to me."

"You mean exactly how you messed up in the first place?" she posits.

"Yes, my missteps have been made painfully obvious through my own realizations and my coworkers."

"It's good to have people around you who call you out when you epically screw up," Gladys adds.

"I appreciate you and them." I clean up and make my way into my studio. It's the second time I've been down here in recent weeks. The last time I was throwing paint onto a canvas, searching for some inspiration. Now I have it in spades. The question is how to get it out of my head and onto the canvas.

I grab the pencil and let it fly across the pad before me. Most of my paintings are landscapes. The only exception is the one of my father and me at the lake. This one will be the second. Near five, I send a text to Scarlett.

Me: Will you have dinner with me so we can talk?

Her response is quick and definitive.

Scarlett: No.

Fuck! Complete and utter failure doesn't begin to cover how significantly I destroyed my relationship. I realize I made a huge misstep, but she won't speak to me. A deeper part of me wonders if I missed something else, something more significant. Undeterred, I make my way to the kitchen and make dinner for us.

After she assists my mother, I knock on her door, which she has locked herself behind yet again. "I made you a plate. I'll leave it out here." Nothing. No sounds come from behind the door. "I would appreciate the opportunity for you to hear me out. I'm sorry I hurt you." Still nothing. Rejected, I set the tray down and make my way downstairs to my studio again.

Hours' worth of inspired painting later, I find the food hasn't been touched, but my note is missing—an invitation to have breakfast with me to talk. Well, for me to talk and her to listen. Without consideration for the lack of sleep, I set an alarm and skip my workout to make sure I catch her before she leaves.

While I'm making breakfast, she greets Gladys and returns back upstairs without a word to me. Rejected yet again, I set the tray by her door and leave for work. I won't give up on Scarlett.

CHAPTER TWENTY-ONE

SCARLETT

The last week has been torture. My heart is shattered, and yet here I am working to brighten the days of young patients. When I submitted my application to work on the pediatric floor, Willa offered me a per diem position until after I take the boards. A few days a week, I work on the pediatric floor and study the other days. At night, I work with Carol.

Overall, she has been awake most nights. If Zack is home, he's either in the basement or hovering when I care for Carol. I haven't allowed him to address our issues. We can't, considering Carol believes we're married. He's seriously making every effort to apologize, but I'm profoundly hurt. I was fine with my past until I let him in.

Sharing the impact of my father's addiction and having Savi raise me as best she could was hard. More difficult was sharing my body with him. I've never given up control in the bedroom, ever. The tiny amount I gave him was indicative of my feelings for him—feelings he disregarded without a second thought.

I push my emotions down and focus on a new patient. Eleven-year-old Elena is here to prepare for a liver transplant. More accurately, her brother is donating part of his liver to her.

"Hi, Elena. I'm Scarlett. Nice to meet you."

"Hi," she mumbles and pulls the pink bunny in her arms closer to her chest.

I take a seat next to her on the edge of the bed. "What's up, buttercup? I'm just here to check on you and introduce myself."

She lifts her eyes to mine. I see fear and trepidation. "I'm worried about Henry."

"Why are you worried about your brother?"

"I don't want him to have surgery for me."

I shouldn't get deeper into this discussion with her without her parents present. They're currently next door with Henry. Her mom, Marci, joins us.

"You should share your feelings with your mom." *Pot— Kettle, Scarlett. Exactly like you should with Zack.*

"I will, Nurse Scarlett."

"Let me know if you need anything, Elena," I add.

"I will."

Smiling, I leave her room and grab my lunch while considering heading outside. The weather forecast calls for a balmy day with highs in the sixties. I nix the idea, wondering if

Zack would show up here to talk during his lunch. I spread my food out on the table in the break room and scan my messages.

Zack: What can I do to get you to allow me to apologize?

I sigh and work on my food. After a few bites, I push it away. I stew on his text a bit more. I should take my own advice. Before I put my phone away, I reply to Zack.

Me: I'm willing to listen the next time I see you. I make no promises beyond listening.

Zack: All I ask is you listen. After we talk, we are up to you.

The gnawing hollow in my chest is deep and dark. I want to forgive him and go back to the way we were before, but I can't. I need to be confident he won't give up on me, on us, ever again. As I'm about to set my phone away, two more texts come in.

Savi: How are you doing?

Me: The same.

Savi: Did you budge yet?

Me: I agreed to hear him out. That's all.

Savi: Own how you feel, Scar. You deserve the world.

Me: I'm trying. LY

Savi: LY

I want the idea of us I had in my head. Perhaps our fake marriage pushed us too far too fast. It feels—felt—right. It felt like my happily ever after could become reality.

Lia: Still waiting?

Me: I'll admit, he's good at groveling. I've rebuffed three attempts so far.

Lia: Ready to cave?

Me: It's not caving. It's being an adult and hearing him out.

Lia: So that's a yes.

Me: Yes. I'm going to listen the next time I see him.

Lia: Just listen. No rash decisions. Deal?

Me: Deal.

I tuck my phone away and finish out my workday. In the parking lot, I take a moment before driving to Zack's.

The knots in my stomach roil and twist. The anger and fear seeps in again. How do I make him understand the gravity of shutting me out? I park, clear my mind, and head inside.

Zack: I'm going to be late. I would leave if I could.

Me: I understand. I'll be here when you're done.

Zack: Thank you.

The knots loosen only slightly. I greet Gladys and get the rundown of Carol's day. She wasn't triggered today but did stumble walking to the restroom. I throw together a light dinner after making Carol comfortable in her room. After verifying the monitor is on, I crack open my review materials in the living room. Near ten, I check on Carol before making my way upstairs.

The draw of Zack has me pausing outside his bedroom longer than it should. True, the guest bed sucks in comparison to his, but the comfy mattress isn't the draw. I may be in his home and caring for his mother and have been each day. The draw is him. I miss him. I miss us. The us that was and the us we could've been. Part of me isn't sure we can get back to the could've been.

I will my legs to carry me to the guest bed and crawl in. At one, I hear Carol talking in her sleep. I make my way downstairs to check on her. She's still asleep. I remain rooted at the threshold for a few minutes before returning to bed. Before I think better of it, I peek into Zack's room. He isn't there. I peer in a bit more and note he isn't home. I curl under the sheets in the guest room and sleep until my alarm wakes me. On my way to the bathroom, I note Zack still hasn't come home.

Dressed and ready for another fun shift with the kids, I brew some coffee and sip it slowly.

"Scarlett," Carol calls. She's up early this morning. It makes sense; she slept almost straight through the night.

"Morning, Carol. Do you know what day it is?"

She shakes her head vehemently.

Her inability to keep track of the day is completely in line with her disease. "It's Saturday. Ready to get dressed?"

"Yes."

I open the curtains and gather her clothes. When I turn back toward the bed, Carol is agitated and visibly upset.

"You lie… t-to me," she accuses.

"No, I haven't. What are you talking about?"

With a shaky hand, she points to my badge. It still says Clemons. *Damn! Think quick, Scarlett!* "I must have grabbed my old one." Not great but might work. I hope it does since there isn't a new one.

"You have t-two?"

I abhor lying, but in this case, I'll make an exception. "Yes."

"Go get it!" Carol's demeanor shifts deeper into agitation.

"I will. Let's take some deep breaths. In." I inhale, hoping she'll follow along. "Out." Carol takes a breath with me. "Good. Again."

With each breath, she appears to calm down. I take a seat on the edge of the bed and set my fingers on her wrist to monitor her pulse.

"Kate… is she?"

As hard as it is to lie again and the devastating pang of pain from what I have to say, I reply, "I'm married to Zack. Kate is married to someone else."

Unconvinced, Carol flails and wiggles out of my hold. I encircle her wrists with my hands to soothe her. Her agitation increases, and she's mumbling. I can only make out a few words here and there. As I formulate a plan, Carol strikes out from the side. The last thing I recall is the searing pain in my head.

CHAPTER TWENTY-TWO

ZACHARY

My seemingly continuous shift has ended. My focus wasn't on the new case but on Scarlett. At a minimum, she agreed to listen. I can't ask for much more. I disrespected her and our relationship out of fear. I rush home and hope I make it before she leaves for work. Though she doesn't have to, she's working shifts to stay connected to her long-term patients while she studies for her exam next month. With a small smile on my face, I park in the garage and take the stairs two at a time, looking forward to a chance to make things right.

After setting down my keys, I hear crying. I hurry toward the sound, and my throat constricts at what I see. Scarlett is unconscious on the floor, and my mother is crying.

"Zack, I hurt your w-wife," she manages and then wails inexplicably harder.

My wife. Her words are a shot to my soul. As difficult as it is, I reach down and check for a pulse. It is steady but she's unconscious. I pull my phone from my pocket and dial.

"9-1-1 Dispatch."

"Dispatch, this is off-duty Officer Smithson, badge number 135. I need two ambulances at 1310 Watercliff Terrace for my mother and her night nurse. My mother, age sixty-two, has stage six Alzheimer's is overly agitated and confused, but otherwise appears uninjured. Her nurse, Scarlett, twenty-four, is unconscious with a steady pulse and appears to have a contusion on her head."

Dispatch replies, "Two units enroute."

The entire call my mother's crying echoes in the background. I rise from beside Scarlett and attempt to calm my mother. In the midst of doing so, I don't hear Gladys arrive.

The horror on her face reflects the feelings coursing through me. "Oh, Zack. What happened?"

"I don't know. I found them like this when I arrived."

Gladys rounds the bed and works with my mother. I drop to the floor and take Scarlett's hand in mine. Fighting the emotions swirling in my body is more difficult than I fathomed.

My doorbell rings, and I hear, "Smithson?" Aside from the fact I called for them, Lacey lives in the unit at the opposite end of my building with her overprotective mastiff, Barkley.

I reluctantly hurry from the floor and open the door for the EMTs, Lacey and Jude, followed immediately by Booker and Penn.

"Any idea what happened?" Jude asks.

"No, I found them like this when I got off shift."

Lacey looks up at me while she takes Scarlett's vitals. "Did you move her?"

"No." I know better than that.

I oscillate between Lacey tending to Scarlett and Penn caring for my mother. Gladys and I are relegated to the threshold of the room. Lacey and Penn spew medical jargon over the radio in concert. It's a jumbled mess, but I heard words like confusion, agitation, unconscious, and possible head trauma.

Lacey and Jude move Scarlett onto a backboard, and Penn and Booker shift Mom to a rolling chair.

After they raise Scarlett, Lacey attempts to rouse her with smelling salts.

Her head moves from left to right, and Scarlett mumbles, "Carol?"

"Carol will be fine, Scarlett," Jude assures her.

Lacey announces, "Ready to move. Zack, you're with me. Gladys, you can ride with Carol."

Either Lacey heard about our relationship or Scarlett's condition is…. Savannah. Without another thought, I run my hands along Scarlett's body to find her phone. It's either in her hip pocket or her scrubs pocket. Her top doesn't have any pockets, so pants it is. Only when I pull it out does Lacey stop glaring at me.

I dial as I follow them outside.

Savannah answers on the first ring. She sounds winded but awake. "Scar, is everything okay?"

"Savannah, it's Zack. There's been an incident with your sister and my mother. They're taking her to York Memorial."

"What happened?"

"I don't know yet."

Savannah replies, "We're on our way."

Then I send a text to Lia too. Scarlett would want her to know.

Me: My mom injured Scarlett. We're headed to the hospital.

As I climb into the ambulance with Scarlett, it dawns on me. The only difference between now and when I was out celebrating with her is the activity. I still trusted someone else to care for my mother when I couldn't be there. I misplaced my anger and guilt on Scarlett. I was angry at myself for choosing to have a life with Scarlett outside our fake wedded walls. When I did, I may have destroyed the best woman to own my whole heart.

"Zack, you good?" Lacey's voice rings in my ear.

"No, not at all. I'm not going to pass out or anything though." The woman I love is injured while caring for my mother. I haven't told her because I'm a complete ass.

Lacey lifts her chin in understanding.

"Zack?" Scarlett's voice is soft and raspy, but hearing it makes my heart skip.

"Yeah, gorgeous." I don't miss the smile on Lacey's face. If she wasn't aware, I confirmed our relationship status for her. Well, maybe, if I'm supremely lucky.

"This is all my fault. Badge not changed, Carol upset."

Oh no! Our marriage charade. "Relax. Everything will be fine." If anything, it's my fault for asking Scarlett to play along from the beginning.

Lacey raises an eyebrow in question but says nothing. We pull up to the ambulance bay, and Lacey wheels Scarlett inside. Penn pulls into the next spot, and Booker tends to my mother.

I'm rooted to the ground, unsure who to follow.

Gladys turns from where she's following my mother and retreats to me. "I know things are strained right now, but Scarlett needs you. You go with her. A man should never choose his mother over his wife, real or not."

Another jab about screwing up from Gladys. I force my feet to move and catch up with Lacey. Carly pushes me aside to care for Scarlett but allows me to stay, though she probably shouldn't. I lean up against the wall with my arms crossed over my chest and one knee bent, my foot on the wall, my gaze pinned to my woman. Scarlett is awake and talking with Carly and the attending doctor. Before I can speak to her again, they wheel Scarlett out of the room. She's conscious, talking, and appears fine. She hasn't, however, spoken to me directly since we got out of the ambulance.

"Where is she going?" I ask Carly.

"They're taking her for a head CT."

"Thanks, Carly."

She leaves the room.

Still torn, I pace between Scarlett's room and my mother's. Through the curtain, I see she's resting.

Gladys steps out and shares an update. "Carol will be fine. They gave her a sedative to calm her down. She said something about a badge and Kate."

"Yeah, she saw Scarlett's work badge and was upset about her name. Then implied I was cheating on Kate."

"Don't beat yourself up. You know it was the right choice."

She means the marriage charade. At this moment, I'm not so sure. I pace until I hear Savannah asking for Scarlett at the desk.

"Savannah."

Her face is pale and concerned. Sam has their son in a stroller and Emme perched on his hip.

"What happened?"

I exhale. "From what I can gather, my mother had an episode, and while Scarlett attempted to subdue her, she struck Scarlett. Then she hit her head. She's currently getting a CT scan." I choose to leave out the marriage charade and cause for her agitation. It's up to Scarlett to share that with her sister, not me. "Savannah, I'm—"

"No. What's going on between you and Scarlett personally is not up for discussion right now. We're going to focus on her injury, then your colossal failure to protect my sister's heart appropriately."

Helplessly, I let my eyes drift closed briefly before suggesting, "There's a waiting room over here with things for the kids to do while we wait."

Sam takes Savannah by the arm and leads her in the direction I indicated while I follow silently. I appreciate her willingness to allow me to stay. She doesn't have to. Savannah can shut me out of Scarlett's room until she can talk to her personally. Hell, she can cut me off completely. I'm grateful she hasn't.

Before I forget, given my current state of worry for Scarlett and my mother, I reach out to Nadine and update her. She asks if I want her to come, I leave it up to her. Then I call Cap and inform him I won't be in tomorrow or the following day. She may not let me take care of her, but I'm going to be available.

On one of my passes across the waiting room, Emme grabs my sleeve. "Who you?"

The truth is the only way to go. I crouch down and extend my hand to her. "Hi, Emme. I'm Zack. Your aunt takes care of my mom, and she got hurt today. I also happen to be madly, head over heels in love with her, but I royally fu—messed up. I hope I'm back to being your aunt's boyfriend today." *And husband. I want the husband title more and to make it real.*

"'Kay," Emme answers and resumes flipping through the picture book.

If only it would be as easy with Scarlett. I don't want it to be easy; I want a chance.

"A second chance will take more than a few meals and pleading texts," Savannah scoffs.

I thought we weren't talking about my relationship here. I shrug inwardly and reply, "I know, and I'll do whatever it takes."

Sam nods in solidarity, which earns him a scowl from Savannah. The door opens, and Dr. Hammerstein enters the waiting room. "Family of Carol Smithson."

"Yes, I'm her son."

As I reply, Nadine bursts through the door. "I'm her daughter."

"Your mother is sedated but otherwise uninjured. I strongly encourage you to find an institutional placement for her."

"She's already on waiting lists," Nadine informs him.

"I see. We'll keep her at least overnight for observation. I recommend you make some calls to local memory centers looking for a bed for her. You can see her now."

"We will. Thank you," I manage.

"Scarlett Clemons?" the same doctor asks.

"I'm her sister," Savannah announces and places herself between me and the doctor.

It won't matter; I'll still be able to hear him.

"Your sister has a contusion on her head. There's minimal evidence of a concussion. She needs monitoring for the day or so, but she can go home soon. You'll be able to see her in about fifteen minutes."

"Thank you," Savannah replies and relief washes over her. Then she turns to me. "I know her injury isn't your fault, but you hurt her deeply."

"Zack, what did you do?" Nadine inserts herself into the conversation.

"Nadine, this is Savannah, Scarlett's sister. Savannah, my sister, Nadine," I introduce them. "This is her husband, Sam, and their kids, Emme and Ben."

"Pleasure to meet you. I would've preferred different circumstances," Nadine offers.

"Same," Savannah replies.

"To answer your question, Nadi, I messed up, and I can only hope Scarlett will forgive me. The fact is, she agreed to hear me out, but I was held up with my new case. When I got home, well, now she's here."

Savannah softens at the reminder Scarlett agreed to hear me out. "You aren't going back in there unless she agrees first." Savannah and Scarlett could be twins. The only outward difference is the wedding ring on Savannah's left ring finger.

"I understand. I assure you, I didn't purposefully hurt her. The issue is mine and mine alone. I only asked for her to listen, and she agreed but…."

"Sam, can you give me a few minutes before bringing the kids over?" Savannah addresses him.

"Of course." He leans closer, kisses her cheek, and whispers for only her to hear.

Savannah leaves. Nadine and I follow as far as leaving the room, but we visit Mom instead. We attempt to anyway.

Gladys greets us when we step into the room. However, Mom is still resting. "She's going to be okay," she assures us. "How is Scarlett?"

I hang my head, and Nadine fills her in. I wear a path into the linoleum, waiting to see Scarlett. I feel helpless and useless knowing she's two doors away and I can't hold her.

After what feels like days, Savannah knocks on Mom's door. "She wants to see you."

"Thank you, Savannah."

"Don't thank me. She's nicer than I am. I would make you squirm longer before forgiving you for your gigantic misstep."

"Understood."

"She never let any man into the deepest, darkest recesses of her heart until you. Don't make her regret it."

Humbled and dumbfounded, I shuffle to Scarlett. Despite the harsh lighting and the IV in her arm, her smile aimed in my direction makes me weak.

Carly is in her room when I arrive. "I'll give you two some time."

Scarlett answers, "Thanks, Carly."

CHAPTER TWENTY-THREE

SCARLETT

"How is Carol?"

He shakes his head and tentatively moves closer to me but doesn't touch me. The last week has been one of the hardest I've ever experienced, at least in terms of relationships. Keeping my distance from him was torture of the worst kind. "How are you?"

"I'll be fine. It's my fault she was agitated."

His response is harsh and unwavering. "No, absolutely not. If anyone is to blame, it's me. I suggested the charade in the first place."

"I agreed, and I forgot about my badge. I had it upstairs and clipped it onto my scrubs early...." I don't need to remind him it was upstairs because of crushed my heart into a millions tiny shards.

"No, if I've learned anything over the last five months, it's her disease is unpredictable and horrible, for her and for her family. I want to make you happy, not drag you down into my family's issues." He's beside me but still hasn't touched me. His eyes clamp closed.

I set my hand on top of his. Immediately, my eyes flutter closed. The feel of his skin beneath mine is a salve to the ache in my chest. I open my eyes and look up at him. His gaze is focused on my hand. "I was happy. More than I have ever been, and it was because of you. Caring for Carol isn't a burden. I chose to care for her. It brought me to you."

He lifts his pained hazel eyes to mine.

"You hurt me. For the first time, I felt like I wasn't enough. I shared everything with you. Only with you, never before. I allowed you to see the darkest corner of my life, and you refused to share yours with me when it got hard. You quit on us."

He takes a seat on the edge of the bed and lifts my hand to his lips. "I'm sorry. You're right. I've spent the last week trying to get you to hear me, to speak to me face-to-face. You continually rebuffed me each time. I understand, I hurt you. I disrespected you and our relationship. I couldn't handle the pressure. I was never angry with you. The guilt… I was out and not at work instead of with my mom, the guilt of that was heavy. I tried to withdraw from the exam. Then this morning, the situation was roughly the same. I trusted someone to care for my mother while I couldn't. Only this time, I didn't feel guilt. I felt shame. Shame for how I mistreated you and realization the guilt was misguided and misplaced."

When I drop my head, he slides his hand to cup my face. I don't pull away.

"I'll keep trying if this talk isn't enough. You'll be sick of me."

I take a deep breath and attempt to settle my trembling hands. I may be hurt and angry, but I'll never be sick of him. I need him beside me.

He continues, "This morning, seeing you laid out and my mother crying because she hurt my wife and waiting for you to talk to me has been unbearable. I love you, Scarlett, and I promise to show you every day if you'll have me back." A single tear falls down his cheek.

I lean forward and kiss it away. "I never thought a love like Mama and Papa Cappelli share was a possibility for me. They are the only stable example I have. My parents may have had the same type of love, but I never witnessed it because she was taken too soon. Then you asked me on a date, sort of, and to be your fake wife. Everything was falling into place for the first time in my life. Then you took it away on one of the proudest days of my life so far."

He exhales sharply, and his eyes snap shut to quell the tears welling in his eyes. The sheer pain vibrating off his body exemplifies his pain and remorse without words.

"Loving you is like breathing. It's unyielding and necessary for my survival. I won't find it again. I will never not put you first ever again." Tentatively, he leans forward to kiss me as if I haven't forgiven him completely.

"Zachary, I need you to kiss me."

He grins and lowers his lips to mine. With slow precision, he kisses me until I can barely breathe. We stare at one another for a long while before he asks, "Will you allow me to take care of you?"

"Yes, though I'm confident I can handle it myself."

He presses a kiss to my forehead and smiles. "Fair enough."

"Truly, how is Carol?"

"She'll be fine. They're keeping her for observation. Dr. Hammerstein suggested we call around for a placement for her."

"I know it's hard, but it's the right choice."

Silence falls around us, but it's comfortable like before.

Carly knocks on the doorframe. "You're free to go, Scarlett. I'm sure you don't need the instructions, but I have to give them anyway." Carly completes the discharge information and looks directly at Zack when she mentions someone needs to watch over me for the next twenty-four hours.

"I'll be glued to her side, Carly."

"I have a good feeling about you two." Carly smiles and leaves.

Savi and the kids return to my room.

"Hey, Savi. Where's Sam?" I ask.

"He's handling a work emergency with a painting in the city."

Emme walks over to the side of the bed and tugs on Zack's pants. "Up," she demands.

Zack lifts Emme from the floor. She sets one hand on his shoulder and the other on his face. "Did you say sorry?"

Zack with a kid in his arms is swoon worthy, especially since she's sticking up for me.

"I did."

She twists to look at me and leans in my direction. Zack sets her gently into my lap. "Did you 'give him? Is he your boy again?"

Oh my heart! I laugh softly. "Yes, I forgave him, and he's my boyfriend again." I feel like I lost the husband part too, at least since Carol may not be coming home for long.

Emme hugs me. "Good. I like him, Auntie Let."

"Me too, sweetie."

Savi is smiling while Ben coos in his stroller. "When you're ready to leave, I can take you to your place, and then you can use our guest room, if you want."

"Thanks, Savi. Zack said he would handle it."

We exchange a few sentences with eye movements and head nods. Amusement dances in Zack's eyes.

"Did anyone tell Lia?" I ask.

Savi states, "I didn't."

"I texted her earlier, but she didn't respond," Zack shares.

"Could you send another one and tell her not to worry and to rock her interview?"

He pulls out his phone and sends the text.

"Thanks. Could you wheel me over to Carol since the nurses won't let me walk before we leave?"

"Sure." Zack lifts Emme from my lap and sets her on the floor.

She tugs on the hem of his shirt until he crouches in front of her. "Good job fixin' Auntie," Emme whispers like only a toddler can—everyone can hear every word.

He smiles at her and offers his palm for a high five. "Thanks, Emme."

"Welcome." She slaps his hand and moves beside Savi. Zack offers me his hand, and I slide mine into his. The heat is impossible to ignore, though I need to for a bit longer.

"Thank you for coming, Savi. I'll call you later when I'm settled at home." I hug her, and she leaves the room. I wave to Sam as Zack wheels me over to Carol's room. Gladys and Nadine hug me when I arrive. Carol is still sedated.

"You don't have to be here," Nadine offers.

"She had no control over her reaction. I'm going to be fine. Thank you though," I offer.

"Zack, take her home. I'll stay until they move Mom. I already placed a few calls at area centers," Nadine directs.

"She wanted to stop by," Zack admits.

"Please call Willa Cappelli directly to ask about a spot in the memory center adjacent to the hospital," I recommend to Nadine.

"I will. No more excuses, go home."

Zack hugs his sister and takes a long look at his mom, then wheels me out of the room. "Do you need anything?" he asks me.

"I need to sign the paperwork at the desk." I ride over to the nurses' station and sign my discharge papers.

With Carly pushing me, Zack is beside me with his fingers threaded with mine. Anguish overtakes his features, as if he failed me in some way again.

"What, Zack?"

"I rode with you. I don't have a vehicle here."

Carly smiles. "It's taken care of. Lacey went back for your car. You were her last call. She parked it about twenty minutes ago. She said something about you taking care of Barkley for her though." Carly drops Zack's spare keys in his hand.

Zack smiles and assists me to my feet. "Thanks, Carly. I'll talk to Lacey later."

Zack drives slowly back to his townhouse—so slowly, cars are passing him as if he were an elderly driver.

"Charming, I'm good. Normal speed is fine."

He ignores my statement and continues at his chosen speed. He parks in his garage and guides me to the couch. After covering me with a blanket and pressing a kiss to my temple, he says, "I'll be right back."

I snuggle deeper into the cushions and close my eyes. Truthfully, I feel okay. I have a mild headache but nothing significant. I didn't see my scans, but I wouldn't think anything of note was evident. If I have a concussion, which I doubt, it's slight. The CT was standard care for a head contusion. He returns with a tray towering with food.

"Are you sharing with me?" I indicate the food.

He smiles. "Yes."

I grab my phone from the tray and sift through my messages while he fusses with setting up the food.

Lia: OMG! Where are you?

Me: I'm fine. I'm at Zack's.

Lia: Do you need anything?

Me: No.

Lia: I'll be there in an hour. LY.

Me: LY.

I scroll through my emails and find nothing of note. Then I send a quick text to Savi.

Me: I'm at Zack's, relaxing per doctor's orders.

Savi: Good. Everything else good?

Me: Very much so.

Savi: Good. Happy for you. Love you. I'll call later.

I dig into the mountain of food Zack brought over.

After a few bites, he asks, "How long until Lia arrives?"

I smile. "About an hour." I have a right to ask, I convince myself. "Did you date Lacey?"

"No. She lives a few doors down. We have keys for each other's places. I take care of Barkley for her when her shifts run over and her brother can't do it."

I quash the momentary jealously gripping me. "She's a great friend."

"She is. Eat, beautiful."

I do as he asks before Lia comes over. When she arrives, Zack makes himself scarce. He doesn't have to, but he does. I appreciate it.

Lia checks me out carefully.

"Lia, I promise I'm fine. A bump on the head."

"You lost consciousness, lovely. It's a big deal." Lia always overreacts to medical things despite having no training at all.

"I assure you, I'm good. To answer the other question you truly want the answer to, yes, I forgave him."

"I'm glad. You were miserable, and you are perfect together."

She's right. He's the one for me. "How about you? How are you feeling about the interview?"

"Excited and terrified about the real world. No, truly the school administrators were great. The space that could be mine is one of the newer ones in the building. I'm hopeful."

"I'm happy for you!"

Lia glances at her watch. "Crap, I have a shift at the brewery I picked up from Bryan."

"I promise I'm good here." Better than good. It's where I want to be. I rise from the couch and escort her out. I find Zack on the phone in the kitchen.

"Sure." He ends the call and stares at his phone for a few moments.

I don't like the look on his face. He's torn about something. "Whatever it is, we can handle it."

"That was Nadine. She's come up empty so far."

"Okay. Gladys and I can handle Carol's care until a bed opens up for her."

"No." His words come out strong and harsh. "I refuse to put you in a position where she could hurt you again."

I step into his space and wrap my arms around him. His fall around me. Being in his arms again reminds me I never want to leave again. Slowly, I lift my gaze to his. "First, you don't get to decide for me. Second, I'll be more careful. I won't quit on Carol because it got harder. It's not who I am. Third, my badge will remain in my car going forward."

"I can't ask you to do that." His words sear into my heart.

"You don't have to. I agreed to care for her, and I will until she has a spot at a center. You know as well as I do finding someone else is going to take time, and by then, there'll be a bed for her."

Logic always settles him. It's why he thrives during his detective assignments. "I don't like it one bit."

"What else?"

Surprise crosses his features. "How do you know there's more?"

I shrug.

"I need to go back to see Mom, but I don't want to leave you either."

My heart squeezes. "Zachary, listen to me. I would give anything for more time with my mother. I would sacrifice years off my own life to be able to talk to her once. I'm a trained nurse. I can take care of myself for a few hours while you go visit your Mom in the hospital."

"Are you sure?"

"I will never lie to you."

The tug of war of emotion on his face is hard to watch. "I'll be back as soon as I can. Please don't do anything crazy."

"I won't. I'm going to curl up on the couch and find a movie."

He drags his thumb across my bottom lip before lowering his lips to mine. I'll never tire of how he makes me feel. I can feel his promises of love in his kisses.

"I'll be back with dinner."

"I'll be here."

He smiles, kisses me again, and hurries out the door. Before I can settle back onto the couch, he bounds back upstairs and is standing in front of me. "I love you, gorgeous."

"I love you, charming."

With one more kiss, he's gone.

I settle onto the couch and opt for a movie I've seen numerous times, *Hitch* with Will Smith. As the credits roll, Zack returns with dinner. We polish off our meals and climb the stairs.

"Can I move your stuff back?" he asks quietly.

"I can do it."

He takes my hand, kisses the back, and guides me to the dressing bench at the foot of his bed. "Please allow me. I caused you to move them in the first place." Within minutes, my hair dryer, makeup, toothbrush, and the remaining toiletries are back in their spot in the master bathroom. "It was a gut check when I came home, found your stuff gone and you locked in the guest room."

"I didn't know what else to do. I didn't trust myself to stay away from you, despite the hurt, and I promised to care for Carol."

"I was upset with me, never you. You were protecting yourself from me, emotionally at least, and I'll never put you in the same position again."

"We should get some sleep. Both of us need it desperately." I strip down to my panties and camisole and slide beneath his ultrasoft sheets. I haven't slept well in more than a week, and it wasn't because of the crappy mattress in the guest room. Although, it didn't help at all.

He slides in behind me and carefully tugs me flush against his hard body.

As much as I would like to ignore his arousal, it's impossible. I slide my hand back and attempt to wedge it between us.

"Not tonight" is all he says for a few minutes. "I missed you so much despite your proximity."

"It wasn't easy for me either. Realizing I'm worth the effort and communication wasn't difficult. Realizing you didn't see it was agonizing."

"I did realize it, a little too late. I'm sorry I allowed you to believe I didn't love you completely, even for a moment. Being without you was hell, and I never want to do it again. You're worth everything I am, and I won't mess up again."

I wiggle deeper into his embrace. The growl under his breath to regain control of himself is heartening. We're going to be fine. With his warmth around me, I succumb to the pull of sleep. It's the first time I've ever been able to sleep deeply in Zack's bed.

CHAPTER TWENTY-FOUR

ZACHARY

At some point in the early hours of the next morning, I wake to Scarlett pressing kisses along my jaw. Her delicate fingers are inching southward, leaving streaks of awareness in their wake until she teases the edge of my boxer briefs.

"Scarlett." My tone is more of a warning than anything else.

Undeterred, she dips her hand beneath the waistband, surrounds me with her soft hand, and strokes me hard twice. "Zachary." She knows I'll fold when she calls me that. It's close to equal when she calls me "charming."

"Are you sure this is a good idea?"

She laughs with her mouth against my neck, her hand still surrounding me but not moving. "Being with you right now is the perfect idea."

"How are you feeling?"

Lifting her head, she meets my gaze. "I'm fine. I willingly let you push me off last night. Not happening again."

Her fiery desire shines brighter than I've ever seen before.

I take a deep breath to soothe myself before rolling to cage her beneath me. "Scarlett, I need you to…."

She stills. An unreadable look appears on her gorgeous sleep-kissed face.

"I need to make love to you, achingly slowly and purposely. I know you asked—"

Her index finger silences me as her sapphire eyes meet mine. "Zachary, make love to me."

Shocked but ecstatic, I lower my mouth closer to hers. I wet her lips with my tongue before delving into her mouth. Her soft whimper urges me to continue. The warmth of her hands heat my back as I kiss over the point of her chin and outward to the thin silky strap of her cami. I rock back onto my heels and lift the offending fabric out of my way.

Only she has ever been comfortable enough with herself to allow me to stare. I cover each breast with one hand and roll her rosy nipples between my thumb and forefinger in opposite directions. Her hips bow off the mattress beneath me while her fingernails mark my shoulder blades.

"What else do you like?" I whisper near the shell of her ear.

"Each time you touch me, you find something I didn't know myself."

"Noted, gorgeous." Maybe she'll allow me to be in charge more often. I appreciate and get off on her assertiveness. I'm going to prove she doesn't need to be in control to chase pleasure ever again.

I lavish attention to her breasts and continue moving down her lush curves with precise, pinpoint accuracy. The moans falling from her lips remind me this isn't easy for her, but I'm not failing miserably either. Her hands twine into my hair as I move between her thighs. I set her feet on my shoulders and lift her heated center in line with my face.

The light caress of my breath alone has her fingers tightening against my head. I drag the flat of my tongue along her folds from bottom to swollen nub. As I move forward to spear her with my tongue, her left hand glides down her abdomen and her index finger advances toward her clit. I lower one foot back to the mattress, take her offending hand, and lift it back up to my head.

She sighs deeply.

"Trust me to make you shatter, beautiful." With a quick glance up, I note her lower lip tucked between her teeth. Patience in the bedroom is not my woman's strong suit. I intend to change that over time until we're at a point where the give and take is balanced. I nip and suck on her folds, earning glorious, pleasured screams and lost hair. I savor her with my mouth and plunge my finger into her heated center, curling them in the exact spot to make her shudder with pleasure. As her inner muscles clench around my fingers, I withdraw and replace one with two.

"Sweet mercy!" She grinds against my hand and face until she surrenders to the waves of decadent ecstasy. Once her orgasm subsides, she grabs and grips at me, attempting to pull me up.

I pepper her skin with open-mouthed kisses until I reach her lips.

"I need to feel you throbbing inside me," she says before meeting my mouth in a soft, sensual kiss.

I reach over to grab a condom, but she stops me.

"Only you. I don't want anything between us."

Her words. Scarlett is her most vulnerable in this moment, and yet she still relinquishes control. I drop a scintillating kiss on her lips and notch myself at her entrance. Her eyelids flutter closed as I bury my hard length to the hilt. Her body stretches and pulses around me.

"Scarlett, look at me."

She complies and moves her hand to cup my jaw as I move within her. Each deliberate thrust increases the intensity of us together as one. Her core contracts around me tighter than ever before. Each ripple of pleasure demands attention. I hammer forward and retreat until we fly over the edge of untethered bliss as one.

Our breathing decreases from frantic pants to normal and measured. I hover over her briefly before gathering her against me and rolling us to our sides. We kiss languidly for a long time before either of us speaks.

"I know handing yourself over completely wasn't easy for you. I can't possibly sum up how I feel right now."

"It was easier than I anticipated. I was never crazy in love with any of my partners before. I never trusted them enough to truly be in the moment and let go. You are in a class all your own."

Content to let our words marinate, I draw her closer and breathe her in. It doesn't take long for Scarlett to seize the opportunity of our nakedness once again. The mere thought of being with her again has me rock-hard between us.

She pushes up to sitting and positions herself in my lap, her legs hooked around my back. With one hand on my shoulder, she braces herself, and with the other, she aligns us. "You good?"

"More than good." I watch with keen interest as Scarlett slides down my length to the root with precise movements. I bruise her hips with my fingers and meet her downward plunge with an upward one. "We feel—"

She crushes her lips to mine, cutting off my words, and tightens her thighs around me.

I break our kiss. "Holy hell! Never felt so... before."

She quakes in my arms as her climax ripples through her, setting off my own. I empty into her in explosive bursts and rest my lips against her neck.

Before I fully grasp the gravity of how I feel, she pulls back abruptly. "What time do you need to go to work?"

"I don't. I took today and tomorrow off."

"You did?"

"I did. You need me here, and I refuse to mess up again."

She's momentarily speechless. "You don't know what it means to me for you to—"

"Yes, I do, gorgeous. I truly do." Putting her first or, at least, tied for first is what she needs to feel secure in our relationship. She will never fall down the list again. A single tear rolls over the ball of her cheek. I dry it with the pad of my thumb. "I love you, and I'll spend each day making sure you trust me without question."

She skims her lips across mine. The look on her face is nothing short of unconditional surrender to her feelings. "I love you." She moves off the bed toward the bathroom. I hear rustling but can't see her anymore. She turns on the water. "Care to join me?" she asks, poised to step into the shower. Red marks from my mouth and hands are evident on her neck, breasts, and hips.

A giddy smile grows on my face. "I thought you would never ask." I hurriedly hop off my bed and join her in the master shower.

I paid for the master bathroom renovation before I moved in. I went over the top with the marble tile and waterfall showerhead.

The floors and towel rack are heated. I added the double vanity and soaking tub as well. It was worth it.

The water sluices over her body, and all I can do is watch. It's almost as mesmerizing as the woman herself. I take the shampoo from her hand and carefully lather her hair. Given we've been together twice already this morning, I'm content with having my hands on her. We finish showering and make a late breakfast. I check in with the hospital. Mom will be released early this afternoon.

"Do you need to do anything before we pick up my mom?"

"Laundry. I'll throw it in later." We clean up and drive to the hospital. "Ready for the questions?"

"Will there be more?" I ask.

"Could be."

"I'll skirt giving details as best I can."

She smiles. "Same."

We stroll to Mom's room hand in hand. Gladys is playing cards with her.

"Morning, Gladys. Thank you for being here."

"You're welcome. How are you?" Her question is directed at Scarlett.

"I'll be fine. Headache is gone, and the swelling has greatly reduced."

"You're a strong young woman," Gladys offers.

Scarlett nods and greets Mom. "Hello, Carol."

Mom doesn't reply. It's hard to know whether she recalls injuring Scarlett or not. Her lack of response isn't out of the ordinary. I've seen some horrific things in my career, but the strongest woman I know lying helpless will be with me forever.

A nurse enters Mom's room. Her name tag indicates her name is Robyn. "Good afternoon. Carol is set to leave as soon as she's ready. Are you her medical decision maker?" she addresses me.

"Yes."

"I'll go over the discharge information with you."

"If you wouldn't mind sharing with everyone here, I would appreciate it. These are my mom's home care nurses."

Robyn shares the instructions, which quite frankly isn't much, while she removes the IV and assists my mother to a wheelchair. The only note that stands out is the stringent recommendation to place her in a memory care facility. The nature of her recommendation angers me. It isn't as if we didn't try as soon as it was suggested. If I could go back and avoid Scarlett being injured, I would without question.

When we arrive home, Gladys offers food to Mom, but she refuses. With assistance from Gladys, she settles into the chair to listen to the news.

"Thank you for sitting with her at the hospital. You didn't have to," I state.

"I wanted to. Besides, Scarlett needed you here more than you needed to be there."

My mind zips through the events of last night and this morning for the first time. I wouldn't dare share, but I'm grateful.

"I appreciate the accommodation," Scarlett answers for me.

Gladys smiles and leaves for the day.

I survey the fridge and turn to ask Scarlett, "Burgers work?"

"Sure. I'm going to see if she wants to turn in. She's dozing in the chair."

"Okay. I'll get started." I pull out the ingredients and wash my hands. Before I think better of it, I follow shortly behind Scarlett and Mom toward her room. Call it fear, trepidation, or love, I need to be close to her to make sure Mom doesn't have another episode and injure Scarlett… again.

After gathering fresh clothes, they shuffle by me again, and Mom steps into the restroom.

"Do you want help?" Scarlett offers.

I can't see her, but I assume she says no since Scarlett closes the door.

"Charming."

I turn to face her more fully.

"I promise I'm fine."

"I'm sure you are. I'm not. If you could simply indulge me for a bit, I would appreciate it."

Scarlett presses a kiss to my cheek before checking on Mom. Only when I hear the click of the rails on the bed, do I turn back toward the kitchen.

Together we prepare dinner, eat, and clean up. After a check on Mom again, we spread our study materials out on the living room floor in front of a roaring fire. It takes restraint not to push our books aside and examine Scarlett by firelight, but I resist by the slimmest of margins. More than before, I'm looking forward to our date on Saturday afternoon.

CHAPTER TWENTY-FIVE

SCARLETT

When I arrive for my shift on Tuesday, Judith sends me directly to Willa's office. I don't have time to drop off my bag.

"Come in, Scarlett," Willa calls from her desk.

"Everything okay?"

She wrinkles her brow. "Of course. I wanted to check on how you're feeling. As you know, word gets around when one of our own gets injured and has a smoking-hot man standing vigil by her bed."

"I'm fine, and my injury wasn't serious. Zack didn't need to stand vigil. I was conscious the entire time I was here."

"So you admit he's smoking hot and yours?"

I drop my head. I walked straight into that one. "I'll confirm Zack and I are a couple, but those details are all I'm willing to share." Between her and Gladys, I don't know who is pushing us together more. Little does Willa realize, we don't need pushing.

"It's so cute you think you can keep your relationship with one of the hottest bachelors in our community private."

I would like to ignore her observation. She isn't wrong. Still, I won't succumb to the pressure of sharing more than necessary. "I don't care if the world knows Zack and I are a couple. Otherwise, the details are ours to divulge or not. Is there anything else?"

"No. Glad you're feeling well. Have a great day."

Needing to settle my nerves, I text Zack on my way to the locker room.

Me: So much for privacy.

Zack: Who?

Me: Willa.

Zack: Interesting. Gladys quizzed me before I left too.

Me: Why? She sees more than anyone.

Zack: No idea. Love you.

Me: Love you.

I stow my phone and bag and make my rounds with my patients. Luckily, I have transient patients today. My chronic return patients are absent. I'm happy both Keegan and Mariah are healthy outside these walls. I have two patients for appendectomies, one for pin removal in her wrist, and one with pneumonia. This is also my last shift before the exam. I've given myself the next ten days to focus solely on studying during the day. The only exception is our date this weekend.

I finish my charting for the morning and make my way outside for lunch. Much to my surprise and delight, I find Zack and Davis heading into the hospital.

"Hey, babe, I didn't think I would see you until later." I kiss Zack lightly on the lips. "Hi, Davis."

"Davis needs to talk to Willa, and I tagged along."

"Hi, Scarlett. I'll be back as quickly as possible, Smithson," Davis states and ducks into the ER entrance.

"What's that about?" I ask.

"He didn't elaborate, and I didn't push. I think Tabi's birthday is coming up soon though." If I recall correctly, Tabi is Willa's bestie.

"Works for me. I'll take any excuse to see you during the day. Will you sit with me while I eat?"

"Of course." We take a seat on one of the benches, and I eat my lunch. Zack only steals a few chips. As my break ends, Davis exits the hospital.

"All set, Davis?" Zack asks.

"Yup. Nice to see you again, Scarlett."

"You too, Davis."

Zack rises from beside me, kisses me again, whispers, "I love you," and scampers away before I can utter a word.

I clean up and make my way back to the pediatric floor for the rest of my day. As I walk through the emergency department, I don't miss the hushed murmurs and stares from the staff, especially Carly. I decide to ignore them and make my way upstairs. The rest of the day passes smoothly, and before I know it, I'm parking at home.

Unfortunately, when I arrive, Carol is already sleeping. "Hi, Gladys. How long as she been sleeping?"

"About an hour."

"What triggered her today?"

"Saul again," Gladys answers.

"Have a good night, Gladys."

"You too, dear. I know this may be overstepping a bit, but I'm glad you gave Zack a second chance."

The mere mention of his name from someone who's seen us together makes butterflies flutter in my belly. "Thanks, Gladys. Me too."

For the rest of the week, I leave as if I'm going to work but instead head to my condo to spend my daytime hours studying on the balcony or in the living room. When she's home, Lia refills my coffee or adds a pastry beside me and slips away to avoid breaking my concentration. I'm tired but also exhilarated. I have a date tomorrow. Seems a bit silly given everything we've gone through so far, but I'll take as much time with Zack as I can. His shifts with the detective division always seem to run over, especially since he gets called in to those on top of his regular ones. I'm sure, after he passes the exam and shifts divisions, it will ease up.

When I arrive at Zack's, Carol is finishing her dinner. I greet Gladys and Carol and stow my study materials. Since we made our agreement about studying and date night, Zack and I have been sticking to it.

Gladys shares Carol had a decent day with only a few minor lapses early in the day.

"Have a good night," I offer as she leaves for the day.

Zack arrives home soon thereafter with bags of stuff. "Hello, gorgeous." He draws me into his arms and kisses me to the brink of insanity with Carol in the same room. That's new. "Hi, Mom."

Carol looks over at him but says nothing.

"What's with all the bags?"

He wiggles a finger in front of me. "Don't you worry. It's painting supplies."

"Can I peek?"

His cheeks turn a light shade of pink. "No, I would prefer to keep you guessing."

I frown but reply, "Fine. Can you cook something while I assist your mom?"

"We can cook later."

Ever since her last major episode, Zack has been beside me. It's protective, possessive, and wholly unnecessary, but also endearing and sweet. He can't be here all the time. Gladys is on her own during the daytime hours. I've attempted to placate his fears, but he stands guard either way. "I can handle my job."

"I have the utmost faith in you. The fault is with me. I can't flush the image of you on the floor out of my mind. I may never be able to. Please let me stand here."

I lead Carol to her room with Zack following closely. I'm resigned to respect his feelings and giddy he willingly shared them. Once she's settled, we make a quick dinner and study the night away. Near five in the morning, I wake alone.

I tiptoe downstairs and search for him. The door to the basement is ajar and the light to his studio is shining brightly. A smile warms my heart. He's painting again. For someone who spent extra money on an expensive mattress, he hasn't been using it enough lately. I return to the bedroom and dress for the day.

The strong scent of coffee fills the kitchen as Zack crosses the threshold. "Morning, beautiful." He presses a tender kiss to my lips, careful to avoid smearing paint on me.

"Morning. How long have you been painting?" Zack's hands covered in drips of colorful paint makes me smile. It means he's setting his emotions out onto a canvas.

"A little more than an hour. Inspiration struck, and I slipped out of bed to start a rough outline."

I smile. "Go get cleaned up. I want as many minutes as I can get today."

He steals another kiss, as well as my prepared cup of coffee, and literally runs upstairs, the sweet sound of his sexy laugh trailing behind him. I built our date into my study plan, and I'm crazy excited.

The last week has been repetitive but hopefully worth it. Zack is beyond capable when planning dates. After a blissful date complete with a mud bath and couples' massages, I have been preparing for my exam nonstop. Gladys agreed to stay for Carol the night before the exam, and Nadine is handling the evening of the exam. It's the big day, and I'm off the charts anxious. My entire career path boils down to this one exam.

I fill a travel mug and grab my review cards.

"Good luck, Scarlett. You'll do fantastic!"

"Thanks, Gladys. I appreciate it."

I follow Zack into the garage. "You've got this, gorgeous! I'll meet you after work today." Zack draws me into his arms. After a possessive kiss, he opens my car door. "I love you. Kick ass on your exam!"

I grin up at him. "I love you. Be safe."

"Always." He closes my door and trots back to the garage. He flashes me one of his trademark, heart-melting smiles before disappearing into his car. I take a settling breath before making my way to the testing site. I check my phone again and scroll through the well-wishes.

Lia: Good luck! You've got this! LY

Savi: I'm crazy proud of you. Love you.

Nadine: Rock it, Scarlett!

Auggie: You've got this, Scarlett.

Sam: Good luck.

Zack: I love you, Nurse Scarlett. xoxo.

I reply to each one before shutting off my phone. I verify I have my ID and stand in the registration line. I wave and hug a few of my classmates who are sitting for the exam at the same time. One deep breath and I begin my test. Three hours later, I take a quick break before resuming my test. When I answer the last question, I note the time and review as many as I can before my time runs out.

I exit the testing site into the early evening. The sun is falling toward the horizon. Before switching on my phone, I drive to the beach and park in my spot. I take in the smell of the salty ocean and the sea breeze for a few minutes of peace on one of the benches instead of my balcony.

"Hey, beautiful. Everything okay?" Zack approaches from my right with a huge bouquet of flowers and a bottle of wine.

"Yeah. I'm taking a minute or five to be proud of myself."

"As you should. You should take as many minutes as you need to believe you rocked your exam, and in a few days or so, it'll be official. Can I join you?"

I motion for him to take a seat beside me and press a kiss to his cheek. I sidle closer and rest my head on his upper arm.

"I'm proud of you, Scarlett."

"Thank you. It means a lot coming from you, even more than Savi."

He takes my hand in his and kisses the back. "Why?"

"You aren't required to be proud of me. Savi is."

"Scarlett, you are the most incredible, strong, smart, and sexy woman I've ever met. I'm lucky to call you mine. I love you."

I lean over and brush my lips lightly over his. "I feel the same way about you, well except the woman part. I love you, Zachary."

He glances at his watch.

"What are you up to?"

He shrugs. "I have a little surprise for you whenever you're ready to head inside."

"What have you done?"

"Let's go see." He hands me the flowers, which are stunning and smell wonderful, and leads me to my condo.

My door opens as I approach, and Lia steps into the hallway. "Yay! I thought I would miss you. I'm so happy for you!"

"Thanks, Lia." I hug her tight, and she's on her way to one of her last shifts at the brewery. She took the teaching job and is taking the rest of the summer off.

Turning into my condo, I find hors d'oeuvres on the island. "Auggie?"

Zack shoots me a surprised look. "How did you know?"

"He wished me good luck this morning. I highly doubt he's keeping track of my schedule that closely."

"Fair enough. Appetizers are only the beginning." Zack wasn't kidding. He managed to set up my perfect date for tonight. The two of us with amazing food and a stunning ocean view. Auggie has seriously outdone himself. My meal is linguine with shrimp. Zack has a filet with asparagus and a cream sauce. Zack has been successfully hiding dessert from me since we arrived.

"Thank you for all of this."

"You're welcome. This is only the start of what you deserve."

There's no response to his statement. All of this is new to me. I can only own how he makes me feel and offer the same to him.

CHAPTER TWENTY-SIX

ZACHARY

Overall, things have been the same with Mom's health. No major episodes have occurred, but her deterioration continues. She's losing her ability to handle everyday things, like dressing and feeding herself. It's distressing to witness. I can't possibly say enough about Gladys and Scarlett. Their care for Mom has been compassionate and unbending. Nadine and I visited one facility, and despite the urgency, we opted against it. It wasn't a good fit for Mom, and it was farther away than either of us were willing to accept. Over an hour away would be impossible for a weeknight visit. Scarlett aced her exam, and she's still working a few per diem on the pediatric floor until her contract starts next month.

Cap has been increasing my time with the detectives. I report to Detective Jones without attending roll call anymore. My new coworkers are great, but I miss my old ones—sometimes. Scarlett may be done, but we continue to follow the study schedule. She's catching up on her lengthy list of Lia suggested romance novels instead.

I park in the lot and cross Detective Jones's path as I make my way inside.

"Smithson, you're with me."

I turn on my heel and follow him.

"We were called to a home invasion on Spring Street," he informs me.

When we arrive, the responding officers have the homeowners sitting in the living room. I'm still in an observing capacity. I note the doorframe is cracked inward, but something is off. We take a walk around the first floor of the home. As I do, I note the broken mug on the kitchen floor, rope hanging from the chairs at the table, and the makings of a school lunch on the island. Before he speaks with the family, we also climb the stairs and check out the master bedroom. Most of the drawers are open, but the jewelry chest is closed. The bed is perfectly made, yet only the teenage son is dressed for the day. I note the location of the bathroom and the son's room as well.

As Detective Jones interviews the couple, their teenage son looks on. He's keenly listening to their description of events. While the homeowners seem on edge but calm considering their morning, the son appears chill and collected, as if he knew something was going to happen. I listen to their responses.

The man of the house is speaking. From the information we received on the way here, his name is Jamal Jeffries. "We were in the kitchen preparing breakfast. Quincy was upstairs getting ready for school. My wife dropped her coffee cup when the masked guys broke down the front door."

As I listen, I take a step back. There's no line of sight from the coffee maker to the front door.

"How did you know there were masked men? You can't see the front door from where you indicated she was standing?" Jones asks.

"She didn't see them, she heard them bust in and dropped her mug," Mr. Jeffries corrects quickly.

While Jones continues his questions, I look around and catalog the room while half listening to their answers. Nothing in the living room is disturbed. Unless Mrs. Jeffries reset the room, the alleged perpetrators never touched anything in here.

"They tied us to the chairs in the kitchen and then ran around the house grabbing things," Mr. Jeffries offers.

"They?"

"Yes, there were two masked men," Mr. Jeffries answers.

"What did they take?"

Mrs. Jeffries answers. "I haven't been able to do a complete inventory, but my wedding ring is gone, my grandmother's pearl necklace, and the display piece for the exhibit at the store set to occur tomorrow. I was delivering it this morning."

"What piece and what exhibit?" Jones asked.

I dig into my mind to recall their professions, which Jones briefed me on as we rode here. Mr. Jeffries is a banker. Mrs. Jeffries works at a prominent jeweler in Boston.

"The piece is a replica of the Pink Dreicer & Co diamond owned by Huguette Clark. The store is participating in an iconic jewelry display. Some are original, others are replicas. Ours was a replica," Mrs. Jeffries tearfully answers.

"Was the stone in the replica real or fake?"

"The center stone was fake, but two accent stones were authentic," Mrs. Jeffries replies.

"Who knew the piece was in your residence?"

"Only my husband, my son, and my boss," she replies.

"Why was it here in the first place?"

"The piece was fashioned by a Maine-based jeweler and only completed two days ago. The timing made more sense for me to keep it here."

"Was it insured?" Detective Jones inquires.

"I assume so," Mrs. Jeffries replies.

"Thank you, ma'am. Do I have your permission to speak with your son?"

Both Mr. and Mrs. Jefferies agree.

Jones turns to Quincy. "Where were you when the door was broken down?"

"I was in my room getting ready for school."

From our tour, his room is the first door at the top of the staircase on the left.

Jones continues, "Did you see the two masked men?"

He looks at his father and then replies, "I heard the shouting, looked down the stairs, and saw the front door broken in. I hid in my closet."

"How many unrecognizable voices did you hear?"

He looks upward as if replaying the voices in his mind and answers, "One."

"Thank you for your time. If you could have your boss contact me at this number as soon as possible, I would appreciate it." Jones hands Mrs. Jefferies a card. "Our technicians will be finished in the next hour or so. Please complete a list of every missing item and forward it to me as soon as you can."

"Thank you, Detective," Mr. Jeffries replies.

We make our way out of the house. My mind is spinning. None of their story adds up. All of them were too calm. Quincy's assertion he hid is fine, but it's almost impossible the perpetrators didn't see him.

It isn't until we're in the cruiser before Jones speaks again. "What is your impression and what do you want to know first?"

Surprise filters through me, but I answer anyway. "At first it didn't make sense the piece was at the residence in the first place. However, given the center stone is an imitation, the sheer value of the iconic replica is less of a concern. Quincy's story doesn't make sense. He's likely an accomplice because he didn't know the center stone was a fake."

"Keep going," Jones urges.

"We know from their story, they were tied to the chairs. Neither of them had chafe marks from struggling against the restraints. I want to know if they are having money troubles or if Quincy is mixed up with drugs or something else and owes significant money to someone."

"Well done, Smithson. You'll make a fine addition to our department when you pass the exam."

"Thanks, Jones."

"We could really use your assistance and soon. No pressure to pass the first time."

I laugh. "I'll see what I can do." There's only one person I want to share with, and now I can. I smile and text Scarlett.

Me: This morning has been fantastic! Can you meet me at the precinct for lunch?

Scarlett: I'll be there. Love you.

Me: Love you.

"Girlfriend?" Jones asks.

"Yeah. How did you know?" Eventually Jones will know our entire story, but for now that answer is enough.

"The goofy smile on your face. Same one I get when I see my wife and kids when I get home each night."

I exit the cruiser when we arrive back at the precinct and make my way to a temporary desk within the detective unit. A few hours later, after gathering more information for the home invasion, I hustle outside to meet Scarlett. I lift her into my arms and hold her close.

She pulls back and sets a sweet kiss to my lips. "Charming, your smile is huge."

I can't stop the grin on my face. "Of course it is. I'm holding you."

She rolls her eyes at me. "Seriously though, I'm not enough for that."

"You absolutely are. However, Jones gave me positive feedback and kudos this morning. I only wanted to share with you. I'm glad you're free today."

"Me too." We eat tacos from the truck.

Hagen and Greyson stop by to say hello as they head back inside from a call. My phone is vibrating in my pocket, but I ignore it.

"You should check your phone."

"It can wait until we're done eating."

"I appreciate that, charming, but it could be Gladys or Nadine."

She has a point. I pull out my phone and see three missed calls from my sister. I dial her, and she answers immediately. "Slow down, Nadi."

"I got a call from the director at the memory care facility adjacent to York Memorial. Can you meet me there tonight at six?"

"Yeah."

"Do you think I can leave the kids at your place?"

I turn to my left and look at my woman as I answer. "I don't think it'll be a problem. Let me ask Scarlett."

"She's with you?"

"Yeah, we're having lunch. Hold on." I mute my sister and ask Scarlett. "There's an opening at York Elm for Mom. Can the kids hang out with you while Nadine and I check it out tonight?"

"Of course. A visit will be good for all three of them."

I kiss her quickly and return to my sister. "Scarlett said the kids can hang out with Mom and her while we check it out."

"Please thank her for me. It's not something she is required to do."

"I will. See you later, Nadi." I end the call and press a kiss to Scarlett's temple. "Thanks."

"No problem at all. York Elm is a great facility and not only because I worked there. It may be a perfect fit for Carol. Tanner and Tallie will be fine for an hour or so with me and your mom."

"You're the best ever!"

She smiles. "I know." Scarlett leaves me, and I head back upstairs to work on my new case. The rest of the day passes quickly. I'm unable to head home before meeting Nadine. I greet her in the parking lot. "Hey there."

"Hey. The kids were super excited to hang out with Mom and Scarlett. Something about attempting to win at cards."

"Ready for this?" I ask her.

"No, but it's the right choice. I can't imagine if Mom hurt Scarlett more severely or injured Gladys. I'm not suggesting they aren't amazing. Given the recommendation of her doctors, we need to make this move. Forgoing the other spot was the right choice. Hopefully this one will work."

"Her resilience astounds me. Scarlett clearly sees the distinct line between our mother and her disease. She doesn't blame Mom at all," I share.

"Scarlett's amazing, and her training offers her a distinct perspective, despite her feelings for you."

I smile and follow Nadine inside. We're greeted by the facility care manager and one of the doctors. As we tour the facility, the manager informs us on their clinical stance, assistance with transportation to appointments, meal preparation, and acute response care when necessary. Each resident—not patient—has private space. I don't need to hear more. The staff is cheerful, the facility is clean, and their reputation is the best in the state.

"Do you have any questions?" the manager asks.

"How does the process work to have Mom moved here if we decide York Elm is a good fit?" Nadine asks.

"Our care team would meet with her and show her the space in the next few days. We would prepare her to move during the visit. Then, within a week, we would expect her to be settled in," the doctor responds. "I understand this is difficult, but your mother's care and safety is our primary concern."

"We know it's time. However, we're breaking a promise to our mother at the same time. It was a false promise, but nonetheless we're going back on it."

"The anguish you're feeling is simply because you know it's the right choice but don't want to acknowledge here is the safest option for her care," the manager offers.

"She's right, Nadine. Can you provide a cost breakdown and give us a few moments?" I ask.

The manager passes a packet of papers to me and shows us to a small conference room. "My office is next door. Please feel free to stop by with any questions or concerns." Silence surrounds us well after she closes the door.

Nadine breaks the quiet. "This sucks."

"It does, but it's the right decision. Isn't it?" Choosing York Elm has repercussions for my life as well. One that didn't strike me until this very moment. Scarlett won't need to live with me anymore. *Would she stay if I asked her to?*

"It is. This is harder than I anticipated."

"Same." I thumb through the packet. The cost is in line with other area facilities. Mom's investments have been covering the cost of her care since her diagnosis. We haven't used any portion of the separate account where she put the proceeds from the sale of our childhood home. Mom wanted the possibility for Nadine and me to get something when…. I push the thought away and focus on the current issue.

"We need to do this for her," Nadine mumbles.

"Yeah, we do. I don't like the guilt welling in my chest, but it's best for Mom."

"Do you have any questions?"

"No. Are you working tomorrow?"

I drop my head. "No. Let's set up her visit for tomorrow if we can." I rise from the chair and hug Nadine. "Why does this feel so wrong despite knowing it's the right choice?"

"I don't know."

We make an appointment for late the next morning. Nadine informs Gladys, and we make our way to my townhouse. When I enter my home and I find my family laughing and playing cards, the tears roll down my face. It's nothing short of cruel that she's having a good day today.

Scarlett looks up from the game and makes her way to me. She kisses the tears away and whispers, "It's going to be okay."

"How do you always know what I need to hear?" I murmur near the shell of her ear while I collapse my arms around her.

"I know you're wishing the decision didn't need to be made and beating yourself up for breaking your promise. Yet you know"—she sets her hand over my heart—"it's the right decision for Carol."

I exhale sharply and tug her deeper into my arms. I never thought I would find the one person custom-made for me. By some miracle of spilled coffee and my mother's illness, she showed up at my door after two years of secretly wondering what could have happened if I could've formed a complete sentence in her presence. "Thank you for staying with them. We're taking Mom tomorrow to visit."

"Why don't you visit with the kids until they leave? We've got all night to talk."

"Aren't you working tomorrow?" I ask.

"Yeah, but you're more important than sleep."

I kiss her forehead and let my hands slide over her hips before joining the kids in the dining room. After they rope me into two games of Go Fish, which I lose handily to Tallie, they head home for the night. I stand guard for one of the last times while Scarlett assists Mom into bed. She checks the rails before leaving the room.

I turn to follow her toward the kitchen.

"Zack," Mom calls me.

Me, my name. Not my father's. "Yes?" I step into the room and stand beside her.

"I like her a-a-nd you."

"Me too, Mom."

"Nadine told me 'bout the center. It's t-time."

"Thank you." I turn and leave the room. I refuse to allow my mother to see me crumble. Why does she need to be coherent today of all days? It's torture. I find Scarlett cleaning up from cards and snacks.

"Do you want to talk or paint?" she inquires.

This stunning woman is more than I ever thought I would find. She didn't run when it got hard. She's willing to allow me to sort through my feelings with a brush if I prefer. "Both." I extend my hand to her and draw her against me. "I know it's the right choice, but it guts me to make it. It isn't supposed to be this way."

"It is for you and Nadine."

"I couldn't handle this without you beside me."

She looks up at me. "You can handle anything. It's one of your most attractive qualities. You're strong, steadfast, and exude grace under pressure, but I'm glad I'm here too."

"Please don't move out. Actually, move in."

"What?"

I tighten my hold on her and ask again, "Will you stay? I don't want to wake up without you nestled against me, despite you stealing the covers."

She smirks at me. "I do not. You throw them to the middle when you get hot. It makes them fair game."

I grin against her forehead.

"Yes, I'll stay."

I kiss her deeply, and we dance upstairs, stripping our clothes off piece by piece. A few hours later, after savoring every inch of her skin I could, I slip out of her hands and pad downstairs to paint. Eventually, I'll figure out how to work, create, and sleep with Scarlett at the same time.

CHAPTER TWENTY-SEVEN

SCARLETT

Half of me is giddy and the rest is sad. Carol settled into York Elm a few days ago. I'm wrapping up packing my stuff with Lia this morning while Zack is working. In order for him to have enough time to study, I tried to push off moving in permanently, but he assured me I won't hinder him from acing the exam next week.

"I'm going to miss living with you so much!"

"We're both moving forward in our lives. You landed your dream job and put in an offer on your first home. It's crazy exciting."

"It is. Are you going to sell this place or rent it out?"

I shrug. "Haven't decided yet. I like owning the view a little too much to sell it."

"You could sell it and buy a better view with Smithson," Lia suggests.

Intriguing idea. "When do you close?"

"Early next week. I'm so excited. The cape is super cute and doesn't need too much work. Tommy said he would help, which is a bonus. My brother-in-law is quite handy."

"Free skilled labor is always a good thing. Plus, Frankie will use your yard as a palette to practice new landscaping techniques."

"True, my sister is a magician with grass and flowers."

We laugh and continue stacking the boxes in the living room. The only thing I have left to do is break down my bed. Sam is stopping by in an hour to bring me the necessary tools. While we wait, Lia and I pack the kitchen, except for one place setting for Lia to use until she closes. Lia is keeping the kitchen essentials, but we're donating the living room and dining room furniture. Both of us are putting our bedroom sets in the guest rooms of our new homes.

Lia answers the knock on the door. "Hey, Sam, Savi. Come in."

I can see the sadness on Savi's face. "No tears, Savi. These changes are good."

She hugs me close. "I know. I'm insanely proud of both of you."

"Hi, Sam. Thanks for coming."

"You're welcome. I'll get to work so you can visit Carol with Zack."

"Much appreciated." While the ladies finish packing the living room, Sam successfully disassembles my bed.

"Lia, do you need yours done as well?" he asks.

"If you don't mind," Lia answers.

"No problem at all." Sam busies himself with that task while we finish the books and games in the living room.

Savi pours four glasses of champagne in solo cups when Sam joins us. "To Scarlett and Lia. Congrats on graduating and finding your path."

We pretend to clink the glasses and sip the champagne.

"Shoot, I need to go. Thank you so much! Lia, I'll see you at dinner next weekend." I hug everyone and dash out the door.

Zack is waiting for me at the entrance for York Elm. "I'm sorry I'm late."

He kisses me all too briefly and links our fingers. "You're not late. I was early."

"What are you nervous about?"

"How do you…?"

"Your hand is shaking."

"I signed the paperwork agreeing to move her here. I broke my promise."

I lead him over to the side of the lobby. It's simple and homey. In fact, the entire facility is comfortable and designed like a living room to ease the transition for the residents. "You knew when you and your sister promised Carol it was a lie. Her living with one of you for the rest of her life was never a feasible option."

He scrubs his free hand down his face. "I didn't see it that way then, and I didn't until now. On the outside, we promised her, but the truth of it is… we lied to her."

"Though true, it doesn't diminish the fact both you and Nadine put her well-being above your own comfort."

He presses a kiss to my head and then my hand. "You always have the right words to soothe my aching soul."

"You do the same for me."

Fingers threaded, we walk slowly toward Carol's apartment. Each resident has their own space and private bath. It's set up like a college dorm but much more comfortable.

Zack knocks on the door and waits. After a solid minute with no answer, he starts getting anxious.

"I'm sure she's fine."

An older lady with silver hair and a name badge approaches from the far end of the hall. "Are you looking for Carol?"

"Yes, I'm her son, and this is my girlfriend."

"I'm Janie. Pleasure to meet you." She extends her hand to Zack.

He takes her hand and replies, "Sorry. Zack and Scarlett."

She then extends her hand to me. "Hello. Carol is in the game room. I can take you to her."

Relief washes over him. "Thank you." We follow Janie to the game room. Carol is sitting at a table with three other residents.

With the help of a staff member, it appears they're playing rummy.

I start to move into the room, but Zack tugs me back.

"We can wait until she finishes the game."

I answer softly, "Okay."

Shortly thereafter, Carol looks up and sends a dagger into Zack's heart. "Saul, see you 'gain."

Immediately I tighten my grip on his hand and look at his distraught face. "Breathe, babe."

He complies and walks toward her. Skipping the pleasantries to avoid setting her off, he says, "Hello. Are you winning?"

Carol frowns and drops her head. "No."

The other players laugh, and Carol folds with the help of the aide beside her. With effort, she stands and shuffles toward her room. Silence surrounds us as we walk. As her disease progresses, Carol more frequently chooses not to talk because she stumbles on her words. I don't know if I could handle the inability to express my feelings. I may be selective, but when I do, it's full-out.

Our visit is short as Carol requests assistance from the staff to turn in. He doesn't speak until we're outside in the parking lot. "Not what I expected."

"How so?"

He takes time to formulate his response. "Everything is the same. She has what she needs, and it's the same but different. I'm not making any sense. Mom has everything here...."

"Except you," I supply.

"Until you started caring for her, I wasn't truly helpful. If I'm being honest with myself, it wasn't until she hurt you that I actually put in any effort to care for her."

"No, you will not blame yourself for acknowledging the fact you couldn't feasibly provide the care she needed and function in your honorable profession. It's unreasonable and unnecessary."

"You would've though," he accuses.

"Maybe true, but Carol isn't my mother. She was my patient. No one expected you to take care of all Carol's needs—not Nadine, Gladys, me, and especially not Carol. You will not diminish the effort made in making sure your mother had care at home and now has appropriate care."

We stand face-to-face with the evening sun setting behind us in stunned silence. A few times, he almost speaks but doesn't. If I've learned anything about Zack, he's precise and thoughtful in his words. Clearly he has been blaming himself for falling short somehow with Carol's care, and choosing to move her here left a scar on his heart.

"No one has been able to succinctly put my feelings into words about my mother's condition and care except you. I'm grateful to have you in my life. I love you, Scarlett."

"I love you, Zachary. Let's go home." His home, which is now our home despite the boxes stacked in the guest room of duplicate items.

CHAPTER TWENTY-EIGHT

ZACHARY

I've wanted this title since before I started in the academy. I have an aptitude for putting pieces together. After over five months of studying, exam day is here. I have to give Scarlett credit. Even though she moved in, she's been a hard-ass about me studying and making sure I'm prepared.

When I silence my alarm for the second time this morning, I notice Scarlett isn't nestled against me. I tug on some shorts and start down the stairs. My gorgeous woman in a barely legal cami and sleeping shorts appears at the base of the stairs with a cup of coffee.

"I tried to make it back upstairs before your snooze expired." She hands me the cup and kisses me softly. "Drink up, then get ready. I'm cooking you breakfast."

"Yes, ma'am." I steal another kiss and heed her request. After the fastest shower I've ever taken, I hustle into the kitchen.

She must've started before because she's plating one of the prettiest omelets I've ever seen. The dish is complete with sausage and toast.

"How did I not know you are a breakfast rock star?"

She smiles and shrugs. "I think you should reserve judgment until you taste it."

"No, it's an actual question."

She sets her plate beside mine and rounds the island. With a sweet kiss, she takes a seat. Her reluctance to answer me is concerning.

"Tell me, beautiful."

"Today is the first time I don't have to rush off to the hospital while you hurry to the precinct, and I don't…."

It takes me a bit too long to fill in the blank. "You don't have a job here anymore."

She drops her head and sighs. "I'm here because I choose us. I'm sorry. I was trying to avoid adding another layer to today."

I rest my head on her shoulder. "Not your fault." I wiggle my fork in the omelet and bring a bite to my mouth.

She's frozen with fear.

"Scarlett, breathe. It's really good."

She exhales and takes a bite of her own breakfast. "Wow, it is!"

I frown. "Have you ever made this before?"

"Yeah, but I failed miserably each time. It must be your influence."

I smile at her and continue working on my food. "This is all you." Finishing the plate, I move to the sink to wash it.

"I'll wash it. You need to go."

Noticing she's correct, I grab my keys, ID, and a travel mug she already prepared for me. When I turn back, she's moved beside me.

"You got this, Detective. I love you."

"Thanks, gorgeous. I love you." After a hot kiss, I bound to my car. The ride to the testing site seems short today. Cap informed me this offering of the test was small. As I park, my phone rings.

"Hey, bro. Good luck!"

"Thanks, Nadine." I attempt to mask my mixed emotions. Nadine has been my biggest and only supporter until I met Scarlett. She doesn't miss the unsettled tone in my short reply. Despite the necessity of moving Mom, making the choice to do it was almost unbearable. The only positive aspect is she's receiving the best care for her condition. I'm not slighting Gladys and Scarlett, not at all. The reality of her care at stage six was never meant to be handled outside a memory care facility. My townhouse didn't provide enough safeguards.

"I know what you're going through right now. Focus on the test and your relationship with Scarlett. The rest will ease as the days continue. I promise."

"I appreciate you, Nadi. Love you."

"Love you too. Rock the exam, Zack!"

I laugh, end the call, and shut off my phone. I settle my nerves, which is an abnormal occurrence for me. Generally, I'm steadfast and calm, except for two things—this exam and Scarlett. She's a paradox for me. Her presence in my life makes me feel unsettled and untethered and yet only she can bring me back to me. I steel my nerves and head inside. Glancing around the room, I note there are five other guys here. None are from my precinct. I suppose that's excellent news for me. The only thing stopping me from attaining the promotion is me not passing this exam.

I take my seat, nod in acknowledgement of my table mate, and start answering questions to secure my career aspirations. The questions seem reasonable until I get about halfway through the test. I fumble through a block of ten questions and rebound for the remainder of the test. I use every minute of time allotted to complete the test. The proctor accepts the booklet and hands me an exam number and website to check the results in the next week.

I exit the room and wander slowly to my car. After settling into the driver seat, I turn on my phone and lean back against the leather headrest. A flurry of notifications pull me out of my brief respite.

Scarlett: I love you.

I check the time stamp. She sent it as soon as the exam started, knowing it would be the first notification when I was done. There's no length she won't go to for me, like there isn't one for me.

I scan through the rest of my texts. The next text holds promising information.

Cap: When you finish the exam, give me a call.

Cap: To be clear, it's a personal matter.

Puzzled, I dial immediately. "Hey, Cap. What's up?"

"Smithson, finished with the exam?"

I scrub my hand down my face. "Yes, I just turned my phone back on."

"How did you find the test?" Cap asks.

"Most of it was as expected. There was a small group of questions that threw me for a bit, but I recovered."

I imagine Cap shaking his head. "Glad to hear it. They need your assistance upstairs. As I mentioned, this isn't a professional call. My neighbor reached out to see if we were interested in their home. We aren't, but are you still interested in the neighborhood? I can ask her to meet with you this afternoon."

Three years ago, when I was looking for a home, I narrowed down the areas I wanted to live to Cap's neighborhood and Nubble Road. The neighborhood provides easy access to the rail trail, stunning water views, and access to a private strip of beach.

It isn't much, but a beach only accessible by a few houses is a plus for me. I'm well aware now, like I was then, affording a home on Nubble Road would cost me a fortune. My townhouse was a compromise of sorts. It was never meant to be a forever home.

"Yes, I'm still interested. Can you have her give me a time to meet later today?"

I can hear the joy in Cap's voice when he responds, "She's free at three."

I laugh. "Thanks, Cap." I end the call and stare at my phone for a moment. Is this really happening? I dial, and she answers on the first ring.

"Hey, charming. How did it go?"

"I'm giving myself a solid B-plus. There was a section I'm sure I completely missed, but overall pretty good. Do you have plans this afternoon?"

"Not other than celebrating with you."

I share the history of my home, how and why I chose it.

"You mentioned you wanted a view but one wasn't available. What does that have to do with now?"

I smile inwardly. "I know you moved in with me recently, but Cap called. His neighbor is listing her home in a few days. He convinced her to allow us to take a look at it first, if I'm still interested in the neighborhood. What do you think?"

Silence rebounds through the line a bit longer than I anticipate. Doubt begins to creep in.

"Scarlett?"

"Oh, charming, I don't know what to say."

"Is that good or bad?"

"You truly hear me, don't you?"

I speed through our interactions. She must know where Cap and Kelsey live. I reminded her our taste in homes is in line and we should look at a home that would meet her ocean view requirements together. "Yes, gorgeous. I do."

"Where are we meeting?"

I glance at my watch and determine I have time to go home first. "I'll come pick you up."

"I'll be ready."

I hurry home and find Scarlett waiting for me in the garage. Throwing open the driver door, I lift her into my arms and turn in a circle.

"I'm crazy proud of you and excited right now."

"Me too." I escort her to the passenger side and close the door behind her.

Her sheer giddiness is rubbing off on me despite me trying to temper my emotions. I don't know which neighbor, but I know the view is amazing from Cap's back porch and master bedroom.

I pull into Cap's driveway. Kelsey and Ben are off to the side on the grassy area with Bear and Knox. They're rolling a ball back and forth. Before I can round the car, Scarlett is advancing toward Ben as he toddles to her.

"Let. Hi, Let!" He throws his arms around her neck.

"Hi, Ben."

"Not at work no more," he accuses.

Scarlett wrinkles her face. "I know, sweetie. I got a new job."

He kisses her cheek and runs back to his ball. Scarlett rises in time to catch his throw.

"Good to see you both. My husband will be right out. He went inside to change. Val puked on him the second he got home."

"Thanks," I reply. However, my focus is on Scarlett and Ben. They're playing catch with the ball and the dogs. The smile on his face is priceless. Hers is more intriguing. I'm on board with a large family, but first we need a home.

"Smithson. Scarlett. Nice to see you." Cap exits the front door and hands Val off to Kelsey. I'll be right back, *querida*." He kisses her softly before escorting us to his neighbor's house.

"Thank you for remembering, Cap."

"You're welcome. It would be nice to handpick my neighbors too." He smiles and rings the bell.

A silver-haired, petite woman opens the door. "William, nice to see you. You must be Zack and Scarlett. I'm Lorraine." She extends her hand to us.

"You as well. Smithson, please stop inside before you leave." Cap requests.

"We will." We shake her hand in turn, then she ushers us inside.

"Please feel free to look around. I'll be in the office," Lorraine informs us before disappearing down a hallway to the side of the kitchen.

"Thank you." I'm overwhelmed. Lorraine's home is spectacular. The foyer is narrow but two story. A wide staircase is off to the right. The main level has an open-floor plan. The living room decorated in soft gray is straight ahead. The eat-in kitchen is off to the right. The cabinetry is navy with brass hardware, and the appliances are all top of the line. We've barely taken three steps into the house, and I'm sold. I don't care if there's only one bedroom upstairs. I'm sure that isn't the case though.

The entire back wall of the house is floor-to-ceiling glass. The view is exceptional.

Her eyes survey the main level slowly and carefully. "Zachary."

"Yes, gorgeous?"

"We should go upstairs before we rush down the hall to find Lorraine."

I laugh softly and lift her hand to my lips. "Yes, we should." We follow the wide staircase to the second level. At quick count, I gather there are four bedrooms and a walk-up attic access. The rooms are appointed perfectly for guests in the first three bedrooms. The master is along the back wall and features a private balcony. The closet is as large as my guest room. The master bathroom is straight out of a designer's fantasy. The Carrara marble shower and floor are complete with a soaking tub, which I'll actually be able to use, making this room a dream come true. It's written all over her face. I don't need Scarlett to say the words. Whatever her price, as long as it's feasible, I'll make this happen for my future.

Silently, we climb the last set of stairs. If the rest of the home wasn't enough, the finished loft in the attic seals the deal for me.

"You could have an amazing studio up here, Zachary. The light is bright and cool. The view is nothing short of idyllic." She's absolutely correct. This space is more than I could ever imagine.

"It's beyond words. Do you love it as much as I do?"

She slides one hand along my jaw, and the other rests on my chest. "I didn't need to see any of this. I was in the moment I looked through the windows at the view."

"Scarlett, let's make Lorraine an offer she can't refuse."

"Yes, absolutely yes!"

We politely hurry downstairs to chat with Lorraine. We approach the office and knock.

She looks up from the book she's reading in the Queen Anne chair. "All set?"

"Your home is stunning," Scarlett replies.

"Thank you. I have years of fond memories here. With my Harry passing and my children across the country, it's time for me to downsize," she shares.

"We appreciate you taking the time to allow us to preview your home. We would like some time to write up a formal offer to purchase it from you."

A mixed smile materializes on her face. "How wonderful." I can only imagine how difficult it was for her to make this decision. She rises from the chair and hands Scarlett a card.

"Here is my contact information, dear. I look forward to your offer. You two are a lovely young couple. This will be an amazing place for you to raise a family."

I extend my hand to her, as does Scarlett. "Thank you. We'll be in touch."

Lorraine walks us to the front door, and we leave. As we walk away, Scarlett glances back at her and offers a cordial smile.

I can barely contain the sheer glee bubbling inside me. Today has been fabulous. Nailing my exam, securing my future with the department, and finding a home with Scarlett is beyond what I imagined for myself. We make our way to the front porch and knock on the Ramirezes' front door.

"Hey there! Come in," Kelsey greets us.

Cap is sitting on the floor playing with Val, and Ben is walking circles around both. "What do you think?"

"Have you ever been inside, Cap?" I ask.

"No. I've seen the back of the house from outside though. I imagine it's amazing."

"It's beyond words from the inside as well. We're going to make Lorraine an offer."

"Yay! I'm so happy for the both of you," Kelsey exclaims.

"Thanks. We're excited too," Scarlett replies.

"Is there something else you wanted to discuss, Cap?" I ask.

"No. I'll see you at the precinct in the morning."

I strain to hear what Scarlett and Kelsey are whispering about but fail. "Ready to go, Scarlett?"

"Yes. All set," she replies and hugs Kelsey.

"Bye, Let. Come back soon," Ben demands.

"Bye, Ben. I'll see what I can do," Scarlett replies. "Bye, William."

Happiness oozes out of her pores as we pull away.

"We need to talk about our current homes and finances a little bit."

Scarlett shifts in her seat to face me a bit more fully. "Okay."

"Mine is worth about three-hundred and fifty thousand, and I don't have a mortgage. What about yours?"

"Mine is worth one-seventy-five or so. I have a small private mortgage to Sam of about fifty. So as far as a bank is concerned, I don't have any debt. I'll reach out to my realtor and list it tomorrow."

"Let's grab takeout and draft up our offer."

"I'm so happy and excited, Zack!"

"Me too, gorgeous. The exams are over, we're buying a home, and the gala is next week. I'm truly looking forward to a getaway with you. We need to talk about the gala more too. Are you okay with staying at Sam's?"

I shrug. "I don't see why not as long as he doesn't mind."

"I think everyone is staying there, all the Morgans plus us."

I wrinkle my brow in confusion. "Are there enough bedrooms for that?"

Scarlett laughs heartily. "There are six, if I recall correctly. Whatever you have in your head as big enough, add at least two or three more when it comes to the Morgans. I'm not suggesting they aren't humble; they are. Their houses, cars, bank balances are merely more than ours."

I laugh at her description. I know in the abstract the Morgans are billionaires, but I never really thought about what that means exactly. Clearly it means six bedrooms in a New York City penthouse as a second home. "Sure, works for me. We're leaving early on Saturday, right?"

"Yeah, Cash is going to fly everyone there, and then we'll return midday Sunday." Cash, Scarlett's brother-in-law, owns an airline. He flies when his family needs to go somewhere or a few of his select high-profile clients request him.

We devour our dinner and work out the details of our dream home offer. A few hours later, with our offer ready, we make our way toward the bedroom. I pause at the doorway to my office. It's barren now. The medical supply company came and removed the hospital bed earlier today. It wasn't until now that I've seen the room empty.

"Want to talk about it?" Scarlett murmurs as she tightens her arm around my waist.

"No. Seeing my office empty doesn't bother me as much as I thought. I'm working on grappling with the fact I signed the papers. That bothers me more than this."

"I'm here if you change your mind."

I press a kiss to the top of her head. "I know, sweetheart. Let's get some sleep."

We climb the stairs, knowing our future is falling into place. The only thing left is to make sure the world knows Scarlett is mine for the rest of my life.

CHAPTER TWENTY-NINE

SCARLETT

I hurry into the hospital two days later and move directly to my floor. Since I'm no longer a student, I don't need to check in with Stacy daily. Judith, my head nurse in pediatrics, only holds one meeting each week unless things go awry. I check the assignments and note I have a light patient load today.

I start my rounds with a new long-term patient. Penny recently moved to the area from Florida. Her father was traded to the regional professional soccer team. She has acute lymphocytic leukemia. The staff is setting up to transfer her chemotherapy here.

"Hi, Penny. I'm Scarlett. How are you feeling today?"

"I'm okay."

"You must be Dad." I extend my hand to him. I'm fully aware of who he is, but I don't intend to go full-out fangirl. Cian Fleming is an Irish-born *futébol* player. He transferred to the United States a few years ago. It's why Judith chose me to run the visits with Marco and his teammates. I'll be discreet. Penny and her father's presence here should be private.

"Pleasure to meet you, Scarlett."

"You as well."

We discuss the tests the team is running today, and ideally, she can continue her chemotherapy regime starting tomorrow. I finish up with Penny and tend to my other patients. Afterward, I decide to take a walk to the food trucks. A spicy burrito is on my lunch wish list today. As I step outside, I hear Zack calling my name. I would know his smooth, velvety voice anywhere. My belly does a flip-flop as I turn around to locate him.

"Hi, baby. How was your morning?"

"Hi. Fine. Is everything okay? Did I miss a lunch date?"

"Not at all. I didn't mean to scare you. I came with news, good news. No, great news!"

"You passed!" I blurt.

"Yes, I did."

I pepper his face with kisses until I can barely breathe.

"There's more," he whispers near the shell of my ear.

"Zachary, you know better."

He winks at me. "Do I or do I purposefully whisper—" He looks around to make sure no one else can hear him. "—to make you wet?"

"Ohmigod! Please share."

"Lorraine accepted our offer, and you have a full cash offer on your condo."

"Really?"

He smiles. "I wouldn't kid about any of that."

I jump into his arms and kiss him again. "Do you think Lorraine will allow us to stop by before closing?"

"Probably, but why?"

"I want to figure out how many lights to order for your paintings."

"We have plenty of time after closing. We should focus on selling my townhouse next."

"Good plan."

He glances at his watch. "I need to get back. Celebratory dinner tonight?"

"Yes."

"Love you." His lips seal over mine before he rushes away, barely hearing my in-kind reply.

Noting I don't have time for a burrito, I head back inside to grab a protein bar and water before finishing out my day. I'm not surprised when I arrive home and find our celebratory dinner is simple and exactly how I like them.

After pizza, we attempt an episode of *The West Wing*. Before we're halfway through, clothes are lining a path to the bedroom.

Too early the next morning, we roll out of bed and finish packing for a quick getaway for the gala. I wasn't worried about this event until Zack parked at the private terminal at Pemberton.

"Good morning, Mr. Smithson. Miss Clemons. Right this way." A steward escorts us from the door directly into the private hangar and relieves Zack of our bags.

"Thank you," I reply and climb the steps of the plane.

Zack dutifully follows me. I can tell he isn't used to this level of luxury. Hell, mostly, neither am I. The attendant hands me a fluted glass, and I take a second one for Zack.

"Morning, Scarlett," Noelle greets me.

"Zack, this is Noelle, Cash's wife. Noelle, my boyfriend."

He manages to shake her hand despite our accommodations.

"It's a pleasure to meet you," Noelle answers.

"Nice to meet you as well."

We take our seats. Shortly thereafter, the rest of the family boards. I introduce Zack to Billie, Sam's sister. Billie in turn introduces her husband, Peter, and sister-in-law, Caroline. Obviously, Zack has met Savi, Sam, and Auggie before. We take off for the gala before ten in the morning.

"Are you okay?"

He turns to face me. His expression isn't hard to read, at least not for me. Zack is floored at the opulence but can't reconcile how my sister and her in-laws act. It was similar for me at the beginning too.

"This is Savi's life, not mine. She went from one extreme to the other. They have extreme wealth, but they don't act as if they do. I don't need or want all of this."

He simply nods, threads our fingers, and reclines in the chair.

The flight is smooth, and we make our way to the penthouse after landing. "Good morning, Miss Clemons."

"Hello, Arthur. Nice to see you again. Zack Smithson, please meet Arthur, concierge extraordinaire."

"Pleasure to meet you," Zack offers.

"Pleasure is mine, sir," Arthur replies.

Luckily, our chat on the plane eased Zack's view of the penthouse.

"Scar, you can take the second room on the right." Savi points in the direction to walk. "We need to be ready to leave no later than four. Sam has arranged for lunch at two."

"Thanks, Savi." I take Zack by the hand and lead him down the hall. "Any better?"

"This home is bananas."

"It is. I focus on the function rather than the luxury of it. We have a soft bed and a private bath to get ready for the gala, as well as a terrace with an amazing city view."

Zack's spirits perk up a bit.

"Come on, let's go check it out." I lead Zack outside onto the terrace.

He circles his arms around me, trapping me against the railing. The skyline is impressive. However, the fall view of Central Park is a sight to behold. The leaves are starting to turn into a kaleidoscope of color. "This is incredible."

"It is. We should come back each season so you can paint it. It's nice to visit, but otherwise it isn't something I want daily."

He tilts his head in question and disbelief. "Do you…? Would Savi…?"

"Yes. All we need to do is ask."

"I would love the chance to paint this view," he whispers against the nape of my neck.

"We can work out a weekend we're both available later in the year or early next year, and we'll make a trip up here."

"Thank you, gorgeous."

We enjoy the view until lunch arrives. I don't need too much time to get ready, unlike my sister. I don't know Caroline and Noelle well enough to say how long they need.

After an insane spread of Italian food from a local mom-and-pop shop is delivered, we join the family in the kitchen to eat. Afterward we get ready to leave. Zack hurries through the shower while I start my hair. His silhouette through the opaque door has me not fully paying attention. Once he leaves the bathroom, I resume working on my hair. If I don't get my act together, I'm not going to be ready on time. But watching Zack get dressed in the mirror is beyond words. I mean, his suits are one thing, but a perfectly tailored tuxedo complete with cuff links and… my word, I need a shower to cool off.

"Stop staring, sweetheart," Zack commands, which only makes me hotter.

"Can't. It's unfair to be as hot as you are!"

He saunters over to me where I'm finishing my hair. "I don't need to wait for you to put on your dress to know you're exponentially hotter than me." He takes my lips in a searing kiss before walking away.

With a deep breath, I rise and unzip the garment bag for my dress. I retrieve my shoes and slip the robe off my shoulders. For years I stole Savi's shoes from her closet. When she started dating Sam, he bought her a pair of red-soled shoes with sparkles on them. I coveted those shoes so much, I splurged and bought myself a pair for this occasion instead of borrowing Savi's. She wouldn't miss them. At last check, most of her shoes have red soles now.

I tug the dress over my hips, fix the straps, and raise the side zipper. "I can feel you watching me."

"Fair is fair." He crosses his arms over his chest and refuses to look away.

I slide my feet into the shoes and turn to face him.

"You look ravishing," he says, softly gliding one hand over my hip and the other around my neck.

"It's the dress."

"No, it's the woman in the dress," he whispers before pressing a light, sweet kiss to my lips. "I love you, Scarlett."

"I love you, Zachary." Our gazes remain locked with one another until there's a strong knock on the door.

"Scar, you guys ready? We need to leave in five," Savi asks through the door.

"We'll be right out."

Zack's hands drift downward before he offers me his arm. "Let's go dance the night away."

I laugh and slide my arm around his. He sets his other hand on top of mine. We join the others in the living room. The lot of us make a fine-looking group.

"Have a wonderful evening," Arthur offers as we pass.

"Thank you," Cash replies, and we ride the elevator to the parking structure and slip into a limo. It never occurred to me until this very moment, the purpose for the gala may appeal to Zack. When I invited him, it was before I knew he was a painter at heart.

"Did I tell you what this gala is for?" I lean closer to him.

"I don't think so."

"It's for the arts. This year's focus is on rising impressionist painters."

Zack gifts me with a sly grin. "Initially my interest was merely to hold you in my arms all night. Now I can also mingle with like-minded painters, thanks to you."

I smile and press a kiss to the corner of his jaw. Luckily, I'm not a celebrity or a billionaire, so Zack and I are able to walk into the gala without a myriad of flash bulbs exploding. I'm surprised Cash didn't request personal security from Blackthorne for this event.

After a glorious, gourmet meal and hours of dancing, we return home and fall into the luxurious bed and drift off into dreamland.

CHAPTER THIRTY

ZACHARY

The last few weeks have been a whirlwind of activity. I have officially accepted my promotion and moved upstairs to the detective division. Mom is stable though deteriorating at York Elm. It's sad but expected. My townhouse is under contract for sale, and we're closing on our home tomorrow.

"Yo, Smithson, wait up," Davis calls from a few spaces over as I head out for the day.

"Hey, Davis!"

I remain still, and he catches up. "I wanted to personally congratulate you on your new gig."

"Thank you. What about you? Any plans for moving to a different division in the YPD?"

Something sparks beneath the surface before he replies, "Not sure yet."

Normally, I would dig more, but I have so much work to do at home. "We should get together for a beer soon."

"We should. Are you sure the missus will let you go out with the boys?"

I grin at him. I have more time to hang out with the guys, but I haven't. "She's not my wife."

"Yet," Davis asserts. He isn't wrong.

"What about you and Tabi?"

"Still going strong without a label, and I'm fine with it."

"Fair enough. Send me some details for the next guys outing," I request.

"Will do. Congrats again."

We bro hug, and I hustle to my car. Thankfully, the attorney's office is only a few blocks away. I pull into a spot and note Scarlett has already arrived.

"Hey, babe," she greets and kisses me lightly. We head inside together and take a seat at the conference room table.

"We're ready to get started," Attorney Kramer states.

Over the next hour, Scarlett and I sign what seems like five hundred pages to buy our dream home. I also execute a contract for the sale of my townhouse. The order worked out well. It gives us some time to paint and make changes without our furniture in the way.

We accept a bottle of champagne from our realtor and cheer when she hands us the keys. As we share a celebratory kiss, my phone vibrates in my pocket. I check the preview before stowing my phone away.

Kelsey: Everything is set. So happy for you two!

I needed an accomplice to pull off my plans for this evening. Luckily, Cap and Kelsey had a spare key from Lorraine. I snuck over to the house at lunch yesterday and set up what I could. Today, Kelsey added the items I needed from the Perk and a few other details.

"Follow me to our house?" I ask when we stop beside her car.

"Sure."

The ride isn't long, but my nerves are getting the best of me. I'm sure about her, but my palms are sweaty and I'm anxious. I shake off my feelings of fear and unrealistic rejection as I open her car door.

She keys open the front door and stops short. Kelsey has outdone herself. There are electric candles lining a path from the front door to the end of our memory tour for this evening. Our new living room is filled with her favorite flowers—burgundy ranunculus—along with quicksand roses, among others. Confused, she picks up the empty cup of coffee with the Perk logo on it from the small table. "Zack?"

"With a little help from our friends, I wanted our first night here to be special. What seems like forever ago, I bumped into a gorgeous woman, spilling hot coffee over her arm and down the front of her jeans. When her piercing cobalt eyes met mine, I was too stunned to speak."

A smile blossoms on her face. I take her hand in mine as we step further into our new home.

"Fast forward two years from our meet-cute mishap, you showed up to help take care of my mom and bail me out. I was in over my head, and you saw fit to care for my mother and help me understand I wasn't failing her despite my adamance otherwise. It got messier when she assumed you were my wife. You also agreed to date me."

She stops our progress and looks up at me with wide eyes.

"I have been working on these as often as possible. Slipping out of bed without waking you is harder than you would think." Releasing her hand, I lift the sheet off the first easel.

"Zachary, it's… me." The painting is a portrait of Scarlett looking over her shoulder from the waist up. I'm not on the canvas, but it was how I pictured her face. "It's stunning."

"I've never felt competent in my craft until you saw all of me. You inspired me to see how my choice to keep my private life, my career, and my personal talent made up different facets of me. It wasn't until I saw myself through your eyes that I saw all of me."

A single tear rolls over the ball of her cheek. She swipes it away with the back of her hand.

I pull a navy box from my pocket, drop down on one knee in front of her and the portrait, and take her hand in mine. "Scarlett, you stole my breath and my ability to see anyone but us the first moment I saw you. Will you marry me and legally take my name?"

"Yes, Zachary. I would be honored to become Mrs. Smithson outside our walls."

I slide my ring on her finger, draw her into my arms, and kiss her until we're both panting for breath. I lower my head to her shoulder and eliminate every minuscule amount of space between me and my future wife.

"What's over there?" She points to the group of easels set up along the back wall of our home.

I smile against the curve of her neck. "Those are a work in progress, but they're for you." I kiss her hand below my ring before reluctantly releasing her from my embrace and leading her over to the first canvas. I reveal a mostly finished self-portrait.

"That's fantastic!"

I kiss her temple. "Thank you. Yours would belong here." I indicate the second empty easel to the left. "The next one will be a painting of our home over the next year. A sliver for each season. I started the fall one as far as the outline in the last quarter."

She's suddenly quiet.

"Scarlett, please say something."

"I'm astounded. These are incredible, and you're not finished. I love your idea, and I can't wait to see the finished series."

"Only you will see it. I may come around to sharing some of my works with our family and close friends. I might be willing to display some of them in our home. But these are a gift to you and only you."

She drops her head in agreement.

"What do you say to a sleepover in our new home?" I suggest.

"Sounds wonderful."

"But…?"

She grins at me. "I'm kind of hungry."

"My love, what kind of fiancé would I be if I didn't make sure you're properly nourished for our first evening as an engaged couple?"

"Not mine?" she quips.

I glance at my watch. "Precisely. Auggie will be bringing dinner in about—"

The doorbell rings.

"Now?" she smiles.

I hurry over to the door and throw it open. Instead of Auggie, Caroline is standing on the other side. "Hi."

"Hi, Zack."

Scarlett sidles beside me near the door. "Hi, Caroline."

"Hey, Scarlett. Auggie is stuck in the kitchen. He asked me to deliver this to you both."

"I appreciate it, Caroline."

"Auggie put instructions for the dessert in the box. Congratulations."

"Thank you. If you could keep that to yourself until tomorrow afternoon, we would appreciate it."

She hands over the bags and zips her lips. With a smile, she turns and walks back to her car. We spread the food onto our waterfall granite island and eat mostly in silence until curiosity gets the best of my woman.

"Who knows our little secret?"

"The jeweler, Cap, Kelsey, Auggie, and now Caroline," I answer.

"Okay, I'll call Savi and Lia in the morning. How did you know I would love this ring?"

"I didn't, like I didn't initially know about your favorite flower."

"It's perfect. What do you say to spending some time where the only stitch of anything on my body is my engagement ring?"

I don't take even a moment to answer her. I throw her over my shoulder and climb two flights of stairs to my new studio and painstakingly explore each inch of her skin with my hands and mouth.

CHAPTER THIRTY-ONE

SCARLETT

More than a month has passed since a mysterious invitation to a book club arrived in the mail for me. It instructed me to pick up a book and read it before tonight's meeting. The novel is set in the early nineteenth century and follows a family looking to marry off their daughter. Generally, I wouldn't consider such an invitation as legitimate until Zack assured me it was fine for me to go. Where he obtained the information, I don't know, and I didn't press. More intriguing is the invitation didn't include a location until this morning. I received a text informing me the meeting is at Kelsey's.

I finish getting ready and shoo Zack out with the guys. He, Davis, Craven, as well as a few guys from the YFD who I haven't met yet, are heading to the brewery for beers and darts.

"Have fun, babe."

"You too. I'll walk you home when I get back," he assures me.

"I can handle walking next door. Besides, you know Kelsey will stand watch on her porch or send Bear with me. Love you."

"True. Love you." He hurries down the hall and through the door into the garage.

Right before six, I grab my book, lock up, and walk over to Kelsey's. She throws open the door before I can knock. Knox and Bear are right beside her and dutifully check me out before they allow entrance. "I'm so excited you're finally here."

Curious phrasing, but I ignore it. When I step inside, I'm greeted by Maggie Washington, Willa, and Carly from work.

"How's engaged life?" Willa asks.

"Fine," I reply.

"When's the big day?" Maggie inquires.

"We want a small, intimate wedding. It'll probably be in the fall." Good job, Scarlett. You shared but not too much. Zack and I have already decided when and where. We simply haven't let anyone else know yet.

A few more women who look familiar from work arrive and grab a place to sit.

Once they're comfortable, Carly calls for everyone's attention. "Good evening, ladies. Welcome to our monthly book club meeting."

Echoes of welcome and nice to have you here surround me. We spend the next hour-plus discussing the book in detail. We share our opinions and objections to parts of the story that truly wouldn't fit in modern life.

After a few more laughs, Carly silences the group and opens the door for two more guests—an older woman introduced as

Lois Canter and Gladys Rhodes. "I would like to call this meeting to order. Please welcome two of our founding members Lois and Gladys."

The newest arrivals take a seat near me.

Carly continues, "I would like to welcome our newest member, Scarlett Clemons. Not only is she a nurse on staff, which warrants inclusion in our group, but she captured the heart of one of our community's most eligible bachelors."

I blurt out before I can process my thoughts, "The rumors aren't rumors. There is a list."

The ladies laugh, and Willa adds, "Welcome. We pride ourselves on keeping our matchmaking a secret."

I swivel in my chair to face Gladys. "Were you in on it the entire time?"

"Yes and no. I assisted with a gentle nudge here and there, but—"

"Like his forced rest at my condo before Nadine's visit?"

"Perhaps. You and Zack didn't need my help at all," she replies with a huge smile on her face.

I suppose she's right. "Thanks, Gladys." It simply took us some time to see it ourselves or, at the very least, be in the right place to be a couple.

"How do you decide who to fix up?"

Kelsey replies, "We have the list, and we work from that. If we see an avenue to assist a person on the list, we do."

"I have a suggestion, but it may seem off the wall to you," Willa whispers.

Maggie and Kelsey speak in unison, "Davis is the perfect choice."

I refocus on Carly. "At our last meeting, we voted to allow women first responders onto the list and create a list of eligible EMTs, as well as increase the overall list size. Are there any motions to be heard?"

The room falls silent.

"No motions are set forth tonight." Carly shares the book for next month and the signups for the charity football game hosted by Santino Gugliotti, which is being held in the late summer instead of early fall this year.

"I shall read the names and adjourn our meeting for this month. The List for the York Police Department reads as follows: Santino Gugliotti, Zachary Smithson, Lachlan Hagen, Donovan Davis, and Piper Montgomery. Former honorees are William Ramirez, Grant Washington, and Luca Cappelli."

I turn my engagement ring on my finger and feel happiness creep into my cheeks as Carly reads Zack's name.

Carly continues reading aloud. "The York Fire Department list includes Bradford Collings, Alden Rhodes, Aidan Madden,

Landry Reed, and Mia Arden. No former honorees to date. Lastly, the EMTs in York County include Séamus Penn, Jude Pascal, Hollis Booker, Lexington Soren, and Lacey Ransom. No former honorees to date. I look forward to seeing each of you next month.

Thank you so much for reading *For Love & Coffee*!

I hope you love The List. Which first responder will find his or her HEA next?

Pre-order *For Love & Basketball* now so you don't miss it!

Ready for a new Cappelli Family novel? Will Lily divulge her feelings to Leo? Find out in *Chasing After You* available soon.

Did you love *For Love & Coffee*?

Thank you for taking the time to read it. I hope you loved it!
If you liked this book or another one of my books, please
consider
posting a review.
A short line or two will be perfect!
I appreciate your support and feedback.

COMING SOON

Two new stories are coming soon!

A York Beach Novel

The Cappellis

Chasing After You

The Matchmakers' Book Club

For Love & Basketball

MY BOOKS

YORK BEACH SERIES:

A New Beginning with You

Taking A Chance on Me

Just One More

Kiss You Like You're Mine

Only with Him

My Once in a Lifetime

THE CAPPELLIS

Chasing Forever

Chasing My Sunshine

Worth the Chase

MORGAN BROTHERS SERIES:

One Unforgettable Favor

Until I Kissed You

Always Have, Always Will

BLACKTHORNE SECURITY

Protecting My Forever

Protecting Our Forever

Protecting Us